Excess Baggage

GW00778200

Also by Jacinta McDevitt

Handle with Care
Sign's On

Excess
Baggage

Jacinta McDevitt

POOLBEG

Published 2004
by Poolbeg Press Ltd
123 Grange Hill, Baldoyle
Dublin 13, Ireland
E-mail: poolbeg@poolbeg.com

Typesetting, layout, design © Poolbeg Group Services Ltd.

1 3 5 7 9 10 8 6 4 2

A catalogue record for this book is available from the British Library.

ISBN 1-84223-144-8

Typeset by Magpie Designs in Goudy 10.5/14.5pt
Printed by Cox & Wyman, Reading, Berkshire.

www.poolbeg.com

ABOUT THE AUTHOR

Jacinta McDevitt lives by the sea
in Malahide, County Dublin. She has sent
two grown-up children and two previous novels
out into the world – a labour of love. The
novels, *Sign's On* and *Handle With Care*,
were also published by Poolbeg

Acknowledgements :

Hi again! This is becoming a bit of a habit, isn't it?

Firstly, thanks to all of you who have read my books. Without a reader, there is no story. Also, thanks a million to all of you who took time to get in touch with me with such lovely messages. I hope you enjoy this one too.

I'm a great supporter of the libraries and I marvel at the events etc. that they run. Thanks to Teresa, Betty and to Marian for making me so welcome.

Thanks to all the lovely booksellers country-wide who promote my books with such gusto.

A big thanks to the wonderful gang at Poolbeg, I appreciate all the work that goes on behind the scenes. Thanks especially to a dynamic duo – Paula and Gaye – who are always so lovely and kind to me. Thanks too to Anne, Brona, Claire, Lynda and Sarah who are always so good-humoured. A very special thank-you to my lovely agent, Jane Conway-Gordon.

A big warm hug to all my wonderful friends who enrich my life so much. Old and new friends, near and dear friends. Hugs all around to the Spilling Ink crew and to the great friends I have met through writing. Thanks too to my friends in Malahide for all their support and generous encouragement.

Lots of love always to Joe and Lucy – good health to you both.

Love and hugs to Eimear and Eoin, who make me feel very much at home. Thank you both.

Soppy kisses and hugs to my darling nieces and nephews: Helen, Sara, Katie, Frank, Ellen, Hannah and Sam. Lots of love, always, to my brothers-in-law, Michael and Tony, and my sister-in-law Maeve – weren't they the lucky ones?

Huge big hugs, kisses and lots of love always to my lovely sisters Margaret, Lucy and Mary and my lovely brother, Frank. We make a formidable bunch.

Lots of love and hugs to Conor, who's been around for a long time now and still keeps Lucy smiling.

Loads of hugs and love to my most favourite daughter-in-law, Maire. She's even more of a

ACKNOWLEDGEMENTS *continued*

treasure and I have to say I think I'm doing a great job at the mother-in-law bit – I'm a natural.

Lots of love and hugs galore to Brian – and here was me thinking it couldn't get any better, but it does, every day, it's just perfek.

Hugs, love and kisses to my parents, Frank and Helen. Thank you both for all the sacrifices you made for me and indeed all your children and grandchildren. I think you're both brilliant.

Endless love, hugs and happiness always to my two terrific children. My son Alan and my daughter Lucy. My geese are definitely swans. The kindness, love and encouragement they give me is truly amazing. Thank you both for making me so happy always. Love the bones of you . . .

Now get reading . . .

Once upon a time . . .

for

Lucy, Alan, Maire

Mam and Dad

Brian

"All of us are in the gutter but some of us are looking at the stars"

CHAPTER ONE

Madame Celeste
Scorpio
October 23 – November 22

Watch your step! There are many paths ahead of you. Only one path is the right one for you. Don't follow others aimlessly on their path. Choose your own path. Make sure it's the right path.

"Well, what do you think that's supposed to mean?"

I held the folded newspaper directly under his nose and stabbed my finger directly at Madame Celeste. Well, not at Madame in the flesh but at Madame's horoscope column. I was hoping it would have the same effect as prodding a voodoo doll with pins – hoping she was feeling my prods, if only indirectly. That was the only satisfaction I was likely to get from Madame Celeste and her column.

1

"What in the Name of God does she mean by that?" I demanded.

When no answer was forthcoming I read my horoscope aloud once more, very slowly this time, then prodded Madame again.

"How the hell is a person meant to figure that out?" I beseeched him. "Why doesn't she write in plain, ordinary English? Something the ordinary man or woman in the street can understand? After all, they're the ones who read it. Then again, maybe no one reads it, except me. Maybe I'm the only gobshite who reads it. What do you think?"

"I'm sure I've no idea."

"You and me both, pal. I have no idea either. Wouldn't it be a turn-up for the books if ol' clever-clogs herself, Madame C, had no fucking idea? Wouldn't that be something? Wouldn't it just? She might be fooling me all this time. Jesus, I hadn't thought of that! What do you think? Do you think it's all a scam? I'd kill if I found out it was a scam and she was only making it up. Someone would suffer. I wouldn't care who. Do you think it's a scam? Do you? Well, do you?" I had the paper rolled up now and was pointing it at him.

"I'd say it's definitely *not* a scam."

He seemed to be trying to back away from me and I could see tiny beads of perspiration erupt like little volcanoes on his brow. He looked a bit frightened, to tell you the truth. OK, so I suppose my voice was a bit raised

2

and I suppose I was overdoing it with the rolled-up paper. Maybe I was verging on the hysterical – but only verging. And I had every reason to be verging. I was on a plane. And I hate flying. I hate it with a passion. I do everything with passion, even hate.

I have always hated flying. I suffer it as a means to an end. If I want to go to B, I have to endure A. Simple maths. But it still doesn't make me want to do A. I only want to do B.

I like talking when I'm flying. It shortens the journey for me and takes my mind off the fact that I am hundreds and hundreds of miles up in the air with no safety net. In a vessel that weighs hundreds and hundreds of tons and has my case in its belly. My case which weighs another ton and is now sporting a large orange HEAVY tag. I'm lucky it's only on my case. I thought the stick-skinny girl at the check-in desk was going to lean forward and tie one out of my fat ear. She was killed looking me up and down. Trying to measure me up.

Then she started asking me so many questions.

"Did you pack your bag yourself?"

The way she asked it, I knew she felt sorry for me. She felt sorry for me because I wasn't as thin as her and I didn't have the glamorous job she had. And I didn't have the brown pencil outlining my lips the way she did. I knew she was thinking my plain old lip gloss was a bit outdated.

3

"Yes." I hung my head in shame. I knew I was about to give her another reason to feel sorry for me. "I did pack the bag all by myself. It was very lonely. Wouldn't you imagine someone would have been with me? I know a pretty, skinny young thing like yourself with those bee-stung lips probably can't understand it, but the answer is yes, I packed my bag by myself, I'm ashamed to tell you."

I could tell she felt really very sorry for me now. I think I even saw her eyes moist over. She tried to pretend she wasn't interested by yawning, but I knew by the very next question she asked that she was more than a little concerned for me.

"Have you anything sharp in your luggage?"

That's exactly what she said: 'anything sharp'.

"Anything sharp? Oh, no, dear, don't worry about that! I wouldn't ever harm myself. It wasn't all *that* bad packing my bags alone! Sorry to have given you that impression. I'm just a little nervous right now because I have to fly today. I don't like flying, but I certainly amn't brave enough to harm myself. Thank you for your concern. I'm touched."

Now my eyes moistened over.

"So you have nothing sharp then?"

"No, but thank you for being so concerned."

She took up a pen which was a major achievement for her. Her false nails were a great handicap. She had to pick the pen up with the soft pads of her fingers and not let her nails come into contact with anything. They were French-manicured, naturally. The nails not the pens. She made several attempts at picking up the pen. It was like being in a funfair watching one of those big claw machines trying to pick up a cuddly toy or a watch. Every part of you knows the claw will never get the cuddly toy but every part of you wishes it could. Just for once. I was wishing she'd get the pen on the next attempt. She didn't. In the end I just leaned over, picked up the pen and handed it to her. She circled my seat number on the ticket and told me which gate I would be departing from.

I never delay at duty free. I never sit and relax in one of the bars or coffee shops either. I never eat before I fly. I just go straight to the assigned boarding gate. I wait until I am told to board the plane and then I take a deep breath and start praying.

As soon as I sit in my seat I fasten my belt and start talking to whoever is nearest me. I love chatting to people on a journey. I like getting the low-down on them. Even though we may never have met before, we have something in common: once in the air we are all in the same sorry situation until the wheels of the plane land on terra ferma. We are all fucked together if the thing takes a nosedive and just does a belly-flop on the tarmac.

I think only people of ten stone or less should be allowed to fly. Of course that would mean that I would have to lose two stone, but wouldn't it be a great incentive to lose weight? And the plane would have a much better chance of staying in the air.

I took a look at the guy beside me. He was over-weight. I am overweight. Everyone on the plane seemed overweight. I wondered if the airline knew they had a plane full of fat people? I hoped they had taken it into account in the calculations for the flight.

"Wouldn't you imagine it would have been in my horoscope this morning that only fat people were getting this flight? I don't know why I bothered reading it at all. Wouldn't you imagine Madame C would have mentioned something about it? It would have been a great chance to show off her psychic abilities. But oh, no, she has to go on ad infinitum about paths. What do I know about paths anyway? I drive everywhere. I'm great on roads. Lousy on paths. I don't do walking at all. I do driving great."

"I'm sure that's lovely for you."

"Today is nothing new, you know. I never, ever under-stand my horoscope. It never has anything good to say. It's always a veiled threat or a warning of doom and gloom. A misery. A confirmation that I'm making a total balls of everything. Do you know what I mean?"

"I'm sure it must be terrible for you."

"It is, it sure is. It's always terrible. Madame Celeste never says 'Wow, Emma, you're such a great person. You have followed your heart and found true, everlasting love. You're onto a winner and about to have such a wonderful

6

life – enjoy it.' Now why does she never say that? It's not as if it would kill her. It's not as if I couldn't have a wonderful life or even a wonderful day, if I tried really hard. If Madame Celeste would only try hard with me I'm sure I could have a terrific day. I feel sure I could have lots of terrific days once I got into the practice of it."

"I'm sure that would be lovely for you."

"I must be a glutton for punishment. Do you know, I'm an addict."

"An addict!" He put a hand up to his mouth in shock.

"Oh, I'm sorry if that upset you. I didn't mean it to. I was merely sharing a little bit of my private self with you. I thought it would be nice for you to know me a little bit better. I can see now I should have kept the addict bit to myself. Maybe that part was a bit too private. But what's so wrong with throwing caution to the wind and revealing my foibles, my inadequacies, my private parts?"

"In the Name of God, woman! I'd feel more comfortable if you kept those to yourself. I am a family man. A very happily married man for twenty-five years. I have six children."

"That's it! Well done, you! You see how much better you feel by sharing and chatting. Now that wasn't hard, was it? Isn't this lovely?"

"Lovely! Lovely! Is that what you call it? You must be a madwoman. You have babbled on and on at me for the

7

last fifteen minutes. You have attacked me with your newspaper and now you tell me you are a drug addict. You need help!"

"I do *not* need help. I am *not* a drug addict. I am addicted to reading my horoscope. I don't harm anyone. I read it every day, no matter what. I suppose I have an addictive-compulsive personality. Personality or disorder – I'm not sure which. I'm hoping it's just a personality. I'd hate to have a disorder. Knowing my luck it's both and I have a personality disorder."

"Well, as far as I'm concerned you're a complete lunatic! I guess that's some sort of disorder all right."

"Well, at least I don't go around hurting people's feelings. My little obsession does no harm to anyone. Once I know where my day is going I'm fine, I can rest easy. I firmly believe that some day all this horoscope thing is going to come together and pay off, big time."

"Yes, yes, yes. I'm sure it will."

"Oh, it will. When the time is just right. I am certain that I am going to be warned about some big disaster like a hi-jacking or a plane crash when everything is in place. When Uranus is hovering over Mercury or whatever it is Uranus does. When Mars has entered Venus and is vying with Jupiter, who is in Pluto or wherever is the best place for all of them to be. When all is so well with the planets and the world that I am heaped with good fortune and love in abundance. The time just isn't right yet. Timing in life is everything. That's what I say. What do you say?"

He said nothing. Absolutely nothing.

"I said timing in life is everything. Did you hear me?
Are you listening to me at all? Well, I don't think that's
very nice. Here I am, absolutely terrified of flying, about
to take off into the unknown and I get to sit beside the
most unfriendly person on the plane. You might be the
last one I ever talk to, you know. I think the least you
could do is be nice."

"Madam. I have listened to you, I have spoken to you,
I have ignored you. Nothing works. Now I have a
headache and my ears are aching. I'm exhausted and my
neck is sore. I am worn out. Totally and utterly worn out
and we haven't even taken off yet!"

"Well, there's no need to be snotty!"

I made up my mind not to speak to him for the whole
flight. He could sit there dying for me to talk to him and
I wouldn't.

Except for one last thing.

"If you're worried that I'm going to read out your
horoscope to you, don't be. I only ever look at my own.
I'm a bit selfish about it. I never bother with anyone
else's. It's enough for me to be watching out all day for
whatever is forecast for myself without having to do it
for every Tom, Dick or Harry, not that I know a Tom, a
Dick or a Harry, unless of course you are a Tom, a Dick
or a Harry? Are you? You're never? Wouldn't that be
hysterical? Anyway, I can see you don't want to tell me

your name and that is your choice. Mine is Emma by the way. I do know an Abigail, a Julia and a Ronan, and I make a particular point not to look up their horoscopes. Ronan, my present partner, lover, potential husband, boyfriend or should that be man-friend (anyone over forty is too mature and experienced to be called boy-anything) doesn't believe in all that mumbo-jumbo even though we'd never have met if it wasn't for my addiction. It was quite funny how we met. I won't bore you with all the details, but it really is a good story."

"Thank you so much for not sharing."

"Ah, I bet you're dying to hear it. Go on, admit it. It will shorten the journey for you. It all started about a year ago."

"Excuse me. I have to go."

"I understand, that'll be your nerves. I had to pee too about five times before we boarded. I never go once I board. I sit in my seat for the whole flight. Sometimes I babble, sometimes I don't. I don't think I'm babbling today though – not really babbling."

He got up and left. He must have been in a bad way because I saw him talking to the air hostess. He was waving his arms all over the place and wiping his forehead and doing all sorts of silly head movements while rubbing his neck.

The next thing I knew he started shaking his head and yelling at her: "I promise I will! I will open the door and jump! I mean it. I don't care how high up we are.

You have to do something!"

She shouted back at him. "Calm down, sir – we are still on the tarmac!"

"I feel dizzy. Let me off. Now! I insist on getting off this plane. I think I'm having a heart attack."

The poor fella must have come down with something. He might have been embarrassed that he would need the loo a lot and it's such a small space. Probably a tummy-bug. I hoped he hadn't given it to me. That was all I needed. You never know who you're going to end up sitting beside on a plane. Pity he had to go just when I was warming up. He'd have enjoyed the story about how I met Ronan. I enjoyed it myself.

As I said, it was about a year ago. I was doing a very nice man's interior. That's what I do, interiors. Not only men's – I do women's as well.

It was great. He was a wonderful client. Very adventurous and not afraid to spend a few bob. He was happy to go along with everything I suggested. Not a lot of clients will give you free rein like that. Clients mostly want to set the rules and give the orders, keep you on your toes and crack the whip every now and again. Do the chest-thumping and the howling bit. If you let them get on with all the animal actions for a while and oooh and aaah while they do it, they usually leave you alone for another little bit. Argue with them and you're dead in the water. *Bang, bang!* They call in every day. They ask a million questions and they delight in telling you

11

that they are paying your wages. Big deal. This client was different – he was very nice and very cute. Very cute and very married.

"I don't care what you do," he said to me as he showed me around his magnificent home. "I don't have time for petty things. That's what I pay you for. I don't want to be asked about colours for the walls or frills on the curtains. I pay you to do all that. I pay you to pick all the little finishing touches that I won't even notice. My wife will notice when she comes back. She is abroad for a week. She is gone to visit her sister in France. I want her to be delighted when she gets back. I want her to think I spent time as well as money on this project. I will pay you a bonus of a thousand euro if you finish the whole job in one week. Another five hundred euro if she has no complaints."

"I'll have to have a look around the house first. A week is a tall order. Pleasing someone I have never met or never spoken to is an even taller order."

"Do what you have to do."

He was a client in a million. By the cut of his suit and the cut of the house I could tell he was a cut above buttermilk.

I decided, in order to save time, that I would have all the walls painted buttermilk then play around with different colours in different areas. The house was mainly green. Green carpet, green patterned wallpaper, green suite, green curtains. As I say it was all green.

Green is not my favourite colour, not by a long shot.

I started with the wife's wardrobe. I didn't try on any of her clothes, although I was tempted. I just sat with the doors open trying to get a sense of her. Nearly every stitch she had was black or white. I guessed she was afraid of colour unless it was green.

Black leather was the obvious choice for the couches and black leather high-backed seats in the dining-area. I worked like a woman possessed. On the last day of the week I arrived at the house at six-thirty in the morning. I pottered around admiring everything. I had transformed the place. It really was magnificent. Very classy. Everything was cream and black. The cream curtains billowed from the windows in yards and yards of luxurious material and softened the room. I knew she'd love it. The final *pièce de résistance* was to arrive at eight o'clock.

It was a very modern piece of sculpture. It was to stand in the hall. It was a vibrant, flowing piece carved from bog oak. It was a shapely woman with her arms extended to the sky, palms open, her belly swollen. She was about six months pregnant. It was supposed to symbolise peace, warmth, fertility, welcome and new beginnings.

The client and his wife were due to come to the house at eleven-thirty to see the fully finished work and I wanted there to be a 'wow' factor in the hallway. The beautiful statue had the 'wow' factor.

13

By nine o'clock the sculpture still hadn't arrived. At five past nine the doorbell rang. A tall man was standing there smiling. I couldn't believe he was smiling – not a word of apology, just a big toothy smile.

"Thank God. I thought you were never coming. You're dead late. Well, don't just stand there smiling – come in. Wipe your feet first."

"But –"

"Yes, you're right, it would be better if you took your shoes off. Well, don't just stand there with your mouth open. Come on, get 'em off ye! I'll just show you exactly where to put my beautiful lady."

"But I don't –"

"Oh, but you will for me. You will put it exactly where I say. It's no good just dumping it inside the door. I could never move it by myself. What do you take me for? Just here, do you see? Not an inch to the right or an inch to the left – just here, in this exact spot. Facing the doorway, but at an angle. I want the light to shine down directly onto her face and her belly. Hey, you don't happen to have a newspaper with you, do you? You'd be a lifesaver if you let me borrow it. There was no shop open early this morning so I couldn't buy my paper."

He opened his briefcase and took out a newspaper and handed it to me. "But, I haven't –"

"Not to worry if you haven't read it yourself yet. I only want to look at one page. My horoscope. I have to read it or I'll get all disorientated and we can't have that now,

14

can we?" I laughed loudly at my own joke.

"I was just going –"

"To read your own? Were you? Well, you can read yours after I read mine. My need is greater." I laughed loudly again.

"No, I was trying –"

"Listen to this: *It's easy to borrow, the paying back bit is harder. Beware of who you borrow from and what they want in return. Make sure they are who they say they are.* Well, what do you make of that?" I laughed even louder. "I hope you are who I think you are!"

"But you haven't given me a chance to say who I am. I'm –"

"The guy with the sculpture. I know."

"There you go again. You don't know. What I'm trying to say to you is that I haven't a clue what's going on and I was just going to leave in this software for my client who assured me he would look at it later if I dropped it off here, at his house, early this morning."

He handed me a package. It was not a five foot statue.

"Oh, I'm sorry. Here's your paper. Thanks. I'm really sorry. Was I babbling? I babble when I'm nervous. The guy with the sculpture is dead late and if he doesn't arrive soon I'll be out a thousand euro."

"Can't you phone and see what's happened to him and his delivery?"

"Great idea." I only noticed now how handsome this guy was. "I'm Emma, by the way. I do interiors."

"I'm Ronan, nice to meet you. I do software."

He was clean-shaven. Black hair, streaked with grey. Tanned skin, small scar on his forehead, above his right eye. Great body. Great suit, slate grey. White shirt, pink and grey tie. Smart. Really smart.

I was glad I was looking a bit smart myself that morning. My cream trouser suit was tailored and the jacket covered my ample arse very nicely. An ample arse is best covered. My black and cream top was tight due to my ample boobs, but it was cut low and gave me a wonderful shape. An ample bosom is best displayed. I was dressed to blend in with the house. I was glad the house was looking so well.

I felt myself go into flirt mode. Doing all the feminine, male-catching things I enjoy doing. Pushing my hair back, adjusting the way I was standing, pulling my stomach in, shoulders back. Pushing my boobs out that little bit further. Making my D cup appear to be a DD or with any luck maybe even an E. Batting my eyelashes and giggling and smiling a big toothy grin. All in all it probably had the effect of making me look like Daisy Duck with a set of falsies – teeth not boobs. God, how easy it is to go into flirt mode. I love it. All feminine and sexy.

"It's on the way," I told him. "It'll be here any minute. Thanks, I'd never have thought to phone them. My nerves are gone. I hope they like it after all this."

"I'm sure they will. Well, now that's all sorted I'd better head off. Nice interior, by the way."

16

"Thanks. I bet your software is good too."

"I hope he likes it."

"Thanks, but it's his wife liking it that I'm worried about."

"Sorry, I meant I hope he likes the software I designed for him. I hope they like the house too, of course. Bye."

He stood on the step putting his shoes back on. They were spotless and shining.

"Wait! I borrowed your paper – what do I have to do to pay you back? "

"What?"

"My horoscope, remember? So what do you want in return for me borrowing your paper?"

"You don't believe all that mumbo-jumbo, do you?"

"Of course I do. So what's it to be?"

"A date?"

"I was hoping you'd say that."

And that's how it started.

We've been dating ever since. For nearly a year now – it'll be a year next month. A year of dating at our age is the same as five years for teenagers.

At our age we have a past. But two different pasts. We have experience. But two different experiences. It makes it more intense. There is a lot to know and a lot to find out. I told him about my crap past and my crap marriage that was way back in my crap past. I told him about Julia, my wonderful daughter. He didn't have too much crap to share. He had never married so that ruled out a lot of crap. He had no children and that ruled out the rest of the crap. One by one, I peeled off all my past secrets to him. Left myself raw as an onion. He was nearly crying at some of the crap.

So I could never give up reading my horoscope now. It had brought me Ronan. God knows what else it would bring me. I was hoping for the lottery numbers.

Once, before I met Ronan, I managed to go without reading my horoscope for a whole day. I decided not to buy a paper with the horoscopes in it so I wouldn't be tempted to take a sneaky look. I survived the whole day. I was charmed with myself.

OK, so I was a bit disorientated and I kept thinking there was something I'd forgotten to do like brush my teeth or put on my knickers. Basic stuff like that. But then when I went to bed I kept wondering what earth-shattering, life-altering pearls of wisdom my horoscope had held that I had completely missed and therefore completely ignored.

I went into panic mode. I couldn't sleep. I tossed and turned and got a rash all over my body and started sweating. So I did the only thing I could and phoned a friend. My best friend in the entire world. Abigail. She's fantastic. A true friend. The sort you can phone any time of the day or night.

"Do you know what time of the night it is? Are you out of your shaggin' mind?"

Not quite the response I was expecting. Obviously,

she wasn't too pleased at my phoning. To be honest she threw a bit of a wobbly and kept asking if I was out of my shaggin' mind.

"I just can't sleep."

"Are you out of your shaggin' mind?"

"Yes, I am actually. I'm in bits."

"Oh God! What's happened? Are you all right? Are you hurt? Is Julia all right? Is she hurt? What is it?"

She was lovely and so concerned. Fair fecks to her, it didn't take her too long to be lovely and so concerned. Ten out of ten for Abigail – yes, a true and loyal friend.

"Actually, I'm not injured or anything like that. I'm fine really. Julia is fine too. Well, I think she is. She's at a party. I hope she's not drinking too much. I hate her getting pissed. She can't hold her drink. She should be home soon and then all will be all right with the world and I can go to sleep."

"Well, I'm delighted to hear that. Thanks for sharing. Now will you just get the shaggin' hell off the phone and let me get back to sleep."

I really didn't think that was a very nice thing to be saying to me. After all, I was supposed to be her best friend in the whole world. Some way to treat your best friend I was thinking.

I went all quiet. It always works on Abigail. She hates the silent treatment. It doesn't work too well on my daughter, Julia. Sometimes it works on Ronan.

"Oh, don't you dare pull the silent routine on me!"

I remained silent.

"I'm knackered."

Still silent.

"You woke me up."

Silent.

"Ah, go on, talk to me. I'm so sorry, I'm so cruel. I know you'd only ring me at this hour if it was an emergency. What's wrong? Why did you ring?"

See, the silent treatment works a treat on my good pal Abigail.

"Please, please, I'm in an awful state. I missed reading my horoscope today. You'll have to read it out to me."

There was silence. Deathly silence. The kind of silence you only hear in the dead of night. Then the silence was shattered.

"Are you out of your shaggin' mind? Do you know what shaggin' time of the shaggin' night it is?"

She was using a bit too much bad language for my liking. I'm not a prude, but she really was just using bad language for the sake of it.

"Abigail, your language is shite. Go on, will you read my horoscope out to me?"

Now it was her turn to be silent.

"Are you still there, Abigail?"

Silence.

I assumed she was gone to get the paper.

"Emma!" She was back. "Let me get this straight. You woke me up in the dead of night to get me to read your stupid horoscope?"

This last remark was cruel. She knew how important it was for me to read my horoscope. Making light of it was very mean. Sometimes my horoscope isn't a bit stupid.

"Yes, now read exactly what it says. Exactly. Go on."

She sighed. Then: *"Do you know what time it is?"*

That was it.

"Is that all? Is that all it says? Wow, that's a bit weird, isn't it? Is that exactly what it says? 'Do you know what time it is?' Are you sure you're reading out Scorpio? Gosh, isn't it so weird? That's so scary. I must've been meant to ring you tonight, in the middle of the night. Can you see the significance of it, Abigail? What does it mean? Oh God, I've just thought of something. I don't know what time it is. Should I, do you think? Oh God, I don't. Wait till I look at my watch. Oh shit, I can't find it. What'll I do? Does it say I should know what time it is or that I shouldn't? Read it to me again. Slowly this time."

I went straight into panic mode and started searching for my watch. Maybe it didn't mean the actual time here and now? Maybe it was to be interpreted in another way. Like did I know what time it was in my life, in the greater picture and scheme of things? Horoscopes are never straightforward.

"It's 3.20am, for God's sake," Abigail proffered.

She also muttered something under her breath about

21

both of us being the worse for sleep deprivation which I didn't quite catch, but there was a few more colourful words in there.

"3.20 a – m. A – M!"

"So now I do know what time it is, what am I to do?"

"Emma, that is not exactly what your horoscope says. Exactly what it says is this: *Someone you know and love is going to kill you, very slowly and very painfully if you don't shag off.* Goodnight!"

To this day I don't believe that is actually what it said. She read it out too quickly. I believe she made it up just to get rid of me. She lied. Imagine her lying to me!

She didn't even bother to discuss it with me. She just read out a death threat and then went off to sleep. Grant it, her husband, Geoff, hadn't helped matters. I could hear him cursing at her, asking her "Who the hell is that?" and telling her to "Shut the hell up!" – which I didn't think was very pleasant of him and no way for him to talk to his lovely wife.

I wished his lovely wife was with me now on the plane. I hated being alone. I wanted someone to talk to. I took out my horoscope again. It was certainly a conundrum. *Choose your own path.* How the hell was I going to make sure I was on the right path? And was this path an actual path or one of those metaphorical ones? I hate metaphorical paths; they are so easy to get lost on. There are no maps and no signposts.

CHAPTER TWO

"Hey! It's never you, is it?" A really gruff, sexy voice was shouting at me all happy and excited, as I sat there on the plane. I knew it was me he was shouting at because I recognised the voice and the very sexy body it belonged to.

Sexy and gruff. Dog-rough.

"Oh, my God, Danny, it's you!!" I replied in a rather high-pitched, overly hysterical voice that I knew he would recognise instantly.

"Emma! I knew it was you." He was smiling from ear to ear.

"What are you doing here?"

"Well, I hope I'm flying back to Dublin. I am on the right plane, amn't I? I barely made it. I was on standby. Someone got off sick and they let me on. A lucky break for me."

23

Danny looked absolutely fantastic. He had looked fantastic way back when I last saw him. But over the years whenever I had imagined him, I had imagined him aging and getting all wrinkly and washed-out looking. Hair thinning, waist thickening. It did me good to imagine him wrinkly and aged, thickened and thinned. But the bastard didn't even have the good grace to do that. He was the picture of youthfulness – and shit, he was still a handsome bastard.

"I can't believe it!" My attempt at witty or intelligent conversation failed miserably. That's the odd thing about witty or intelligent conversation – you only ever think of what you could have said after the event. When the opportunity has passed.

It's also the weird thing about meeting ex-boyfriends you've bonked a million times till you're blue in the face. It's hard to make small talk when you meet them years later in a public situation when you're both fully clothed. It's the knowledge that they have seen every bare square inch of you – even bits of you you haven't seen yourself – that's a bit disarming.

"I can't believe it either. Well, well, Emma!" At least his attempt at chit-chat was as bad as mine.

"Yeah. Well, well, Danny. " Another failed attempt. This was painful stuff.

"Ah, Jesus, Emma." He relaxed and stretched out his arms. "Come here an' gimme me a hug, don't go all shy on me."

He broke the ice and nearly one of my ribs at the same time, he squeezed me so tight. To tell you the truth I thought he overdid the squeeze. Maybe he wasn't as relaxed and nonchalant as he wanted me to think.

"It's years since I've seen you. How's it going?"

He seemed genuinely pleased to see me. Really pleased. Maybe it was fate. Maybe we were supposed to meet again now. Then again maybe I was on the wrong path. I sure as hell wasn't going to be led down the garden path again by Danny, no matter how fan-shaggin'-tastic he looked.

I decided to play it cool.

"Absolutely great, really wonderful, terrific, fine. Everything is fine with me. How about you?" I babbled. I don't do cool very well. I do babble great.

"Fine, yeah, terrific, wonderful, great, absolutely fine with me too."

He grinned from ear to ear. He was mimicking me. I think he was teasing. I guessed he was only putting on the awkwardness, it came so naturally to me. He was laughing at me. So some things never change. He was always laughing at me, but not in a cruel way. He was a kind bloke. That's what was so hard about it all.

I had always hoped I'd never set eyes on him again. I always knew it would be a hard and very awkward situation. I was right. Sometimes I hate being right.

Oh well, how bad could it be? I suppose it was inevitable that I would bump into him sometime,

Ireland being a small place and Dublin being a very small part of it. I suppose it was weird that we hadn't bumped into one another a lot sooner. That was partly because I avoided everywhere I knew he would be. I had never gotten over him. I avoided all his usual haunts and kept my distance. I really didn't want to see him ever again. I think I was afraid to.

In all fairness it was more a matter of self-preservation on my part than cowardice. I was trying to preserve my broken heart. A broken heart can only stand so much abuse. Not that I know anything about medicine, but I was wise enough to know that a poor broken heart can only take so much pulverising.

So here he was now and there was no avoiding him. I was captive. If only I didn't still fancy the bastard so much it wouldn't be so bad. If only my heart hadn't mended so well. If it was still even a tiny bit cracked I would have been more cautious. But my heart was in good condition. A little bit bruised all right, but manageable. My heart was feeling so good that I could feel myself going into flirt mode.

I suppose meeting him here was for the best – we wouldn't be able to talk for too long. Sex was definitely out of the question, which is just as well because I might have been tempted. Well, I am only flesh and blood. Unless, of course he had ambitions of becoming a member of The Mile High Club. Knowing Danny, he and his member were already members.

So, safe in this confined space I could have a bit of fun and flirt a bit and it would be no harm. He might even feel he could flirt a little bit with me too. Then he'd have to go back to his own seat, fasten his own seat belt and I could stay here, safely held in mine. Great. I gave him my best doe-eyed look and my best toothy smile.

He reached up and opened the compartment above my seat and pushed his hand-luggage in tight beside mine. All snuggled up together for the journey to Dublin.

"Looks like we're going to be sitting together. What a stroke of luck! You get to chat me up all the way home." He patted my knee as he sat into the seat beside me and fastened his seat belt. I had the window seat and he was in the middle seat.

"You can't be sitting beside me! There's a man sitting there – he threw a wobbly and went down to talk to the air hostess."

"He was sitting here? Well! That's a double stroke of luck then. I was on standby and some guy, must be him, just got off in an awful state. He really looked in a bad way. He was shouting "People like her should be locked up! They certainly shouldn't be allowed to get on a plane!" One of the air hostesses, I suppose. The poor guy, I thought he was going to bust a gut. Poor sod. I felt sorry for him. But his loss is my gain and I get his seat."

"He was in a bad way. I felt sorry for him myself. I

wonder what happened to him?"

"Well, let's not worry about that — we'll be taking off any minute now."

"Jesus, don't tell me that. I'd better get into position to kiss my ass goodbye."

I was hemmed in by Danny. He smelt gorgeous. All Aramis and peppermint. Thank God. There is truly nothing as bad as sitting on a plane with someone who smells. Sitting beside someone on a plane is a very intimate experience. Parts of you are touching. You can smell their scent. I would rather their scent be out of an expensive bottle than be their own brand.

"Ah, no. Please tell me you've gotten over your fear of flying."

"Nope, I can't tell you that because that would be a blatant lie and you know me, I don't do lies."

"You were always too honest for your own good."

He stared at me.

I stared at him.

I started to rummage in the pocket on the back of the seat in front of me. Just for something to do. I hit the jackpot. A magazine some passenger had left behind. I flicked the pages, quickly. Then hit the jackpot again:

Marvin's Mystic Musings
Scorpio
October 23 – November 22

Your head is in the clouds and it's no good to you there. The sky's the limit for you if you'd only keep your feet firmly on the ground.

Well, it made a bit more sense than Madame Celeste, but not much.

"I see some things never change. You haven't stopped reading your horoscope."

"Yeah, I'm still a masochist."

"You must be if you're flying and on your own."

"Actually, I fly all the time now, but I still haven't got used to it. Each and every time I board a plane I have a huge urge to go deep into a fit of projectile vomiting. Oh, don't worry, it's all right. I won't be sick. I promise you."

"Well, it's not exactly you getting sick that I'm worried about. Remember our trip to Vienna, many moons ago or don't you want me to remind you?"

"That was a long time ago." I was scarlet now, remembering a little fainting spell I had on a flight from Dublin to Vienna.

But I had every reason to faint. I had never seen a lightning storm at such close quarters before. There was such a lot of turbulence. I seriously thought we were going to be struck by lightning and die. I most certainly knew that there was no escape. It was the loss of control that hit me hardest – that and the smack on the face the air hostess gave me as she tried to get me to stay in my seat. Whenever we hit turbulence I felt an overpowering need to get out of my seat. I hated being strapped in like a lunatic.

"I'm sorry, Miss," the well-versed, well-dressed, well-made-up air hostess said. "The fasten-seat-belts light is on and you must remain seated. We are experiencing a little turbulence."

"A little turbulence? Are you out of your mind, you foolish woman? This is not a little turbulence. A little turbulence wouldn't bother me. This is a lot of turbulence. I want to use the toilet."

"Well, I'll have to ask you to wait for a couple of minutes."

"Well, I just can't wait. I have to go now."

"Well, you can't."

I guess she knew my plan.

I had decided to have a word with the captain. I wanted to go into the captain's cabin or quarters or whatever official name they give to the place where all the decisions are made about all the lives in the other part of the plane. It wasn't as if I was panicking. I was doing great. All I wanted to do was to get to the captain and tell him in a calm and reasonable way to land the shaggin' plane or at the very least to turn the bloody thing back and let me off.

When the air hostess wasn't looking I made a run for it only to be intercepted by another very glamorous air hostess with a tackle as good as Jonah Lomu. You know him, the good-looking rugby guy. Does great things with odd-shaped balls.

Anyway she floored me and started shouting at me. I knew she wasn't a bit worried about the turbulence. She was only dying to put all the safety measures she had beautifully demonstrated earlier in the flight into practice.

"You can't go into the cockpit! It's out of bounds!"

"That's it, that's it – the cockpit. Cock! Pit!" I shouted and banged my fists off the floor. "I suppose it's an all-male pit too. I bet there is not even one level-headed female in there – not even one lone female voice in the male wilderness to tell them to land the bloody plane. All testosterone and muscle pulsating to prove how brave we all are. Well, feck that – I'm not brave." I shouted this last bit at the door of the pit housing all the cocks. "Do you hear me? *I am not brave!*"

"It's OK. The captain is very competent – she's been flying for years. She can handle a little turbulence. It'll all be over in a minute. Take it easy. Relax."

"Will you stop saying 'little turbulence', please. I'm no fool. *She?* Did you say the captain is a woman?"

That's the last thing I remember. Immediately after I assured everyone I wasn't a fool I foolishly fainted. It was after she said the words easy and relax. I took her at her word. It was easy when I knew there was someone with a bit of cop-on making the decisions, but maybe I overdid the relax bit. Anyway, it was a release for all concerned I can tell you. Not least Danny.

Obviously he still remembered it. His slant on it might have been a bit different to mine though. Romantic trip to Vienna, girlfriend throws a wobbly, mortifying trip to Vienna.

He had been really good to me throughout the fainting episode. He had held my hand the rest of the way to Vienna. Maybe because he loved me and wanted to reassure me that I was safe in his manly hands or maybe it was just because he didn't want me to leave my seat again and make another show of myself and him. Anyway, for whatever reason, he held onto me all the way there and I have to admit I liked it. They wheeled me out in a wheelchair just to make sure I'd be OK.

They made a bit of a song and dance about frightening all the other passengers and in particular the group of young schoolchildren who were on the plane. They said I'd put the kids off their wonderful adventure. They were representing Ireland in some sort of world choir competition and, according to the powers that be, half of them were so terrified that they'd lost their voices.

I didn't believe it. I guessed the kids were just looking for an excuse not to sing – they wanted to do a bit of sightseeing and no singing. I was a kid myself once, I know every trick in the book. Although I did see at least one of them pointing at me and crying. I have to admit, I felt a bit ashamed. But Danny told me not to worry, that it would give them something to tell their friends –

if they ever got their voices back.

"Yeah, that sure was some flight, Emma. I hope there's no 'little turbulence' on this flight. Anyway, you made up for your misadventure. We had a terrific time. It was a great time wasn't it, Emma?" I knew he was talking about more than just the trip to Vienna.

"We always had a terrific time, Danny."

"Yeah, we did. Didn't we? We were terrific together, Emma."

"I suppose we weren't too bad."

"You know we were great. A match made in heaven. Have dinner with me, will you? We could talk about old times and broken hearts. Are you still unattached?"

"Let me think about it."

"Think about having dinner with me or whether you're still unattached?"

"Both."

"Have you noticed we're airborne?"

I hadn't, nor had I noticed when exactly he had taken hold of my hand.

"Thanks, I never felt a thing," I said as I pulled my hand away from his.

"I'll be here for the landing too so don't sit there fretting for the whole journey, will you?"

"I'll be fine."

"Hey, isn't this fate? I mean us crossing paths again like this."

Thoughts of my horoscope raged through my head.

"I'm trying not to pay any attention to fate these days. Now I'm going to have forty winks, that's how I deal with flying now. Wake me up when we're in Dublin."

"OK. Sweet dreams."

I closed my eyes not so much to fall asleep but more to gather my thoughts. There were so many of them to gather I wondered would I ever be able to gather all of them into a neat pile. None of my thoughts were neat so I guess one big neat pile was out of the question. Maybe lots of little piles might work. Little piles. All sorted under different categories. The more I tried to gather and sort the more I realised that one big huge messy pile was the best I could do. All filed under the 'Crap' category. All to be dipped into and thought about at random and in no particular order.

I squinted my eyes a little so they looked like they were still closed, but at the same time I could still see Danny. I wanted to take a good long look at him without him knowing I was looking at him. I stared at him through the slits.

"Not able to sleep then?"

God, I was caught. My eyes hurt from squinting.

"It's OK. I'm just getting comfortable." I wriggled a bit and then closed my eyes properly this time. But not before I had a good look at him. He did look older than I remembered him. But then again so did I – or maybe I didn't. I just always assume the worst of myself.

"Do I look different?" I asked him straight out.

"Not much."

Except for the maze of wrinkles all leading to nowhere, I guessed he was thinking.

"You look practically the same, but your hair is a different colour."

I ran my fingers through my hair. I was blonde. I had been blonde for exactly six weeks. Blondes don't have any more fun than brunettes – take it from me. It's all a myth perpetrated by blondes to make themselves appear more interesting and more desirable.

"But do I look older?" God, I'm such a masochist. I wanted him to say no. To lie and pretend I didn't look any older than the last time he saw me. Ronan always told me I looked younger than I was.

I know I looked as well as I could, barring major surgery, which I am too much of a coward to ever contemplate. I was wearing a pale pink linen trouser suit, a pink and white tee-shirt and pink shoes. Pink is my colour. Now that I am blonde it is even more my colour. Linen might have been a mistake for travelling. I was all creased, but at least I was a designer crease. My eyebrows and eyelashes were still dark though. I wondered if that looked odd, but Abigail and Julia assured me it didn't.

"No. You don't look a bit older. Your eyes are the same as ever they were. I always loved them. You're the only woman I know with violet eyes. Except for Julia, of course, she has them too. All in all, Emma, I'd have to say you look exactly the same. Maybe even a bit younger." Danny was terrific. You could always rely on him to say the right thing. He always knew exactly what you wanted him to say and he always obliged. He was such a lick. He was a master at it. It was a major buzz.

I still didn't believe that I didn't look any older though.

"Well, you haven't changed a bit." I laughed. "You're still such a bloody charmer." I reached out and hit him on the arm.

"It's self-protection." He held his hands up to his face.

We both laughed.

"How's Julia?" he asked.

"She's as wonderful as ever."

"I miss her, you know. We really got on well. She's a great kid. So listen, you still haven't answered my question: are you unattached or what?"

I pretended I didn't hear him.

I felt my eyes getting heavy and closing.

I felt him tuck a blanket in around me.

"You look exactly the same as the last time I saw you," he whispered. Then he pecked me on the cheek. The cheek of him! It was lovely. Just what I needed. I didn't know I needed it until he did it.

"You look beautiful," he added.

"You're a terrible liar," I said as I drifted off to sleep.

CHAPTER THREE

I had last seen Danny four years ago. Four years, two months and three weeks ago to be exact. I guess it must seem that he was very important in my life for me to remember the exact time I last saw him. Well, he was important to me. But the real reason I remembered the exact time I last saw him was because I last saw him on my thirty-sixth birthday. At my birthday party. In a moment of madness I had decided to have a party. I invited everyone I knew and some turned up that I didn't know, friends of friends. It was to be a brilliant night. All my work colleagues, friends and family were all there to wish me well. For once I wanted to be the centre of it all. For once I wanted everything to be just right.

The first indication that it was all going pear-shaped was when Julia rang me the night before the big event. She was crying her eyes out.

"Oh, Ma, I've gone and spoiled it all. I have ruined your birthday and it's not even your birthday until tomorrow."

"Julia, stop crying. You have ruined nothing. Where are you?"

"I'm still in Galway. I missed the train. There isn't another one until tomorrow. It'll take me ages to get home. I won't be able to help you prepare anything or clean or do your make-up or do myself up or do anything. It's all a mess. I should never have come here. I should have stayed in Dublin – at least that way I'd be with you now."

"Now, listen Julia, everything is in hand. You stop worrying and just get home whenever you can. Was it good?"

"No, it was shit. They were dreadful. It was embarrassing. I should have stayed at home."

"Well, there's no good saying that now. Just look after yourself. Can you stay in the hotel with the others for tonight?"

"Yeah, that's where I am now. I'm so sorry, Ma."

"I know you are. Hey, see you tomorrow – and keep smiling. Promise. Love you loads."

"Me too, I love you and I will. Bye."

I could have told her this would happen, but if I had told her she wouldn't have listened to me. Only other people's kids listen to their mothers. Sometimes other people's kids even listen to me. But my kid listens to no one. She certainly never listens to me. She doesn't have to. She knows it all. The only thing she didn't know was the timetable for the Galway to Dublin train. I knew she's miss that bloody train. Pity she just hadn't given the gig a miss. But oh, no! she couldn't discommode her friends. She couldn't miss the gig. Her friends were relying on her. To listen to her talk, they would all be suicidal if she didn't go. Part of me was delighted to hear that she was so popular, the other part of me had to question what type of friends she was hanging around with if they would be prepared to commit suicide if she didn't turn up to their gig. It was a bit worrying.

A group of her friends had formed a band and whenever they had a gig the rest of their friends went to support them. A bit like Rent A Crowd. The gig never looked a total flop even when it was a flop. There were always a core bunch of fans there. According to Julia the core bunch of fans were more important than the band. In all fairness to her the band were brutal. But the fans enjoyed the craic and the travel. But where did it leave me? Having a party with no one to help me. That's where it left me.

This was the worst thing that could happen to me. I had been relying on her to give me a hand. Abby wasn't even around, she had to bring one of her boys to a football match and would only be back in time for the party. She couldn't even give me a hand. There are times when the only hands you can rely on are your own.

I had decided to cook a big dish of chicken in wine and a huge dish of garlic potatoes to go with it. With Julia and me doing it together it would have been easy. We were a good team in the kitchen.

The menu was a big mistake. I had heartburn in no time. Not from the food. I hadn't even started cooking it. It was from the thoughts of it. I just got heartburn thinking about it. I should have prepared it the day before, but I thought there would be two of us doing it. I should have done what my mind told me to do in the first place and got a caterer in to do it all. But the price of that gave me heartburn too.

I took out the chicken fillets and washed them. I dried them off and started to chop them. Five minutes into it I wanted to stop. But I had started so I had to finish. You would not believe how long it takes to chop thirty chicken fillets. One hour and seventeen minutes. Well, I had to cut them into very small pieces. If I never saw a chicken fillet again it would be too soon. I also chopped a chip of mushrooms, a mound of garlic and a net of onions. My arm stayed in the chopping motion for about a half an hour after it had finished chopping. I had no control over it. My clenched hand kept going up and down and up and down. Handy enough if I had anything else to chop, but after searching the presses I discovered that I had chopped everything choppable.

My eyes were watering from the onions and the despair I was in.

The house was a mess and I was hoping the 'black sack trick' would cure it. It was my magic trick. Anything that was not where it belonged got dumped into a black sack and shoved under the stairs. The place was spotless. The 'black sack trick' is fantastic. Sometimes the 'black sack trick' has a great secondary interest. If I forget to get the black sacks out from under the stairs as soon as the visitors are gone, I forget about them altogether until someone else is calling to the house and I have to deploy the 'black sack trick' again. I sometimes find sacks that have been under the stairs for weeks. It's brilliant. It's like getting a load of presents when it's not even my birthday or Christmas when I find a black sack that has been left under the stairs for a while.

The black sack area under the stairs also doubles up as a lost property area. When I thought I had lost my watch a while ago I looked in a black sack under the stairs and I found it. I hadn't lost it at all. Just cleaned it away. As luck would have it, when I was looking for the watch I also found my tickets for the Garth Brooks concert. I might never have found them before the concert if I hadn't put them in the black sack. Abby would have killed me if I had lost them.

On the day of the party I filled two black sacks. Books, nail varnish, a couple of forks, a vase, a packet of Alka-Seltzer (I made a mental note of these as I had a feeling I might be needing them after all the garlic I had

41

put into the chicken), two magazines and several pairs of shoes. Most of the shoes were Julia's. She leaves them in the hall all the time.

Danny arrived really early to give me a hand.

"The place looks great. What's cooking? Great smell. Jesus, you look shit! Were you crying?"

"Thank you, Danny. Thank you so much for that. No, I wasn't crying, but I just might go into a burst of tears right now. Just to keep you happy. The reason I look shit is that the place looks great and the feckin' chicken feckin' fillet smells so feckin' well. Two out of three ain't bad."

"You just look a bit blotchy, that's all."

"Well, if you had had to do to thirty chicken fillets what I had to do to them today you'd look a bit blotchy too. So now, Mr Bloody Perfect, you can get out the booze and the glasses. I haven't had five minutes to draw breath, never mind take a pee. I have to get myself ready. Oh, Jesus, what have I done? I should never have decided to have a party. It was a silly thing to do. I'm full of silly ideas. Suppose the whole thing is a flop?"

"Don't be ridiculous. It can't be a flop. It will be brilliant. Here, have a drink. I'll set up the bar and it'll be fantastic."

He did. He set up a little bar at the end of the sitting-room. I thought it looked tacky and spoiled how nice the place was looking. He said it was great and that everyone would love it. They did, of course. Particularly the friends of friends. They had no taste.

Julia arrived home just as I was getting ready to leave. I had decided to leave my own party. Not to stay for it at all. I had left everything ready for everyone to have a good time and I was just going to bow out gracefully. I was wrecked (because no one had helped me) and I knew I looked crap (because Danny had told me) and I had a terrible sense of foreboding (for no reason at all). I knew something was about to happen. I just didn't know what. I wondered would they notice if I just went up to bed and slept through it all? Knowing my luck some randy couple would find my bed and think they had hit the jackpot when they saw the potential for a threesome. I'm sure the fact that I would be sound asleep would only be a minor discomfort for them.

I was never so pleased to see anyone in my life as Julia that moment. There was one other moment in my life that I was desperate to see her. It was at her birth. I was truly never so happy to see anyone in my life as Julia at that moment too.

I remember thinking during the labour that if she managed to squeeze her way through my birth canal without the use of a miner's helmet she would be able to survive anything. I also knew that as soon as she squirmed her way out of my dilated bits they would be able to undilate and go back to normal.

The nurse giving me a running commentary on how far dilated my bits were was of no help to me. "Good girl, four centimetres. Well done!

"For fuck sake, only four! I've been lying here in agony all day dilating to the best of my ability and you tell me after all this time that it's only four? Could you not lie? Could you not say eight? Please, please lie! Take another look and lie to me."

"OK, another contraction. Ready with the breathing, good girl."

"Why don't we just call it pain, plain and simple. Let's cut the crap here. Cut out the major deception. Call it as it is. Pain coming, pain, pain, *p-aaaaa-i-n*!"

After that I kept quiet. Nothing like a good dose of pain to keep you quiet.

I knew as soon as the baby appeared the contractions would stop. I badly needed the contractions to stop. By that time I didn't care if my bits never undilated again. I just wanted the pain to stop. I reckoned I would never be using my bits again anyway. Never again. It might make me think twice before I let anyone near my bits again if I knew that it was still dilated. Especially if it was the full ten centimetres.

It didn't take that long for Julia to appear and put me out of my misery. She was a beauty. It didn't take all that long either for me to be delighted that all my bits were back to normal and I could enjoy using them to their best ability.

"Oh, Julia, Julia! I'm so glad you're here!"

"Happy Birthday, Ma! I'm sorry I didn't make it back

to give you a hand. I promise I'll serve the food and do everything for you all night. You just enjoy it."

"Oh, Julia." I burst into tears.

"You're worn out. You go up and have a soak in the bath. I'll take care of things here. Where's Danny? He can greet the people when they arrive. Now go on, get ready!"

I managed to clean myself up and look less blotchy before everyone arrived. I wore a red and white spotty halter-neck top knowing that if the blotches returned I would blend in with them.

I also wore my classy black trousers and bright red high shoes.

"Wow! You look fantastic, Ma."

"You look great yourself, Julia. Come on, let's party!"

"Hey! You both look great." Danny had learnt his lesson. I was hoping he wasn't just saying it. I was hoping I did look great.

I was, if not the hostess with the mostest, certainly a terrific hostess. I was only short of doing cartwheels, handstands and the splits all in the one go to please my guests.

They were all having a terrific time. I was making sure they did.

"Great party, Emma."

"This is the best, Emma."

"Well done, Emma!"

I was lapping it up. Danny was coping very well with

45

the bar. The night was a fantastic success.

"Ma, have you noticed Danny? He's tasting more booze than he's serving."

"Don't be so silly, Julia. He doesn't drink that much."

"Well, it's my guess he'll be pissed in no time."

"Now you are being silly."

I should never have spoken.

Without one word of warning – without even a nod in my direction – Danny got pissed out of his head. He didn't often get drunk, in fact he usually didn't drink all that much. But he certainly had a skinful that night and, boy, did he choose the wrong night to do it! If I had noticed earlier I could have stopped him. But the first inclination I had was when he fell over. Flat down onto the floor. He dragged a lamp down with him. It lay on the floor and shone onto his face like a spotlight. Everyone was waiting for him to sing or say a little recitation. I felt really sorry for him even though I wanted to kill him for making a show of me.

I stopped feeling sorry for him when he made an even bigger show of me. Right there and then, while sitting among the debris he had created. It wouldn't have been so bad if I was the only one within earshot. But he chose the very moment that the CD had finished. The Bee Gees, like the rest of us, were having a bit of 'Night Fever'. Belting it out and fair play to them. Everyone was standing around waiting for the next bit of music. There was a lull in the room.

A hush descended and Danny's voice ascended from the spotlight: "I feel so hemmed in and tied down, Emma!"

That was it.

His party piece.

It was a great party piece all right. He stole the show. Everyone was gobsmacked. Everyone was very uncomfortable. Not least of all, me.

Maybe if he hadn't gone for an encore it mightn't have been too bad. But just for good measure he continued entertaining the crowd. He could have just played the piano. So what if he couldn't play? The cringe factor would have been just as bad. But I might have been saved a big dose of humiliation.

"I just feel I'm too young, Emma! You know what I'm saying? I'm far too young to be tied down and I think I need to spread my wings and do a bit more exploring and travelling around before I buy into all the domestic bliss bit ..."

The big bastard. He had never done any exploring or travelling. In fact, he still lived in the same village that he had been born in.

Julia ran over to me. "Don't listen to him Ma! He's just a big bastard. How could he do this to you? How could he do this to me? Jesus, I'm so mortified. I going to tell him to get the hell out of here. Who does he think he is mortifying like this? Let me hit him, Ma! Let me at him!"

I had to grab hold of her to stop her. I had to put a lid on this whole mess. The loud whisper is the only thing that Julia finds threatening. She knows I mean business when I deploy the loud whisper. I leaned over and whispered loudly into her ear.

"Now listen to me, Julia. He might be making a show of us, but you sure as hell aren't going to join in!"

She turned to me to protest.

I cut her off. I went into a more threatening whisper: "Dust lissen to me, Dulia. Say noting. Asolutely noting. Kee smilin an I'll ge tru dis. If you can't dust say notin den ge u-stairs."

I said it all between clenched teeth. I wasn't sure if she understood me. We were like the ventriloquist and his dummy. Julia kept opening and closing her mouth. I was only glad I didn't have to ask her for a gottle of gear. God knows what she would have produced. She was raging. She was dying to give Danny loads, but fair play to her she kept quiet. Not that Danny made it easy on her.

"I love you and your violet eyes and your soft body and that cute bum of yours – I could eat you. But I can't do the whole 'til death do us part' routine. I love Julia, she's a miniature of you, you know. A little miniature. But I'd be a lousy father to her."

"I am going to kill him. I am going to slowly kill him. I am going to think of the most painful way to do it and I am going to do it. Because it is your birthday I will do as you ask and I will not do it tonight, but tomorrow he is a dead man. Do you hear me, Ma? He is a dead man."

I was a bit frightened by her, to tell you the truth. She was smiling at everyone as she was talking. She looked a bit unsettled.

"You know what I'm saying, Emma, don't you? You do, don't you?"

But all I knew was that every head in the place had been staring open-mouthed at him. Now every head in the place turned from him. They were turned directly towards me, me and Julia. Open-mouthed. What did they want? A return match. They were all waiting for me to serve Danny with the kick on the arse he deserved. I was powerless to do anything. Julia was holding her napkin in a very threatening manner. Her fist was clenched. Her teeth were clenched. She was getting into the attack position. I wanted to defuse the situation.

"Emma!"

All heads turned to Danny again.

"Yes."

Back to me.

"Tell me you understand."

Back to Danny again.

Back to me for my reply.

I felt I was in the singles final at Wimbledon. All heads were staring at me waiting for me to serve an ace. I couldn't let myself down. I thought this was a love match. The crowd held their breath. I held back my tears.

"Of course I know what you're saying, Danny." I used a soothing, relaxed voice that I didn't recognise as my own. My real voice was shouting in my head: *'You big bastard, Danny!'*

Julia was shouting in a whisper at me: *"The big bastard!"*

I looked at the crowd to make sure they had only heard my soothing chat. I was good at this. They were all fooled. They hadn't heard Julia either. She was good at this too. She must've got that from me.

"Sure, it never even occurred to me that you and I would have domestic bliss! I'm far too young to be tied down too," my soothing voice continued to the admiration of the audience.

'Especially to a big bastard like you!' the voice in my head was shouting hysterically now.

"Not to a big bollocks like you anyway!" Julia whispered to me.

Still no one heard. The crowd let their breath out. I still held back my tears. All heads turned to Danny.

"I bet you want to call me a big bastard, Emma?" He knew me too well.

"I bet Julia wants to call me a big bollocks?" He knew her too well too.

And with that Danny passed out. There was no point in talking to him any more so I didn't. It would have been easy to form a queue and play a party game. Pin The Tail On The Donkey. Danny could be the donkey and we could use a very sharp instrument to pin his tail on. We could have lots of goes at it. It would be great fun. Julia would have loved it.

I was so hurt. I was gutted. Any moment I felt I would go deep into a huge cry and never come out of it. I could have cried my eyeballs out into a pool of tears. Maybe that would have been a good distraction for people. I could have cried endless tears and drowned myself in front of everyone in the salty water. Give them more free entertainment. A party to remember.

"Hey, come on!" I shouted as I saw the little clusters of people just standing whispering together. "This is supposed to be a party. One drunk does not a party make. So fill your glasses. Put on some music someone, I feel like dancing and singing. Hey, did you hear the one about –"

My best pal, Abigail, grabbed me by the arm and whispered in a very loud whisper to me. The loud whisper thing was catching on at a great rate. Very soon no one in the room would be talking normally.

"Shag him! Now, you don't start telling jokes and singing and dancing and doing the all round, all singing, all dancing, all entertaining Emma just to distract everyone and make them have a great time! Just let it go. Leave it. For God's sake, Emma, don't start. Just leave it. There's been enough of a peepshow for everyone without giving them extra value for money. You've supplied good food, good wine and a bloody stand-up comedy routine by Danny – what more do

they want? They've got their money's worth."

"Emma? Emma? You wouldn't want to tie me down, sure you wouldn't?"

All heads turned again to Danny.

Then back to me again.

I still said nothing. I couldn't. I was far too upset.

Maybe it had something to do with the fact that I had been expecting a sparkler from the drunk on the floor for my birthday present. He didn't know I was expecting a diamond. I thought he would surprise me with it. I could have told him my favourite diamond in every jeweller's shop in Dublin. I had taken to diamond-gazing. I was torn between a solitaire and a three-stone, depending on how much he was prepared to spend. Either one very large diamond or three very large diamonds. I didn't mind which. Any diamond would have made me happy. Large diamonds would have made me very happy. When it comes to diamonds, I like large.

So he surprised me all right.

He struggled up off the floor to come over to me. He missed me and flopped into an armchair. He passed out again and this time he stayed down.

"Come on, everyone! I thought we were here to have a good time. Get the music going." Abby took control.

I started dancing. Wild exotic dancing. A mix of salsa and belly dancing. I was really letting go. I stood in the middle of the floor and gave it my all. I tried to do an impression of a happy person. A person who wasn't humiliated. A person who didn't want to just grab her boyfriend's balls in one hand and twist them until his eyes watered. I had the need to do physical damage to him. I was wondering if I'd get away with dancing over beside him and, in a dramatic dance-move, kick my leg up in the air and get him right on the chin. Do a quick twirl with my arms stretched out wide and slap him in the face. If I twirled really quickly I could get him twice.

"Abby, I think I am going to do severe damage to Danny. He is not safe. Keep me away from him."

But it was Julia who stopped me. She knew exactly what to do. She put on a Garth Brooks song and we were off. Abby and I hooked our thumbs into our bra-straps and pushed our heels out in front of us. We were brilliant line-dancers. Electric slide and all.

"Look at him." Julia shouted over the music. "I could easily give him a dig and no one would notice. He's a sitting duck."

"Leave him," I whispered. I looked at the sitting duck. He was slumped in the chair and there was a cute half-smile on his face.

We left the sitting duck in the armchair all night.

I wanted to leave him there forever to rot. But Abby said he'd start to smell after a few days.

Anyway, he got up the following morning bright and early and brought me breakfast in bed. There was a small, black, square jewellery box on the tray.

"I'm so sorry Emma. I made a fool of myself and you.

Please forgive me. I drank too much and I overheard someone say that it was about time we got married, that we weren't getting any younger. I just panicked. I love you. You know I love you, don't you? I should have given you this yesterday, but I didn't get a chance."

He handed me the little square box. I nearly melted. Who couldn't forgive him?

"Don't mind them. Of course I forgive you. You had too much to drink and you're not used to it. I love you so much."

I put my arms around him and he was such a good kisser and he loved kissing my boobs and he was so good at it. He loved looking at me and touching me. Before I knew what had happened he was in the bed beside me. I wrapped myself around him and he kissed me long and hard.

"You're beautiful."

He was always telling me I was beautiful. God help him, I think he believed it. He rolled over on top of me and he watched me as he made love to me. He loved watching me. He came quicker than he wanted to. He said he wanted to last all day. He held me and ran his hands all over my body. Touching me. Feeling every bit of me. Kissing and touching me everywhere until I couldn't stand it any longer. I was on the verge of fainting. Inside my head was going black. I felt the rush of pleasure he was giving me all over my body. I was beyond all control now.

Then at last it was over.

"Jesus, you're good!" I said as I kissed him.

"I know."

We laughed and then I went to open the little gift box.

"Hey, Emma, will you –?"

Holding the box, I said, "Yes, yes, yes. I will!"

"Thanks. I'm having a shower then. I'll be ready in no time."

He jumped out of the bed and ran into the shower.

"But, but ... wait, I haven't even seen the rin –"

I could hear him singing.

This was not how I had imagined it.

I had imagined him down on bended knee. Pushing the ring onto my finger. Me admiring it. Me crying. Him nearly crying. Us kissing.

I opened the box all on my own.

The most beautiful pair of earrings shone back at me. Sapphire and diamond. Really large. Really beautiful. I started crying.

Danny came out of the shower. Whistling.

"I feel human now."

"You were asking me something before you went into the shower, what was it?"

"Will you give me a lift home? That's all. Did you not answer it. I thought you said you would."

"Bugger off!"

"What?"

"Go on! Bugger off out of here!"

"What the hell is wrong with you?"

"Nothing. I just want you to bugger off and never come near me again."

"Jesus, what have I done? Everything was all right just before I went into the shower. What changed?"

"I shouldn't have forgiven you so easily for last night."

"You know what, Emma? You are just weird."

He glanced down at my hands. I was still holding the open box. I could see the penny drop, the light come on, the clueless bastard copping on to what had happened.

"I'm not as weird as you," I said. "Will you just go? Go on, bugger off!"

So he did. He just buggered right off.

I have to admit I expected him to put up a bit of a fight, but he didn't. A decent bloke would have put up a fight for me. Would have done anything to be with me, but he just buggered off into the sunset. I was broken-hearted. I could actually feel the break. If I had been able to get a plaster cast on my heart it would have been fine. It would have been healed in six weeks. It took a lot longer without the cast.

Only for Julia and Abby I'd never have got out of bed that day. I'd still be there.

This was the first time I'd seen Danny since then. The first time I had seen him since he broke my heart. Wouldn't you imagine he'd have the good grace to be even a little bit embarrassed?

But he wasn't. Maybe that was because he had been right all along. The timing was wrong. He was right not to propose back then. It was nice to see him again. It was nice to have him sitting beside me at such close quarters on a plane, our legs touching. Our arms tight up against each other. Shoulder to shoulder. All the old electricity came charging back through me again. I tried to keep my feet on the ground, but they were tingling. All my bits were tingling.

He noticed I was awake again. "Well? Will you have dinner with me?"

He obviously thought the statute of limitations was well up on the buggering-off bit. God, he was cute!

Why not? I thought.

"Why not? That would be lovely. I'd love to go out to dinner with you."

"You still haven't answered my question."

"I just did. Yes. I will go out to dinner with you. I just said I would."

"Not that question. The other question."

"What question was that?"

"Are you attached?"

"Nope."

Which was, of course, a lie.

I was attached to Ronan. Ronan had been the man in my life for the past eleven months. From the moment he appeared at the door of that client's house and I thought he was the statue-man, I liked him. It wasn't quite love at first sight. At first sight it was a very healthy like-a-lot. It definitely was love at second sight. The second time I met him he was dressed semi-casual. Jeans and a jacket. He was wearing a white shirt. He has a penchant for white shirts – so do I. The second time we met he called to collect me and we went out for a drink. It was good fun. We talked for ages or should I say I talked and he listened. We had a good laugh and then he offered to drive me home. Julia was away. Need I say more? I couldn't help it. He couldn't help it. We were parked outside the house and I could see all the net curtains twitching in the neighbours' house. I could see everyone looking out to see what I was up to. So I did the decent thing and asked him in for coffee. We never got as far as the kitchen. We did not pass the stairs. We went straight to the bedroom. I was charmed with myself that it wasn't too messy. Although I don't think he would have noticed what state the room was in he was in such a state himself. So over the next couple of hours we discovered that we had a lot in common.

I like sex, he likes sex. I like eating, he likes eating. I like sex, he likes sex. I like cinema and theatre, he likes the same. We both like sex. Sex is a very important part of our relationship. For the first couple of months after we met it was sex first, talk later. Then as time went on we started having little conversations before sex.

"Hi, Ronan, how was your day?"

"Fine, Emma, how was yours?"

"Fine."

"Jesus, you look fantastic!"

"God, you're a ride!"

"Do you fancy it?"

"Do I what? Like mad I do!"

Then we'd both fall into bed and bonk the bones off each other.

When we got to the stage where we were staying overnight in each other's houses we started doing all the normal things. Long in-depth conversations, watching telly, going for walks and then we'd fall into bed and bonk the bones off each other.

Up to a month ago that was pretty much how wonderful it all was. How wonderful we were together. We were very firmly attached. We were having all the fun in the world.

We did have a good balance. We weren't attached at the hip, every night of the week. Only some nights. The nights he stayed over with me. The nights I stayed over with him. It was safe and exciting. He was steady and reliable. He was good for me. He was good to Julia. The sex was great. What more could a girl want? What more could a mature sensible woman who had fallen madly and completely in love with the man want?

Lots. I wanted lots more.

We had a good thing going, Ronan and I, just before I spoiled it. Just before I got greedy and wanted more. I made a big mistake. I'm always making mistakes. Big ones, little ones. Mistakes and men.

We were together changing the sheets on the bed. Each of us standing safely with the bed in between us.

"What would you think about us moving in together?" I pounced the question on him.

"Us? You mean us? As in you and me?" He was pointing at himself and then at me over and over again.

"No, us as in you me and the whole Manchester Untied team if they'll come with you."

"Live together? You mean you and me live together in the same house? Like a couple?"

"Well, that was the general idea. I thought we already were a couple."

"We are, we are. But you mean a couple type of couple."

"Is there another type of couple?"

"Well, yes, there's the dating couple, the living-together couple and then the really extraordinary couple – the ones who get married."

"I take it you don't want to be one of the really extraordinary married type of couples?"

"Steady on. You've only just mentioned about the living-together bit and now you want to marry me!"

"I never said that. You were the one who brought up marriage. But at least now I know where I stand on that score."

I shook out the duvet cover and started shoving the duvet into it. I was doing it a bit too violently. The quilt wasn't going in the way I wanted it to. Nothing was reaching the corners. Nothing was working for me. Everything was going against me. I pulled the whole thing out again in a temper. I held the top two corners of the duvet and took a dive into the duvet cover.

"Now you're getting all upset. Just because I'm not ready to get married."

"Upset? Upset?" I shouted from inside the duvet cover. "What gave you that idea? Fuck this fucking thing!"

"Here, let me do it."

"Bugger off. I have it done now."

"It's just a bit of a shock that you want to get married, that's all."

"For the last time. I don't want to get married. I was just asking you if you thought it would be a good idea for us to live together. It was a simple question. If it bothers you, we needn't do it I just wanted to see what you thought. It's no big deal."

"Well, it sure as hell is a big deal now! It must've been a big deal for you to ask me in the first place. I had no idea you were thinking like this. I didn't think either of us was ready for that sort of commitment. It's something I thought we'd talk about in a year or two."

I finally got the duvet right. It was taking a bit longer to get the moving in together bit right.

"Right, right, forget I asked. It was a silly thing to do."

"No, it wasn't. It's just that it's a big step. We've only

61

been dating for a short while. We should think about it. Will we do that? Will we think about it? Isn't that a good idea? I think that's the best thing. Let's leave it for a bit and if we both feel that moving in together would be the right thing to do well then we can do that, in a year or two. I can't understand how you're thinking of this now, all of a sudden."

"Well, it's not all of a sudden really and Madame Celeste thinks the timing is right. Timing is so important, Ronan."

"Who the hell is Madame Celine?"

"It's Celeste. Remember my horoscope woman. Look!"

I showed him:

Madame Celeste
Scorpio
October 23 – November 22

The timing is just right. Romance is in the air. If you've been thinking about a change on the home front, now is the time.

"That's a load of mumbo-jumbo. I know you like to read it, but I don't believe in it. Anyway, that could refer to changing the colour of the loo paper or the colour in the hall."

"I don't think Madame Celeste would waste her time talking about loo paper or paint. I can see you're not taking this very seriously. I shouldn't have said anything. I thought you'd be delighted."

"I'm delighted that you asked me."

He put his arms around me and gave me a hug and for a tiny second just as he was kissing me I thought he was going to change his mind. I thought he was going to tell me it was a terrific idea. I thought he'd move in bag and hopefully not a lot of baggage by the next morning.

"I am really delighted that you want us to live together. I do think it's a terrific idea, just a bit too soon. As for Madame Celine, I'd prefer if her mumbo-jumbo wasn't a factor in our major decisions. We don't even know her."

"It's Celeste and I know her very well. I have known her for years. Actually I know her longer than I know you. By the way, that will be the last time I'll ask you to move in with me. I will never ask you again, ever. The next time it can be your big idea."

I punched the pillow and imagined it was him.

I was pissed off with him.

So I put all thoughts of big white fluffy, meringue-type dresses out of my head and tried to continue along the way we had been.

I was gutted. I pretended I wasn't too upset because I didn't want him to bugger off. But I really should have told him where to go. Things changed. Not for him, for me. I couldn't get over the fact that he didn't jump at the chance to live with me. We had been drifting along ever since then. I should have had the guts to finish with him and salve any bit of dignity I might have had.

But I am not great at finishing affairs or anything else for that matter. I hate letting things go. Saying good-bye. Breaking hearts. So I plod along hoping things will turn out all right in the end.

Now we were only loosely attached, Ronan and I. We were so loosely attached that I was thinking he'd just dangle off completely soon and we'd become detached altogether. I was hoping that we wouldn't become totally detached. I was hoping that if we did become detached it would be very gently. That we would just drift away slowly from each other so that neither of us would notice. Neither of us would be broken-hearted or inconsolable. I couldn't do the whole broken-hearted thing again.

Now we were in a rut, a furrow. Ronan didn't know we were in a gaping furrow. I was the only one with that privileged information. I was finding it tough to forgive him for not moving in with me. I needed something to get me out of the rut.

I wanted commitment. He chose caution. Maybe I should try a bit of excitement. A romantic gesture. Maybe this would be the answer – I could have a bit of excitement for the both of us only with someone else. Maybe inject a bit of romance into my life. So what if it was with the wrong man? It could even improve my relationship with the right man no end. It could cure my need for commitment. So I wouldn't be doing anything wrong. I certainly wouldn't be doing anything to hurt Ronan. I'd never do that. In fact, it could be a really great thing to do for him. In fact, I'd be doing a really good thing for our relationship.

Jesus, I'm so good sometimes.

CHAPTER FOUR

"I'm home!" I shouted as I threw my suitcase down onto the hall. I pulled the HEAVY tags off it. They had really screwed me for excess baggage too. For someone who travelled as much as I did, I really hadn't got the knack of packing. I always brought too much with me. Shoes to match every ensemble and an ensemble for every day and every night.

It wouldn't be so bad if I didn't buy stuff everywhere I went. Tons of stuff. Most of it was for work. Bits and pieces for various clients. If I see materials I know will look well on a job I know is coming up I buy them there and then. It's partly the reason my business is such a success. I have a knack of picking the right thing for the right place. It has taken me years to get my business to the success story it is now.

It started when I bought a house. Up to then I had been renting and it was a total waste of money. Also, I felt I could do nothing to it. It wasn't mine to chop and change the way I wanted to.

Then one day when I was driving back from town, there was a big tail-back of traffic. To avoid sitting in the traffic jam for hours I took a turn off onto a little side road that would eventually bring me out onto the main road again but way ahead of the traffic. At least that was the intention.

Halfway up the side road I saw a *For Sale* sign on a wonderful house. I stopped and got out. It appeared run-down and uncared for. But there was a charm about it. It was obvious that, at one time, it had been much loved by someone. There were all the little tell-tale signs. A hand-painted sign saying '*Welcome*' had fallen down and was lying neglected on the ground. Pink, scented climbing roses formed an archway over the door. They were overgrown, but the smell was amazing.

I made an appointment to view it and next day went there with Julia.

All the interiors were well worn, but they had been well looked after at one time. All the furniture and fittings came with the house, though no one in their right mind would want any of them. But I was taken with all the fine details. The little window seat where I imagined children sitting watching for their mother or father to come home. The little markings on a post outside the back door with heights and dates nearly worn out now. Faded marks on the walls where pictures had been hanging. There was a feeling of love inside the house. This had been a happy home. I loved it instantly.

"I suggest you use the old furniture as firewood." The poor estate agent was nearly embarrassed showing me around the house. You'd think the poor git had lived in and neglected the house himself.

"Who lived here? Do you know?"

"A lovely old couple. They reared a big family in this house. The old couple are in an old folks home. They didn't want to burden any of their children by living with them. They wanted to be independent. If you ask me they didn't want to be readymade baby-sitters. The children fought with them to come and live with one of them, but they said no. Now they want to sell this house. They'll never come back to it. They're a nice old couple. They have one stipulation to the house being sold though."

"What is it?"

"It's a bit weird and normally we wouldn't agreed to any stipulations, but they are such a nice couple and they are old. Just call us suckers, but we agreed. They want the house to be sold to someone who's perfect for it. It's been on the market for a while. I don't think they'll ever let it go. No one will ever be perfect for it."

"And who's to say who's perfect?"

"That would be me. Look! I have other properties in the area I could show you."

I wondered, if I gave him a quick shag would he think I was perfect?

"How do you know who's perfect?"

"Well, if I think you're perfect I go back and tell my clients all about you and they make the final decision about accepting your offer. I have to tell you your offer is very much lower than a couple of others we have received and they didn't take those."

"It's all I can afford."

"Mammy! Mammy! Look at me!" Julia was calling me.

The estate agent guy and myself went out the back to Julia. She was sitting on a tiny little garden seat. It was as if it was made for her. On her head was a big floppy straw hat. Her face was hidden. The hat was right down to her chin.

I heard a strange noise behind me. I turned around and the estate agent guy was in convulsions. I thought I would have to do mouth to mouth. Then I realised that the guy was just laughing. Laughing at Julia. I started to laugh myself.

"She's perfect. Just perfect!" he said.

So I got the house at a bargain price and all because I have a perfect daughter.

I stripped and painted anything made of wood. I threw nothing out. Lots of the furniture was hand-made. I cleaned and covered everything. The finished house was a total transformation. Everyone that saw it went mad about it.

Then my friends started asking me to help them revamp their houses. I loved doing it. Spending other people's money and transforming mediocre houses into fantastic houses. I didn't charge my friends, but they always gave me lovely gifts when I had finished. But most important of all, friends of theirs saw the job I had done and asked would I do theirs. I did, but this time I charged a fee. I got most of my jobs by word of mouth. I have been working constantly ever since. I still work by word of mouth and I'm busier than ever. I don't have to watch every penny any more.

I dragged my case into the living-room and opened it. Stuff vomited out all over the floor.

"Hi, Ma!" Julia flung her arms around me and I gave her a hug.

I had missed her and I was delighted to see that she had missed me. "Hi honey – well, did you miss me?"

"Loads."

"I'm glad to hear it. So, come on, give me all the news. What have you and that boyfriend of yours been up to while I was away?"

Julia had been dating Colin for about eight months.

He was a weed. Weeds are two a penny. He even looked like a weed. He was about nine feet tall – well, not quite nine feet but as near as hell to it. Put it this way, if the circus came to town he was guaranteed a job. He had spiky red hair and had decided to put black streaks in it. He was like one of those oranges you see on food displays at parties, the ones with the cloves stuck in them. He liked the designer stubble, but to have the designer stubble you have to have stubble in the first instance. The designer fluff didn't have the same effect. He grunted at everyone and had a mesmerising way of walking. He put his right leg out and his right shoulder went with it – his left leg and the left shoulder went with that. I was always hoping he'd have to run some day when I was around, but short of me shouting at him to leave Julia alone, which I was often tempted to do, I never saw him run. I regretted that. It would have been fascinating.

Julia was too nice for him. It's not that I am foolish enough to think that she is too nice for any bloke, just this one in particular. There was nothing about him I liked. She loved everything about him. What could I do?

"I have loads to tell you. First, how did the trip go?"

"Great, but you tell me your news first."

I was hoping she had dumped Colin.

"Colin was a total toe-rag to me. I had a huge fight with him the other night."

My prayers were answered. There is a God.

"In fact, I nearly dumped him, but I just couldn't. I didn't have the heart to finish with him."

"Well, if you feel you should then you should. You have to be cruel to be kind sometimes."

"It's OK now. We made up and he's so cute."

Oh you foolish girl! Where did I go wrong? Maybe I shouldn't have led by example. I was a very bad example for her where men were concerned.

"It was all over something so stupid. I had to go to a party in college and he didn't want to come with me. He wanted to go to the pub with the lads and watch some stupid football match. I was being silly. I ended up going on my own and meeting up with him afterwards. "

I wanted to tell her that it was mean of him not to go with her. But mothers can't always say what they think.

"I don't think that's silly, in fact I think it was mean of him not to go with you."

There are certain times when mothers have to say what they think.

I try, God knows I try, not to say what I think, but I never succeed. Especially when I think Julia needs to hear what I have to say.

"I was so furious with him. I wanted to ring you. I wanted you to be on my side. I knew it would have been stupid to ring you about a silly little row so I sat on my hands for a solid hour to stop myself. Then when I gave up and decided to ring you my hands were so numb from sitting on them that I couldn't push the buttons on the phone so I couldn't ring you."

"Oh, honey! Poor you! I wish you'd rung."

"Abby came to the rescue. She called at the right time for me and the wrong time for her. I poured my heart out to her."

"I bet she was delighted she called – she would never think it was the wrong time."

"She was great. She brought me for pizza and ice cream. She just sat and listened while I ranted on and on and then cried a bit."

"Abby cried a bit?"

She laughed, I knew she would.

"You know Abby – as soon as I started crying she started. So the two of us just sat there crying. Then Abby said 'Oh shit! This isn't at all what your mother would do is it?' So she wiped away her tears and tried to be you."

"Was she any good at it?"

"Well, she could've done with a blonde wig, but other than that she was fine. In fact, she was better than fine. Abby put on a voice like yours and started telling me jokes and had me laughing in no time."

"Hi, you two! What's that you're saying about me? Good trip?" Abigail came in and gave me a hug.

"Great. Paris has to be the most wonderful place ever."

"Well, it's the most romantic anyway. Pity Ronan wasn't with you. So no romance for you then." I saw her winking at Julia.

"Well, now that you mention it. You'll never guess who I met on the plane."

"Oh, Ma, do we have to guess? I hate when you do this. We haven't a clue who you met, just tell us."

"Yeah, Emma. We're wrecked so just get on with it. By the way, we missed you."

"So I hear. Thanks for stepping into my shoes."

"It was a pleasure." She smiled at Julia.

"I made dinner for you," Julia said.

"What culinary delight is in store for me?"

"A delicious lasagne, even though I do say so myself."

"I'm starving. I might have to have two pieces."

"Abby, do you want some?"

"How can I resist? But first I want to find out who your mother met. Come on, Emma, tell us."

"Danny."

"Danny!"

"Not our Danny!"

"Yes, our Danny. Him that does the great party trick. He asked me to have dinner with him."

"And you being my sensible mother said no thanks very much and have a nice life."

"Well, eh!"

"Oh shit. You didn't? Did you? You agreed to meet him. Oh shit, Emma, will you never learn?"

"Abby, you say shit far too often. Ma, I can't believe you agreed to meet him after all that shit we went through before. Me and Abby had to pick up all the pieces after that big bastard buggered off. We won't do it again, will we, Abby?"

"Most certainly not."

"Well, you won't have to because this time there aren't going to be any pieces. I know exactly what I'm doing."

"What about Ronan?" Julia chipped in.

"What about him?"

"Well, do you think he'll like you going out to dinner with someone else? Don't hurt him, Ma. He's too nice for you to treat him badly."

"Look, Ronan won't mind. I'm just meeting an old friend. What's wrong with that? What can Ronan possibly think is wrong with that?"

"Just make sure you know what you're doing."

"Well, I think I do. Anyway, Ronan said he wasn't ready for commitment. So now he can have a taste of what an uncommitted woman does without a commitment. Maybe this will make him sit up and think. I was the one who was all set to buy the big white meringue dress and whisper 'I do' or at least share a tube of toothpaste with him. He was the one who didn't want to. Well, now he'll just have to suffer the consequences. What is it with me anyway? As soon as I get ready to commit to a guy he gets cold feet. What's wrong with staying with me for the long haul?"

"Maybe it's not you. Maybe it's the guys."

"Ah, no. I've heard that one before. But the common denominator is me. What do you think it can be?"

"This is all getting a bit too serious. Come on and rummage in that huge suitcase and show us some of the things you bought in Paris."

I always brought Julia and Abby something back whenever I was away.

"Here, this is for you." I gave Julia a bottle of her favourite perfume. Kenzo. It was her trademark.

"And one for you." I gave Abby a bottle of Estee Lauder – Beautiful. She had worn it for years and it suited her. She was beautiful. I was so lucky to have a friend like her. She was the sister I never had. She had wonderful pitch-black hair. Shiny and silky. It fell just to her shoulders. Her dark brown eyes were always sparkling. She had a sallow complexion and was a natural beauty. "Here, Abby. Try this." I threw a snow-white halter-neck dress at her and she ripped off her top to try it on. She was like a child. But her body was all woman in the halter-neck dress. I didn't envy her fabulous figure. I could never envy her. I just wished mine were as good.

Julia clapped her hands while Abby modelled the dress up and down the room.

"You might need these."

I threw her a pair of strappy white sandals.

"Oh, Emma, you're too good. I love it. I love all of it. Thank you. Wait until Geoff sees it. He'll be drooling."

"And this is for you, Julia."

I pulled out a parcel and she tore at the paper. There were layers and layers of tissue. A turquoise dress with little shoestring straps. She pulled off her clothes and pulled the dress on. It was as amazing as I knew it would be. It was covered in tiny little violet beads. All hand-sewn. All glittering as she moved. I gave her another parcel and she was thrilled at the matching sandals and bag. All covered in the same tiny violet beads as the dress. Her face lit up as she twirled to show Abby and me how she looked.

She looked magnificent. She swept her long blonde hair up onto her head and twirled again. Smiling. She was still tanned after spending her Easter break in Crete working in a resort hotel and having fun. The only student to owe more money than she earned when she finished working. She was a free spirit, but nothing is free. So someone had to pay for it and it was always me. But I didn't mind. Isn't that what all us parents do? I just wanted to know when it would all end.

I had visions of myself at a hundred years of age still handing out money at a rate of knots. I could not even contemplate a life where the only one I had to pay out for was me. When I could do what I liked with my own money. I suppose she was thinking that she couldn't wait to earn her own money so she could do what she liked. So the two of us would be happy. Her with her money and me with mine, all mine. I wouldn't even need her to pay me for board and lodgings. The savings I'd make by not having to give her money constantly would be enough for me. It would make me a very wealthy woman.

I knew that one day soon she would fly the coup. But she had two more years in college to do and I knew she'd be around for at least that time.

"Oh, thanks, Ma! It's terrific. It must have cost you a fortune." She hugged me.

"Well, only a small one and you're worth it."

"I know. What's this?" She was picking up a big square box.

"That's for Ronan. It's a fantastic globe. He'll love it. It's pewter and enamel. Now look what I got for myself."

I dug down deep into the case and pulled out a large painting. It was modern.

Just a deep canvass of shapes. Misshapen shapes. All exactly the right shape. All in exactly the right place. A wild mix of colours. In the bottom right-hand corner there was a big blue dot. I am not an artist. Because of my job I have to have a knowledge of art, but it is limited. I am not an expert. I know what I like. I liked this. I felt this was special. Daft as it sounds it was as though the artist was baring his soul to me alone on the canvass in paint. It was full of passion and very intimate. Two things I liked.

I would have sold everything I owned just to have it. But it was a bargain. It should have been way out of my reach. I just happened upon it. I thought I was meant to have it. I had wandered into a little curiosity shop in Paris. It was in the Pigalle district. I had just climbed down the steep narrow streets from Montmartre. I had spent a stolen afternoon watching the artists painting in the square. I saw some bits and pieces in the window of the shop that I thought might be nice to have in store for my work. I went in.

The little shop was packed with souvenirs and tack, but it was good tack.

There on the floor, leaning against some ugly-looking stone replica of the Eiffel Tower was the painting. I picked it up and stared at it. I was staring at it so long it came to life. For some inexplicable reason I started to cry. It was a bit embarrassing. A big grown woman like myself brought to tears by a painting. It made me feel lonely. All the familiar, strong colours and gentle brush-strokes. Blue. Violet. Turquoise. Vermillion. Wild.

"Wow!" Abby stood staring at it now the same way I had been staring at it in the shop. Seeing the same passion I saw.

"It's fantastic!" Julia saw more than the two of us put together. She had the advantage of looking at it with the same free spirit as the painter.

We hung it on the wall alongside another painting by the same artist. Yes, I already owned one. I noticed the other painting had a matching big blue dot in the bottom left-hand corner. They were a pair. They belonged together.

We opened a bottle of wine I had brought from Paris and sat eating delicious lasagne, salad and garlic bread while gazing at the two paintings.

Danny had bought me the first one years ago. It was on our trip to Vienna. He told me it would always remind me of a time when I was happy. It did. I nearly told him when I met him on the plane from Paris that I had found another one. But I didn't. He'd have wanted to see it. I wasn't ready to share it with him.

I showed Abby and Julia the other bits and pieces that I had bought in Paris. A wonderful black skirt with a hem like a switchback railway. A black and red sexy strappy top to match. Red sandals finished the ensemble. I was a bit plump, but it looked good on me. Well, at least Abby and Julia thought so.

Abby was my best friend in the entire world. She had seen me through thick and thin. Although I was rarely thin. Not for the want of trying. I was just born plump and was supposed to be plump. It was just the way things were. I'd see a doughnut. I'd eat a doughnut. I'd see a bar of chocolate. I'd eat it. I loved food and I loved cooking and Julia loved cooking. She loved me eating what she cooked. I was her mother and it was my duty to eat each and every delicious calorie she cooked.

Even though we were mother and daughter we had grown up together. I was only nineteen when I had her. She was never a mistake. OK, so she wasn't planned, but once I saw the cute little button she was, I was smitten. I dressed her like a doll and delighted in bringing her everywhere with me and teaching her things. She was a quick learner. I was always glad I hadn't given her up for adoption.

Her father was a year older than me, but still only a child to be a father. We adored each other. We mistook it for love. It was passion. It's easy to mistake passion for love when you're only learning about it and eager to experience it. The passion could have turned to love if we'd been given half a chance.

He was stunning-looking. He had cheekbones any woman would envy. We got married in the smallest little church in Dublin. St Finian's. It was a very small wedding. My parents, his parents, his best friend who was also his best man and my best friend who was my bridesmaid. It should have been intimate and romantic. It wasn't. I was two months pregnant as I marched up the aisle.

It took him about three weeks after the wedding to realise what a big mistake we'd made. It took me a week longer. We would have realised it even sooner except that his parents gave us a two-week holiday in Benidorm as a wedding present. It's hard to realise you've made the biggest mistake of your life while lying on a sun-soaked beach in foreign climes.

It was the first time I was on a plane and I puked all through the journey.

We had a great honeymoon. The hotel was fabulous.

The sex was uninhibited. Once I got on the plane home I puked again. I continued puking for the rest of the nine months. Not only in the morning, but in the evening and night too.

Alex, my poor unfortunate husband, didn't know what to make of it. He asked his mother what she made of it and his mother told him exactly what she thought of it.

"She might be looking for a bit of attention. She should be over all that getting sick by now. It would be better for her if you didn't fuss. Just ignore her."

We mothers have a huge influence over our children. We don't even realise the impact we have. How easy it is for us to sow little seeds of doubt in our offspring's minds and hearts. How important it is for us to only sow seeds of love. It is our duty to make our children responsible for their actions not to back out of any consequences of those actions.

Alex's mother was different. She was a law onto herself. Maybe she thought she was only using the law of the jungle. Protecting her young at any cost. But she smothered Alex. He had a wonderful shot at happiness with me and a terrific daughter, but before he had the chance his mother took it from him. Filled him with doubt and cut the balls off him at every opportunity. I know the law of the jungle too. It applies to grand-children as well as children. Alex's mother was a peculiar breed. She had no gra at all for her first grand-child.

I am a bit wiser now than I was then. I have come from the school of a past filled with mistakes. A great learning curve. I try not to dwell on past mistakes, not to make the past be my future, but my past has shaped me and I cannot shrug it off that easily. Nor do I want to. Sometimes I take comfort from it.

I often wonder would we have made a go of it if I had been wiser way back then. If I hadn't believed that everyone has at least a bit of goodness in them. Even if that goodness was buried deep. I believed it was there somewhere in everyone only looking for an opportunity to escape. I think I waited too long for the goodness to show itself in Alex's mother. It was buried so deep you'd want a water-diviner to find it. God help her, she thought she was doing the best for her son. Maybe she was. She thought he'd been trapped. Maybe he was trapped. He was a free spirit, he was only a kid. But I was a kid too. Two of us had tangoed. Two of us had created a life. Was only one of us to be held responsible?

Maybe things would have turned out differently if Alex had been encouraged a bit more. If he'd got the support he needed. The same support my parents gave me. The silent tower of strength that they both were for me. But Alex's mother was vocal. Very vocal.

"Make your stand now, Alex. You've been trapped into this marriage. I only hope this baby she's expecting is yours and that you're not being taken for a ride."

It was the bloody ride that got us into the mess in the first place.

"It could be anybody's child, you know. I hope you found out for certain if it's yours," she said one night when she thought I couldn't hear.

"Of course it's mine. Don't let Emma hear you saying that."

But I did hear. In those days, in my innocence, I always kept my ear to the ground. I got to hear everything about everyone and loads about myself that I didn't like. I don't have my ear to the ground so much any more. It's kinda painful with your ear to the ground. You hear things you shouldn't. Sometimes you hear things that squeeze your heart.

The first time I heard Alex talking to his mother about me my poor heart was squeezed tight – big time.

"She's just tying you down. I think you should come back home to us for a while and see how it goes. I'm not telling you to run away altogether. I'm just saying don't be wasting your life. I want you to go to college. Everything I wanted for you can still happen. You just have to talk to Emma. She'll understand. She can go to her parents and you can stay here until you finish college, then decide what you want to do. I honestly thought you'd do better than this, Alex."

"Look, Ma. I'm trying to do my best for everyone. Will you just give me a break? I don't know what's right any more."

The rot started that day. He was starting to waver. I thought I had married a man. I had only married a kid.

It's tough being pregnant and devastated. I should have confronted him there and then. But I was pregnant and I'm a coward. If I confronted him I would have had to do something about it.

His mother was always there for Alex. She called to the house often to see him, sometimes with his father in tow. Whenever I left the room to make tea or puke she would give Alex the benefit of her small little mind. She had a loud voice. I always heard her. My heart squeezed each and every time.

"You should be out playing football and training, son. You're far too young to be cooped up indoors night after night. Make your mark now. Emma will understand you need to get out and about. It's ridiculous that job you've taken. Working in a pokey little gift shop is no sort of work for you to be doing. It was fine for summer holiday work, but not as a full-time career."

"I like what I do, Ma. I work in the biggest craft centre in Dublin. I have a good salary and I enjoy it. What's wrong with that?"

"You'll never make anything of yourself. I still think you should go to college. I know, I know you'll say you don't have the money to support Emma and yourself and keep this house and go to college, but you know your father and I will support you. Isn't that right, Harry?"

"Of course we will support you in any way son. But

your first priority should be Emma and the baby when it arrives."

"Oh, keep quiet, Harry! What do you know?"

And poor Harry, so used to a lifetime of keeping quiet did exactly that, kept quiet. Maybe if he'd started speaking out when he was younger he would have been well practiced at it by now. Maybe Alex would have been able to speak up to his mother now if he'd ever seen anyone else do it. But Harry's gentle manner was easy to squash. He made a stand once though. It was for me and Julia.

Alex didn't stay around for the birth of our child. In fact, he was on the other side of the world when Julia was born. Harry, on the other hand was outside the delivery ward the whole time I was giving birth and was one of the first people in the world to see Julia. He took her photograph when she was only a few hours old. I know how difficult it was for him to be there.

"Let her follow her dream, Emma, and you make sure to follow yours. It's a little life you have there in your arms. It's precious. You'll turn around one day and she'll be all grown up. Give her love and values to hold on to and she'll be able to fly, to soar above all the mean-spirited do-gooders and find her own spirit."

He pushed an envelope into my hand with a cheque in it and written in a scrawling print on the outside was:

Let her soar and fly, Emma –
love Harry (Grandad)

I kept the envelope. I gave it to Julia on her thirteenth birthday. The money is long spent. The sentiments on the envelope kept me going on many a sad and lonely day. Sometimes, when I had nothing else to cling to I held tight to that envelope.

I wished Harry had been allowed to find his spirit. Maybe when he was younger he should have shared his dream with his wife. Maybe she'd have listened. Maybe she would have helped him. She didn't realise he had a dream. She never realised he wrote beautiful poetry, that he had a magical way with words. She found all his poetry after he died. It broke her heart that she never knew. Maybe Harry was wrong to keep quiet. A lifetime of maybes.

I loved him. I cried for days after he died. Julia was only six months old. I cried for the loss she would have in her life from not knowing him. I cried for the loss of the last thread of contact between Alex and me. I cried because I knew that with Harry gone Alex would have no knowledge of his daughter's life. He'd never get in touch with me to ask. That would be the brave and moral thing to do and Alex was neither brave nor moral. I hoped that age would change him and some of Harry would rub off on him and that someday, somehow he'd contact Julia. I hoped that some day he'd want to know if she had a dream.

It made me sad that Julia never knew Harry. I knew she would have liked him. But that's the way life goes.

She never knew Alex either. Some things we have control over and others we don't. Some things we should make an effort at. Some things we leave too late.

CHAPTER FIVE

Madame Celeste
Scorpio
October 23 – November 22

Watch out today for objects of desire. Remember they are only objects. There are more important things than objects.

"Hi, Emma, any news?" Abigail had called in after school.

"Nothing much. I have to watch out for objects of desire today so I hope you have brought me at least one."

"Sorry, I only brought myself."

"And a very nice object you are too, if not an object of desire."

Abby worked in the local school and had been Julia's favourite teacher. Her husband, Geoff, was the headmaster at the school and they usually travelled in and out to work together.

"What are you doing here at this time, anyway? This is a pleasant surprise. You look great. You give me a pain in the ass. I look like crap."

She did look great, stunning even, but she looked a bit paler than usual. Her eyes looked tired and I couldn't help noticing little dark circles under her eyes. Like smudged eyeliner. She never wore eyeliner.

"You OK?"

"Yeah, I'm fine."

"Well, how did the last day go?"

"Great. The kids were all talk about where they were going on holidays, Florida, Africa and God knows where. Does no one go to Spain for a fortnight any more?"

"I'd go if I got the chance. So where's Geoff?"

"I got a lift home off one of the others today. Geoff stayed behind to sort a few things out before he turns his back on the place for the holidays."

She sounded bland and uninterested.

"Are you sure you're all right?"

"Yeah, I'm fine."

"Could you be a bit more enthusiastic? You're on your holidays."

I worked from home and so I was never on holidays. I never had time off and when I did, I felt guilty that I wasn't working. Working from home is a 24/7 job. Only a crazy person would do it.

"Do you want to go to the cinema tonight?" I asked her.

"Yeah, but only if you drive. I'm knackered."

"Of course I'll drive."

Abigail was distracted, even a crazy person like me could see that. I started to put away all the bits of material and sketches I was working on off the table.

"Did I show you these?" I held out the pieces of material.

"They're nice." She was miles away.

"They're the ones I got in Paris."

"That's nice."

"I had to sleep with the fabric guy to get the samples. I had to bonk him for hours. Him and all his brothers."

"That's nice."

"His father and two sons."

"That's really nice."

"I think even a few uncles."

"Nice."

"I drew the line when he brought in his wife and all her sisters and behind them a herd of camels."

"Very nice."

"Abigail! Abby!"

"Oh, I'm sorry, I was miles away. What were you saying?"

"Nothing – just talking about my sexual escapades and you missed it."

"So I missed nothing!"

"Look, let's have a coffee before we go – we've plenty of time."

"That'd be nice." She was back to 'nice' again. Her voice was too even.

Normally when I offered her coffee she complained that I only offered her instant.

I decided to brew some fresh even though she hadn't asked for it.

She watched me going through all the motions. Coffee in. Water in. Wait.

She didn't even notice that I had a small carton of cream to put into the coffee.

This was serious. A lot more serious than I thought.

"Spill your guts."

"What?"

"Come on, Abigail. I've known you most of your adult life. I know when something's wrong."

"You know me too well. But, to be honest with you, I don't want to think about it and if I talk about it I'll only think about it and I don't want to."

"Not even to me?"

"Not even to myself."

I poured the coffee.

We drank it. In silence. Wherever Abigail was in her head she wanted to be alone. But not quite alone. She wanted me to be there with her but silently.

I sat for the longest time in complete silence.

I went through a mental list of things that I wouldn't have minded being wrong with her. The usual suspects with Abby were:

1. She'd been invited to a party and didn't know what to wear. But her wardrobe was even fuller than mine.

2. She'd broken another nail. I checked her nails. They were all present and accounted for.

So it had to be something else. By the look of her I was guessing it was a lot more serious than I would like.

I ran up the stairs and into Julia's Room. I stopped dead in my tracks. Someone had been in it and ransacked it. There were clothes everywhere, hanging out of everything. Clean and dirty all hanging around together. Make-up was strewn on every available surface. Sticking to the mirror was a yellow post-it.

'DON'T TOUCH ANYTHING, MA.'

I didn't often venture into Julia's bedroom. Whenever I did, I got an overwhelming urge to clean. Which just goes to show how bad it was because I hate cleaning. With a passion. Julia hated when I cleaned. She said she liked doing it herself. She never did it.

I opened the only drawer in her room that was closed. I sorted through the various bars of chocolate and picked Abby's favourite. I made sure to close the door on my way out to cover my tracks. Also I didn't want anything escaping from her room. I didn't want the dirty clothes to get the idea that now the door was open they could all pick themselves up and come down the stairs and throw themselves into the washing machine in a desperate effort to get clean.

I ran down the stairs. Abby was sitting exactly as I had left her. She hardly noticed I had gone.

"Here you go, Abby, this'll make you feel better."

"Thanks, that's nice."

When Abby hit rock bottom she hit it with a vengeance. There was no talking to her when she was at rock bottom. You just had to sit it out. Wait until she was ready to deal with whatever it was that had brought her that low. The only way to deal with it was to wait for her to start talking. I would just have to sit it out because I could see she was at rock bottom, again.

I was also hoping that it wouldn't be a repeat of what happened a few years ago. Apart from all the hassle for poor Abigail, I didn't know if I'd be able for that horrible mess to repeat itself. Call me selfish, but I really couldn't go through it again. As for poor Abigail, it would kill her altogether.

The whole incident had been terrible. It seemed to drag on for days. It all started when Abigail found a pair of knickers at the end of her bed. Not all innocent on the top of the duvet, but hidden away. Tucked up inside the bed, at the end of it. She was distraught. She rang me and I couldn't make out what she was saying.

"Oh, Emma, Emma, what am I going to do? I found a pair of knickers."

"And?"

"And they're not mine!"

"Whose are they then?"

"That's the problem. I don't know whose they are."

"Do you want to come over?"

"I'm on the way. Jesus, what will I do?"

"Just come over and we'll sort it out together."

To my horror and surprise she brought the offending knickers with her. To call them knickers was an exaggeration. A knickers should have two sides and a gusset. These had only one side, a front side, and it was tiny. The rest was all string.

Thanks be to God she had put them in a clear freezer bag. She put them on my kitchen table and stood there with her arms folded and her face as long as the piece of knicker-string. She started stabbing the air, pointing at the knickers.

A fly flew past. The bloody thing had been bothering me for days. I couldn't swat it. I had tried everything. The marks of my shoe-heels were still on the walls from where I had tracked and hunted it one day. I think it had come out of Julia's room. It was too robust to have come from anywhere else. Obviously it had been living in grave conditions to have got that robust.

I was hoping the poor unsuspecting fly would fly past Abby any time now. It would have been great timing. Abby was stabbing the air at a wild rate. If he came by now he would meet a sorry end. He would be stabbed to death. He would be impaled on the end of Abigail's very well-manicured nail. I wondered if she would even notice the poor dead fly's body on the end of her nail. We could have laid him out beside the knickers. We could have had a legitimate crime scene. The knickers were already looking like evidence. Exhibit A. The dead fly could be Exhibit B.

"Well? Well? What do you make of those?"

I didn't know what to make of them.

"What do you think?"

I didn't know what to think. I didn't even know what she wanted me to think.

"Well! Are you just going to stare at them? Have you no opinion at all on them?"

"Well, I honestly don't know what else to do only stare." And pray for inspiration.

I had no opinion on the knickers except that they were expensive and sexy. All silk triangle that there was of them. They were a wonderful shade of midnight blue. There was a tiny diamante bow on the back. These were a knickers to be worn with nothing else. An outfit in their own right. An outfit that would only look like an ensemble on the right arse. A small arse.

"Well? What do you think?"

"God, Abby, I don't know what to think."

"Well, you must be thinking something."

"I'm actually thinking that I hope I say the right thing to you. That's what I'm thinking."

"Well, rather than the right thing I'd prefer you to be your usual blunt self. Don't start going all nicey-nicey on me now. This is my hour of need for fuck sake. Don't desert me now. Exactly what are you thinking? I don't care how bad a thing it is you're thinking. Just tell me what it is."

She was pointing her finger at me this time. Stabbing at the air close to me. Very close to me.

"Well, exactly what I'm thinking is … that it's a small arse fits into those knickers."

I thought this might have made her laugh, even giggle a little bit, smirk even, but it didn't even merit a smile.

"I'm thinking the same thing myself. Now what would they be doing in my bed?"

"Are you sure they're not yours?"

"I wish they were."

"What are you thinking, Abby?"

"I'm thinking someone's been sleeping in my bed and it's not Goldilocks. I am also thinking that Geoff better not be the Big Bad Wolf. If that horny bastard has even looked at another woman he's dead. Dead. Do you hear me, Emma? I'll have his balls. Imagine it. In my bed."

I just couldn't imagine it. Geoff was a nice guy, if a bit ordinary and predictable. He even had a bit of a pot belly. Geoff was what I would call safe. Tweed sports jacket, grey trousers, blue shirt, plain tie. The sort that you could bring home to Mammy and she'd be pleased as shit with his pensionable job and his clever way with money.

Now there is nothing wrong with safe and predictable. It can keep you warm on many a frosty night. Safe-and-predictable never forget to pay the phone bill or the heating bill. Safe-and-predictable are great for the long haul. You could do a lot worse than safe-and-predictable. Abby could do a lot worse than Geoff.

You could set your watch by everything Geoff did. He left the house at the same time every morning and returned at the same time every afternoon. He mowed the grass on a Saturday and played golf on a Sunday. He went to the driving range on a Wednesday. He went to the library on a Friday. Not that I watched Geoff all that much, but Abby filled me in. Funny thing is Abby never noticed how predictable Geoff was. If he was out playing golf on a Sunday she'd tell me he was playing golf. She'd say it as if he had only just taken up the hobby. As if it was an impulsive act on Geoff's part, but Geoff had never done an impulsive or spontaneous thing in his life.

I once asked Abby if they had sex on the same day of every week. She told me not to be so ridiculous, that they had it whenever they wanted it. But I didn't believe her. I bet they had sex on a Monday, Tuesday or Thursday. They were the days that Geoff did nothing. Well, nothing I knew about anyway. Geoff was a safe bet. There was safe and then there was Geoff.

Safe is good. Safe is where you feel someone loves you so much that they wouldn't allow man or beast to harm you. Nor would they harm a hair on your head themselves. They minded you and because they minded you so well you just wanted to mind them right back. You aped them. I liked safe. Geoff was very safe about himself and that's the bit I didn't like. I liked it for Abby because she loved it. It worked for her. She liked the fact that he wouldn't do anything exciting or out of routine or out of the ordinary.

"What will I do if it's Geoff?"

"Don't be ridiculous, it can't be Geoff. He'd never do anything out of his routine."

"What routine? Geoff doesn't have a routine, does he?"

"Well, he might have a little routine going in his life. He likes things the same all the time. He'd never do the likes of this – it's too spontaneous."

"How else do you explain it? The turd, the toe-rag! He's dead. Dead. Do you hear me? He is so, so dead."

"You're not being rational, Abby. Geoff wouldn't have the balls to have anyone in your bed. He's not that stupid. It's something else. There is a perfectly good explanation and it isn't Geoff."

"I will have his balls, Emma. I will have them on a skewer if he has anything to do with this. The evidence is overwhelming."

The thoughts of Geoff's balls on a skewer was doing

nothing for my stomach which was feeling very sick looking at a pair of knickers that weren't mine displayed on my kitchen table. It was a very good table. I had slogged and saved for months to buy it.

I was also thinking that not a lot of women would find Geoff attractive enough to be in bed with. I didn't want to tell Abby this. I wouldn't hurt her feelings. I was thinking that if it was him I would have to do a whole rethink on the type of man Geoff was. Maybe the tweed jacket and the timetable were a cover-up for a wildly passionate man. Maybe our Geoff was a bit of a dark horse. A bit of a raver in the bedroom department. I know he always pleased Abby in that department and she had a fairly hefty appetite. She always said he was a good ride. I decided now was not the time to remind her that he was such a good ride.

"If it's not Geoff, then who else could it be. Rip Van fucking Winkle?"

"What about one of the boys? Would they belong to one of the boys?"

"Well, if one of my boys wears these, good luck to him. Anyway that wouldn't explain how they ended up at the end of my bed. It would also mean I had done a terrible job as a parent if I didn't notice one of them dressing up in women's clothes before now. They are definitely women's, aren't they?"

"Most definitely. Look! What I mean is, could one of the boys have used your bed when you were out? You know, taken a girl in there and had a bit of fun with her and she went off bare-arsed with no thong between her legs. Not noticing she had left her knickers behind. After all there's not much of them to miss now, is there? So, instead of it being Geoff, why couldn't it be one of the boys doing what you think Geoff was doing?"

"Are you joking? Are you for real? These are my boys we're talking about here. There is no way I want to even think about them doing that. That's disgusting."

"Maybe one of them got carried away in the heat of the moment."

I couldn't believe that she was perfectly willing to believe Geoff had a woman in their bed but was totally unwilling to believe it could be one of her boys.

"I hadn't thought of that. Well, I suppose that could have happened. So what do I do now? Do I confront them? Jesus, that's disgusting that they'd use my bed. What's wrong with their own?"

"Well, for a start yours is a double bed and they all have singles."

"Yeah, that, added to the fact that no self-respecting girl would even enter one of their rooms. The poor bitch would need a map to find her way beyond all the mess of dirty clothes, dirty books and dirty magazines."

"Well now! There's your answer."

"No. It still doesn't make sense. I don't believe it."

Abigail had four boys. All stunning-looking like their mother. Girls had been known to parade up and down outside the house for hours in a very put-on nonchalant way in the hopes of bumping into one of them.

All Abigail's boys had done well. They were clever and hardworking and genuinely nice guys. The oldest, and my personal favourite, Dylan, had lived a charmed life. Good sportsman, great student. He had studied pure Mathematics in college.

A month after he got his degree he was spotted by a modelling agent. They liked his rugged good looks, easy smile and firm muscular figure – didn't we all? They made him an offer that his mathematical brain couldn't refuse. He reasoned it would take him two lifetimes of working with figures to earn the figure they were offering him for showing off his own figure to full advantage. He was good at modelling. Abigail encouraged him – after all he had his degree and could always get a "proper" job if the modelling didn't work out, she reasoned. She still got all excited when his picture was in any magazine. She had scrapbooks full of him.

It never went to his head. My Julia made sure of that.

Julia and Dylan were inseparable when they were young. Julia was a little bronze, blonde-haired baby. She wore frilly dresses and frilly knickers. I put bows in her hair. At five she was a pretty young girl. Chocolate-box pretty. She had long blonde curly hair. She wore short skirts, matching tops and canvas ankle boots. Then at eleven something happened. At eleven Julia started her 'I am master of my own destiny' phase. It was to last exactly three years. If someone had told me it would only last three years I would have blissfully ignored it and let her get on with it. But I thought she was in it for the long haul.

Part of being master of your own destiny requires you to wear the ugliest clothes possible. You also have to have short hair. If possible it should be streaked with exotic colours. Pink, red or orange. When Julia was fourteen I went through the 'battle of the hair dye' phase. I wouldn't allow her to put anything in her hair except shampoo. How was I to know you could get coloured shampoo?

Everything Julia wore when she was eleven, twelve and thirteen was baggy, everything looked old and everything was black. Dylan thought she was great for wanting to be master of anything, especially her own destiny. She persecuted him for any old clothes he had grown out of and fair play to him he gave them to her. I never forgave him for that. He was a terrific friend to Julia and I knew she talked to him about things she couldn't talk to anyone else about. I loved him for that.

"Well, I don't believe it." Abby was adamant. "None of the boys would do that to me. Think about it, Emma – they are all really decent kids."

"Less of the 'kids', Abigail. They are all adults. Maybe they got carried away in the heat of the moment. You don't know."

"Oh, but I do know. If they just got carried away

they'd have gone into the guest room downstairs. There's a double bed in there and it's private. Why would they use my bed?"

"Well, if the guest room was in use by one of them, I suppose one of the others could have used yours. God, Abigail, you could have a right little knocking shop going on over there and never suspect a thing."

"Jesus, you don't think that really, do you? A knocking shop! I hadn't thought of that. Oh my God! What am I going to do? This could be worse than I thought."

"I don't think you have a knocking shop, Abby. I was just trying to bring a bit of levity into the situation."

"I really don't think this is the time for levity, Emma. My life is falling apart. I have found a pair of knickers in my bed and you talk to me about levity. Get a grip, will you, Emma. You're supposed to be my friend."

"I still think it's one of the boys."

"The boys being rampant sex maniacs is not the explanation. I feel there is something else. Something obvious that we're missing."

"Well, anything is better than it being Geoff, isn't it?"

That night she confronted Geoff.

"Do you know who owns these?" She held out the offending knickers. They were still secure in the bag. I was only delighted they had left my kitchen. I thought she was going to ask me to hold onto them for safe keeping.

"Well, do you know who owns them?"

"You?"

"That is the wrong answer. I would like to think you'd recognise my thongs, Geoff. Try again."

"Well, it's very hard to remember them all and anyway there is no one else in the house who wears them."

"That is precisely my point, Geoff."

"Well, I don't know whose they are."

"Do you want to know where I found them?"

"Well, I suspect you're going to tell me. I don't like the tone of this conversation by the way. How the hell would I know where you found them or whose they are?"

"In our bed."

"What? Who put them there? That's disgusting."

"I was hoping that's what you'd say. Do you promise it wasn't you? That you aren't having an affair and using our bed?"

"How can you think such a thing? I think you're losing the plot here, Abby. It might have been one of the boys though, have you thought about that?"

"Yeah, it's a horrible thought, but I suppose it would be better than it being you."

"Look, boys will be boys!" he said and laughed.

"I don't know what you find so funny. Your boys might be boys, but my boys will certainly not be boys."

"Well, I think you should leave it. Say nothing."

"No, that's too easy. I'll bide my time. I will wait until

they are all together. All sitting around the table for dinner or something. Then like Marvin the Magician I will pull out the knickers and dangle them in front of their astonished faces and let the investigations begin. I will confront them, Geoff, make no mistake."

"Ah come on, Abby. Let it lie. You'll only cause the lads to be embarrassed and for what? It's not as if any of them are too young to be responsible if they are sleeping with women."

"Well, I'm going to get to the bottom of it, if you pardon the pun. No one, except me, is having sex in my bed."

"Not even me? Listen, leave it to me. Let me have a word with them. Man to man. I'll sort it out. I won't even mention the knickers. I'll just tell each of them that our room is out of bounds. What do you think? It's the best way to deal with something like this."

"Are you sure? I think doing my magic act would be much better."

"Well, I think that will get you nowhere."

"Right! Do what you want to."

"I promise, I'll sort it out, I promise. Now come here and get into bed. It's my turn to show you something! I was thinking you should get one of those diamond thongs yourself. You'd look terrific in it. I could have great fun getting it off you."

"Once I was the only one you were gettir, any off."

"You're the only woman for me, diamon¹ thong or no

thong. Come on, give me a kiss."

Abby gave in. I was disappointed.

I was enjoying the idea of her magic act. I had been hoping for a ringside seat.

We didn't have to wait long before The Curious Incident of the Knickers in Bed, or CIKB (pronounced 'sick-bee') debacle as we called it, was finally put to bed. We didn't need Agatha Christie or Morse. It was solved when the culprit made a mistake. A second one. Bigger and better than leaving their knickers behind.

It was unbelievable stuff. Only I was there myself at the time I'd never have believed it.

If I had only known what would happen that day I'd have stayed in bed, my own bed. Pulled the duvet up over my head and slept through it all. Instead I was in on the horrible nightmare.

Abigail and I had decided to go shopping. I had made a mental note not to go into any lingerie shops. This was a big sacrifice as we always treat ourselves to a nice bit of underwear when we go shopping. But as the purpose of the exercise was to help Abby forget her worries and not to dwell on them I decided that anywhere that sold thongs was out of bounds.

As I arrived to collect Abigail from her house the cleaner was just letting her self in so she let me in too. I liked Martina. She was always friendly and bubbly.

"Hi, Martina."

"Hi, Emma. Beautiful day isn't it?"

I'd been in that much of a rush I hadn't even noticed. She was right though, it was a beautiful day.

"Yes, it is isn't it? A terrific day."

"You waiting for Abigail?"

"Yes, we're going shopping."

"Abigail! Emma's here!" she shouted as she ran halfway up the stairs.

With that Abigail came down the stairs.

"Are we off then, Emma? Under starter's orders. I mean to do some serious damage today. Hi, Martina, how are you this morning? Would you be a pet and peel a few potatoes before you leave today. I'd be very grateful. I'm going to be home late."

"Oh, that's no problem." Martina took out a box of cleaning equipment from under the stairs and an apron off a hook. She put it on over her very tight jeans. She was wearing a tight little pink T-shirt that she was obviously intent on keeping clean. She was in her late twenties and was a mature student. She came to Ireland from Croatia as an au pair for one of the teachers in Abby's school. She wasn't here too long when she discovered that she hated minding children. She was very unhappy. She was great at organising and cleaning. So she returned to college and cleaned a couple of houses a week to keep her going financially. Abby was very good to her. She gave her generous bonuses and birthday and Christmas gifts. Abby felt sorry for her so

110

far away from home. She had been working for Abigail and Geoff for about six months. She was good at her job.

"Right then, Martina. Is everything good with you today?"

"Yes. I am fine, Abigail, thanks."

"I left your money on the press in the kitchen, Martina. Dylan is here, still asleep, so you needn't do his room. He has a photo shoot in town later this morning. The rest of the boys are upstairs in various stages of getting ready for work. They'll be out of your hair in no time. Geoff is in school even though it's a free day. He's preparing for the open day in the school tomorrow. There's lots of stuff in the fridge for your lunch. I'll see you on Tuesday."

We hit the shops – big time. The plastic was flying – big time. Do you know how hard it is to avoid thongs? They were everywhere. I was worn out avoiding them.

We were laden with bags when we finally admitted defeat. Neither of us could walk another step.

"Hey, Emma. I have an idea. Instead of going in somewhere crowded for lunch why don't we get fish and chips and bring them back to my house to eat them. We could kick off our shoes and really relax."

"Well, I'm shagged and I've spent all I can so I think that's a great idea."

"We'd better get Martina some fish and chips too. I'd die if she got the smell of them and I didn't bring her any. It'd be terribly mean. Maybe we'll open a bottle of wine, really push the boat out."

We let ourselves and the cod and chips in. They were dripping with salt and vinegar. I dumped my bags in the hall and went straight into the kitchen with the chips. I put on the kettle.

Abigail dumped her bags beside mine. She was bursting to go to the toilet and she went rushing up the stairs. It was then that I heard all the running around and screaming. I ran up the stairs and stopped dead in my tracks. Abigail had stopped dead in her tracks just ahead of me. Martina was running up and down the landing in a midnight-blue thong with a diamante bow at the back. Exactly the same as the one Abby had found in her bed. It looked absolutely amazing on her. Her body was golden and soft. Her breasts were firm and she had huge nipples. I was gobsmacked. I wanted to giggle. She kept running up and down as if there was something chasing her. She looked so silly. Maybe if she'd stopped screaming she wouldn't have looked so silly.

So she was dusting and rubbing more than the fixtures and fittings. I just kept staring at her. So did Abby. Apparently Abby had come up the stairs just as Martina was coming out of the bathroom. The poor girl took one look at Abby and took off like a woman possessed up and down the landing. Not knowing what to do. She just kept doing it.

We held our breath wondering which one of the boys

she had been with. Abby's bedroom door was open. The next thing I noticed was Geoff at the bedroom door.

"What's all the commotion. What's going –"

He stopped dead in his tracks. He was stark naked. Bollocky naked. Naked as a newborn.

He just stood staring. From his wife to the nearly naked woman, Martina.

His mouth was opening and closing, but nothing was coming out. I nearly felt sorry for him. I'd say he was sorry I was there.

"Hi, Geoff." I thought I should be polite to him in his own home no matter what the circumstances.

He nodded in my direction. He couldn't wave. He was holding his two hands, crossed almost religiously across his dangling willy. No doubt lamenting how quickly it had gone from one extreme to the other.

"Get out! Get out!" Abigail started shouting at Martina.

"What the hell? What's going on? Jesus, what's all the commotion?" Geoff found his voice at the same time Abby found hers.

He really looked so silly standing there with his belly hanging out and his dark chest hair sprinkled with grey. He looked like a raw pastry man about to be cooked. All he needed was three little raisins down his belly. He was trying to hold it all together. I bet he was trying to hold it all in as well. It was very undignified for a headmaster. He was afraid to move his hands. Really, being honest about it, the naked body can look awfully silly some-times. Geoff's looked silly.

It really depends on the circumstances. When you're actually participating in sex or about to participate it looks fantastic. You get to see all the dangly bits in a wonderful light. When all your hormones are all in tune and all your loins aching for a great session with a partner the naked body looks terrific.

I'm not saying that a perfect naked body hasn't got the potential to look great. But how many perfect exam-ples of the naked body are there? Even then it only looks great when poised or posed in a certain way. Even the perfect example of nakedness looks silly doing some things. Running is one of them. Bits flying everywhere. Martina looked silly. Small and all as her bits were they were still flying about a bit.

Geoff too looked really silly even though he wasn't running anywhere. I don't know why he was bothering to hide his willy at all. Everyone had already had a good look at it except me. I had only got a quick glimpse of it when he first opened his door. What would it matter now if I got a good look at it? I was dying to see it. I was dying to see what he had that would entice this young girl to want it.

Martina ran into the bathroom. She locked the door.

Abby started banging on the door.

"Get out of there, you slut! Do you hear me? Get out of there and out of my house!"

"I did nothing!" Martina shouted back.

"With nothing on."

"Please, don't be angry. We didn't mean any harm. We were only having a bit of fun."

"Fun! Fun! I'll give you fun. Geoff, stop standing there like a guard on duty. Get some bloody clothes on and give your prick a rest. I want her out of there. Do you hear me?"

Abigail marched down the stairs.

I marched down after her.

A few minutes later Martina marched down.

I couldn't help but notice that she was carrying the apron.

So the Curious Incident of the Knickers in the Bed was finally solved.

The culprits were caught redhanded and bare-arsed.

Poor Abigail went through a terrible time. Even though it was blatantly obvious to all concerned what was going on, Geoff denied it. He told a bare-arsed lie. Even though Abigail had a witness: me.

Geoff was really upset. Abby was absolutely gutted. I was in a state of disbelief.

So gutted was Abby that she made Geoff move lock, stock and barrel into the spare room. She made him tell Martina they no longer needed her. Either to clean the house or give him a shag on the shag pile or a bonk in the bed or a ride on the rotary line whenever the fancy took him. He was also sworn to secrecy.

"You're no example to your sons. I don't want them to know about this, do you hear me? Not until I decide to tell them. They'll think it's open season on having a shag with everyone and anyone. Here we are trying to drum a few morals into them and you're playing away from home in our own home."

Geoff did all she asked. He protested his innocence throughout.

"I swear I did nothing. Absolutely nothing. As God is my witness, nothing happened. I am an innocent man. I don't even know how she got onto the landing. She appeared from nowhere. I only saw her when you did."

"Well, Emma was a witness too and I think there is no denying that what she saw was you having an affair with what would appear to be the ultimate feather duster."

"Well, not exactly, Abby – I just saw her in her thong and him in the nip."

"Exactly."

"I swear nothing happened. Sure what the hell would a man of my age want with a slip of a thing like that? For God's sake!"

"This is not the first time, is it Geoff? How long has it been going on?"

"I think I should leave." I felt very uncomfortable.

"You'll go nowhere. Are you on his side now? You are the main witness."

"No, I was just being an independent witness."

I didn't want to stay. I didn't want to be a witness.

Witnesses have a habit of disappearing. I wanted to disappear.

"Abby, will you listen to me? I came home with a thumping headache and got into bed. I've been in bed ever since."

"Listen to that, Emma, he's admitting it."

"I'm admitting nothing. Will you listen to me?"

"It better be good, Geoff"

"I never saw Martina or anyone else in this house until you started shouting. As God is my witness I came home with a raging headache. I took two tablets in the kitchen and then came up here and got straight into bed. I never even knew she was in the house. She certainly never hoovered while I was here."

"And you want me to believe that. Only an idiot would believe that. Emma, you don't believe it either, do you?"

"I do. I believe it."

"Emma, you are such an idiot sometimes."

"Well, it sounds like something that might happen."

"To think I paid her good money and all the time she was shagging him! She must've thought she had won the Lotto, getting paid so well."

"Why won't you believe me, Abby?"

"Why would he make up a story like that?" I tried my best to convince Abby that he was innocent.

But Abigail could only believe what her own eyes and my own eyes saw.

"To cover his arse. Pity he didn't think of covering it a few hours ago. I don't believe a word of it. That's it, I'm finished. Why don't you just admit what you were doing?"

"I'm sick of being accused of something I didn't do. I won't admit to doing what I didn't do. I didn't do anything. How many times do I have to tell you what happened?"

"You have to keep telling me, Geoff, until you get it right."

"Are you sure he did it? I'm not convinced. How can you be so sure?" I asked her later when he wasn't around.

"Well, I saw what I saw. You saw it too."

"What are you going to do?"

"The bed will be the first thing to go. My skin crawls when I think of it."

"I think that's a good idea. Get rid of the bed and the thong. But what about Geoff? You won't throw him out too, will you? I think you'll only regret it."

Fair play to Geoff. He kept up the 'it wasn't me' routine for weeks. He never deviated from his story.

"He says he's sorry. It's no good, I just can't look at him right now. He says I should know him better and he can't believe that I think he did it. He says he's never looked at another woman. That he loves me. Says at his age he's blissfully happy and that he'd be a lunatic to look at a silly young girl when he has me. He keeps talking about his age. I know I'm being weak. I know I should shove him out and tell him not to look back, but I don't know if I could cope without him. This is all I know, Emma. Him and me and the boys. It's a package. I bought into it. I can't give it all up just when it all goes belly-up, can I? The boys would be affected too. If only he'd admit it, we could deal with it. But it's just hanging there."

"Well, I think you're doing the right thing. Don't give up your family lightly, Abigail." She was hurting badly.

Sometimes when you're not the one directly hurt you can be even more hurt. I was hurting for my pal.

"It hurts, Emma."

"I know. He's probably hurting too. You know you can always count on me. I'll support you and help you anyway I can. Except financially, of course." I joked. "Just don't turn your back on me because I know too much, will you?"

"Never."

And there it was. The true value of each of us to the other. She wasn't afraid that I knew her deepest darkest days. She knew I'd never throw them back at her. Deep dark days are like diamante thongs and objects of desire – they should never be thrown back at anyone, least of all your best friend.

As far as I was aware that was the one and only time Geoff had strayed. As far as I knew Geoff had kept his pecker in his trousers ever since then except when Abby requested the pleasure of its company a few times a week. It took a while for her to make the first request after the CIKB, but he won her over. Also the fact that she was a very sexual woman and she began to feel that if she didn't have a good ride soon she'd hang herself. Rather than leave the boys with the mess of her suicide to cope with, she and Geoff had a ride and a half.

He was a terrific husband and father now. Maybe he always was, but it took something like the CIKB mess to bring out the best in him. It had also made Abby see how easy it would be to lose everything she had worked hard to build. She knew how fragile life was. How families can be devastated in a moment. She just never thought it would happen to her little family.

CHAPTER SIX

So, was Geoff up to his old tricks? Or had he learned a few new ones? I sat in silence drinking my coffee. Abby hadn't touched hers. I looked at her. Tears were rolling down her face.

I held her tight.

"There, there, hun. Cry if you want. Don't bottle it all up. Let it go."

"Oh, if only it were that easy. I can't. I can't." She gulped for air. Gulped again.

I held her wrecked body. There is nothing as bad as holding someone who is so desolate that their own body won't hold them up. Something eerie and lonely about feeling all that pain knotted in someone's body. Feeling it unravel and seep from them into your very being. Any heart would break.

"Come on, hun. Cry it all out. Get rid of it, Abigail.

Tell me what it is. I'll never talk about it if you don't want me to, just don't bottle it up – let it go."

"Oh, Emma. I can't talk about it. If I talk about it it will be a reality. I just can't. Can you understand?"

"Of course I can. I'm Emma, I understand everything."

So I held my pal closely to my heart and rubbed my hand along her hair. Soothing. I loved this woman so much. Not in a physical sense – two tits too many for my liking. I loved Abigail the same way I loved my parents and my daughter. Wonderfully platonically. There was a certain freedom about it. Never having to preen, pluck or puff just because she was coming over. There is no physical letting off in our friendship. No venting of energies. Just the spark and sheer light-headiness of the secrets and the baring of souls instead of bodies. It is mostly easier to bare your body than your soul. Maybe Geoff had only bared his bum again.

And then she whispered so softy I barely heard her.

"I think Geoff is having an affair again."

"Ah, no, Abigail!"

I was right then. It left an awful taste in my mouth. I didn't like being right in this case. I took no pleasure in it.

"Yes. I think he is."

"Are you sure?"

"No, I'm not sure. I wasn't lucky enough to find knickers in the bed this time. This time it was a telephone call."

"Go on."

"No. I can't. It's too awful. What am I going to do?"

"Well, I'm sorry to say it, Abby, but first you've got to make sure that he is having an affair. I really think he learnt his lesson after the CIKB."

"I know, but when you hear what happened you'll know what I mean. A woman rang from the Damison Hotel and said she needed to check the details on Geoff's credit card in order to book the special suite he wanted."

Well, then that was that then. Nothing could be more obvious. Was the man all balls and no brain? Had he learned nothing?

"Well, now, it'll be all right, you wait and see." I was trying to comfort her. This was the last straw altogether. I tried to give her some hope, something to hold onto while she got used to the idea that he had blotted his copybook again. It was very hard to find anything. Even a straw would have done.

"Look, Abby, the Damison Hotel is one of the best hotels in Ireland. He'd never do anything silly there. Maybe he had to go up there for some conference for the school or maybe he's playing golf and forgot to tell you."

"It's not school stuff, I'd know about that. He'd tell me if he was going off with the lads playing golf. I never stopped him having golf trips, so why wouldn't he tell me about that?"

"The Damison is awfully posh, you know. It's the lap of luxury. Maybe he thinks it's a bit of an extravagance for a golf trip and is building up to telling you. Or maybe he simply forgot."

"Or maybe he doesn't want me to know he's going or who he's going with."

"Ireland is a small place, he'd be an awful gobshite. Someone will see them if he's taking someone off for a dirty weekend. Even the Lesser Spotted Geoff will be spotted by someone. People talk. The rare sighting of Geoff with a chick on his arm will be noted. You won't have to wait long before some well-meaning do-gooder anorak gets in touch with you to tell you they just happened to bump into Geoff and his lady friend. Geoff knows that. Unless he's a total prat, you're wrong."

"Maybe he didn't think it through."

"I don't think so. Do you think that it could be for you? That he could have booked the room for a very romantic weekend away with his darling wife."

"He never bothers his arse to bring me to places like that so why start now? If it is me he's bringing, it's to cover a guilty conscience, so, one way or the other he's fucked. It must be costing him a fortune."

"It is expensive."

"Who the hell can she be? It's not someone from school. The rest of them would have dropped not so subtle hints and then sat back and watched all the skin and hair flying."

124

"Well, there now, that's good, isn't it?"

"It could be someone less obvious. Someone who's around the house all the time. Roz is around the house a lot even when Dylan isn't there. Geoff and Roz get on really well, you know."

"But she's his son's girlfriend," I objected.

"But maybe to Geoff she's just a fantastic-looking woman that he fancies the arse off. I don't know any more. All I know is that they're always talking and laughing and he loves her being around the house."

"Yes, because she's his son's girlfriend. She's the last one I would suspect. It's never Roz. How can you think such a thing?"

Roz was Dylan's girlfriend. She was a nice girl as far as I was concerned. Abby didn't know what to make of her. She thought she was a bit possessive of Dylan. Abby thought she mothered Dylan a bit too much. She tried her best the poor girl, but the truth was that Abby was a bit possessive of all her boys. She rarely saw the bad in them and if she did she was the only one who was allowed to point it out.

Roz spent a lot of time in Abby's house and that got on Abby's nerves. She never knew where Roz was going to hop out of next. Roz was a nurse and shared an apartment with two other nurses. It was easier for her to stay with Dylan than for Dylan to stay in the apartment. Abby noticed that when Roz stayed over Dylan always stayed in the guest room. It was becoming such a habit that lately they had been very blatant about it. Abby was mortified. They'd just say goodnight and head off together into the double room. Abby felt she had gained a lodger.

"Look, Emma, I know you mean well, but I can't help remembering that you defended Geoff the last time too and you were wrong."

"Well, this time I'm defending both of them and this time I am absolutely right. There is no way, no way in hell that Roz would go away for a weekend with Geoff. It has to be someone else. It could be someone you don't even know. Then again it could be someone right under your nose."

She stared at me.

I stared back.

We both started laughing.

"I promise it's not me. Although I wouldn't mind a weekend in the Damison myself. But not with Geoff. Not that I don't think he's lovely and all that, but he's yours so I never think of him in that way. You know I like him, but not in a man-woman way more in a friendly sort of way. But that's not to say that –"

"Stop babbling, Emma, I know it's not you."

"God, I do envy whoever it is all the same."

Abigail stared at me again.

"I mean that I envy her getting to stay in such a classy place. It's not that I envy her getting to stay with Geoff. Although, as I said, he is lovely. But you know how much I love places like the Damison."

I love nice places. Nice places bring out the best in me. I should always be in nice places. I'd sooner have a shortbread biscuit and a cup of tea for my dinner in nice surroundings than have a big slap-up four-course meal in some mediocre place. The minute some doorman opens the door for me, nods his head at me and makes me feel like I belong then I'm away on a hack. If there are chandeliers, cut glass and cut-throat staff all queuing up to serve me some delicious delicacies then I'm way in there. I reckon I can fill up later on tea and toast in my own humble surroundings at home. But when I'm out why not do it all differently and go posh. I had enjoyed afternoon tea in all the best places. So what if I couldn't afford dinner. I still got to eat there.

"Well, don't forget that whoever she is she'll be with my husband. I have to find out who she is."

"We could be completely ignoring the obvious, of course."

"Go on!"

"Suppose it's Martina, back on the scene."

"Jesus, I never thought of that. The little thong-losing tart. This time we aren't even getting the house cleaned. Imagine that tart going to the Damison. She'll never be let in. I'm sure the only time you'd see a tart up there it's covered in custard at afternoon tea. I'll have to keep my ear to the ground and watch every movement. I should never have trusted him after the last time. I let him off too easy. But I thought all that was over. I thought we were happy now."

Abby started crying again.

I knew enough not to say anything.

I gave her a tight squeeze.

We sat again in silence.

Maybe she was right and she should have dealt with it better years ago.

Maybe a kick in his bare arse would have done the trick.

"Jesus, Emma, I really thought we were happy."

How wrong can a poor bitch be?

CHAPTER SEVEN

"Be careful in the kitchen, Ma. I dropped a carton of apple juice all over the floor. The bloody carton was full. It went everywhere."

"Shit. It's a mess."

"I mopped it up as best as I could. I put the newspaper over it to stop someone slipping."

I was knackered. I hadn't slept last night thinking of Abby. I had to get up early this morning to show fabric samples to a new client. The day seemed to drag on. I had been dying to get home all day. Now I was home I was sorry I wasn't still out.

I walked slowly along the kitchen floor. Very slowly. I wasn't afraid that I would slip. I was afraid that Julia had drowned Madame Celeste in apple juice. Then I saw it.

Torn from the rest of the paper and held onto the fridge with a magnet.

Madame Celeste
Scorpio
October 23 – November 22

Things conspire against you today. Go with the flow and admit to your inadequacies. People will admire you for being honest.

"This is a total mess, Julia. Dumping newspaper all over the floor isn't doing any good. Have you no intelligence? Have I to do everything?"

I was skating around the floor trying to pick up all the sodden paper. Little bits of print were all over the white tiles. White tiles are a stupid colour for a kitchen floor. In my line of business I should have known that. But I thought they'd look great and that, as there were only two adults and no small children or animals living in the house, we could keep it clean. We couldn't. White tiles need clean adults – that's where I made my mistake.

Julia was up on her feet. Stomping mad. "I was only doing my best! Jesus, your best is never good enough in this bloody house!" she was ranting. She had a plastic bag and was shoving the lumps of wet paper into it. She kept missing the bag and the sodden paper was landing in a plop on the floor making a bigger mess.

"You're making a bigger mess," I pointed out to her.

"Well, if you're so bloody great, do it yourself then."

So much for people admiring my honesty. Things were definitely conspiring against me. I would have to find a few inadequacies before I could admit to them.

I brought a cup of tea in to Julia. She was glued to the television. She had a face on her that only a plastic surgeon could fix.

"Thanks," she grunted when I handed her the tea.

I thought if I told her about Abigail she might feel better. So I poured forth. It didn't make her feel any better. She just felt worse. Julia is a very feeling sort of person when she feels like it.

"Pool Abigail!"

"I didn't know what to say to her. I hope I said all the right things."

"I'm sure you did. She must be in bits."

"She's in so many bits that I'm afraid she's bordering on Humpty Dumpty. It might take all the king's horses and all the king's men to put her together again."

"Ma, they never succeeded in putting Humpty Dumpty together."

"Well, he was an egg. Abby's my friend. She'll be back together in no time. If I was around for poor old Humpty I'd have made bloody sure to get him together."

We sat in silence sipping our tea. I was thinking that the king's horses and the king's men must've been useless.

"Here's another thing –"

131

"Ma, if anything you're about to say contains the words Humpty or Dumpty I don't want to know."

"It doesn't, although –"

"Ma, please! I know you can fix anything. Can we leave it at that?"

"Once you know. Anyway, what I was going to say is that Abby seems to have got it into her head that if it's not Martina Geoff is fooling around with, it could be Roz. What do you think? You know Dylan better than me. What are he and Roz like together? They always seem mad about each other to me."

"That's mad. Roz wouldn't even look at Geoff in that way."

"That's what I told Abby."

"To be honest, all is not well in the Dylan and Roz Paradise. Roz wants to go away as a volunteer nurse for a few years. There's this new project being set up in a group of villages somewhere in Africa, I forget where. To tell you the truth I don't know all the ins and outs of it. The gist of it is that there will be a small team of doctors, all with different medical expertise, attached to about ten widespread villages. The doctors will divide their time between the villages treating the people, doing minor surgery and that sort of thing. The nurses will stay in the villages all the time and give the patients the aftercare they need. It sounds like a brilliant thing to be involved in."

"It sounds marvellous. She's great to do it. It sounds

like you think Dylan isn't all that convinced?"

"It's not so much that. They have decided to have a clean break before Roz signs up for it. Abby doesn't know yet. I only heard it myself while you were away and I was afraid to tell Abby. Dylan should tell her."

"Too right he should. If he knew what his mother was thinking, he'd go ape."

"Big time. Roz really gets on with Geoff, but not in that way. Do you know she was asked to be involved in this project? She's a brilliant nurse. She says she just can't turn her back on it."

"But why are they breaking up? I don't understand that bit."

"I don't know. He says he wants her to follow her dream and go. But ..."

Dylan was a man I really liked more and more.

"But he never asked her to stay or said that he'd make time to go over to her or that they should make some sort of a commitment to each other. Do you know what I think?"

"I have a feeling you're going to tell me, Julia."

"How right you are! I think she wants to get engaged or married and Dylan doesn't even know that's what she wants. She said something the last time I was talking to her about men being paranoid about commitment and Dylan was no different. I told her he wasn't a mind-reader."

"Christ, I know I'm always whingeing about males not

making a commitment but he's a bit young isn't he?"

"Yeah, I know – crazy, isn't it?"

"So, what's the bottom line on them then?"

"Dylan and Roz are easy. They're in lust not love. They just think it's love."

I was gobsmacked. "When did you get so sharp?"

"I don't know. I just woke up one morning and there I was: a real clever bitch. It's just that they don't seem to do the little things for each other the way people do when they are in love."

"Like?"

I was fascinated. This was my own flesh and blood and she knew things I hadn't taught her. Granted, she probably knew a *lot* of things I didn't teach her, but none that could be used as coffee-table conversation. What is suitable coffee-table conversation these days anyway? "Hello, coffee table. You're looking considerably well polished today."

Imagine Julia being wise to the ways of lust and love. About time for her to be sharing it with her mother. She'd shared everything else in her life with me, her ironing, washing, cleaning and her debts. She'd kept this little gem all to herself.

After all I'd done for her over the years and here she was knowing all about love and not telling me. Children can be so ungrateful sometimes. Really thoughtless.

"Well, it has come to my notice that people who really love each other do all the little things for each other. People who only think they are in love miss all the little things. Oh, they do all the grand gestures! But they miss out lots."

Such a gem, and from my own flesh and blood's lips. I was beaming. My only child was such a smart child. If my smart child was so smart why didn't she apply this little rule to the boyfriend from hell, Colin? He was a master at doing nothing.

"Well! Well! I am impressed."

"It's nothing. You just have to think about it logically. All relationships are based on love. Therefore they should all be the same. Like take for instance you and me. We love each other right?"

"We certainly do."

"So you do things for me all the time without even questioning what you're doing. And, even though you might not think it, I do things for you all the time that we don't even notice. Like tearing your horoscope out of the newspaper before I put it on the wet floor."

"Thank you for that, by the way, and I did notice."

"Now if we were to translate that into a lover-type relationship all you would need to add would be the physical bits. See, it makes sense."

"Perfect sense."

And for some reason it did.

"Hey, Ma, shouldn't you be getting ready or have you had a change of heart?"

"Oh, shit. Look at the time. Come up and talk to me

while I'm getting ready, will you?"

"I suppose you'll be wearing a pair of baggy trousers and a polo-neck jumper."

"I would, but I don't have any. Actually, I was thinking of wearing my little black leather skirt and the halter-neck top that goes with it."

"The little flimsy one?"

"What's wrong with that?"

"Well, it depends on what message you want to give him."

"Something like 'look at what you missed out on, you big bastard'."

"Well, that's all right. I'd hate for you to give out the wrong message. One like: 'Here I am on a platter for you.'"

"Don't be so ridiculous! Anyway, Danny is lousy at reading messages. Even if they are in big bold print."

"Or little flimsy tops?"

"Do you really think it'd be a bit much?"

"I think your little blue dress and matching cardigan would be perfect. You look great in it."

"You're right. What would I do without you?"

"See all the little things I do for you!"

The phone rang.

It was Ronan.

"Hi, honey. This is the first chance I've had to ring you. How are you?"

"Hi, Ronan. I'm great. How's it going?"

"It's going really well. They loved my proposal. I think I have it sewn up. I have a dinner with them tonight and I think they'll shake on it then. This is the big one, Emma. If I pull this off we'll be on the pig's back. Wish me luck."

"Good luck. I'm delighted for you. I hope it goes brilliantly for you. That's great news. Well done. I knew you could do it."

"I miss you. How did Paris go?" He genuinely sounded as if he missed me.

I felt a bit guilty, but only a bit. I was only going to meet an old friend. I was hoping he wouldn't ask what I was doing tonight.

"Great, I'll fill you in when you get back. I miss you too."

I did miss him. But I didn't just miss him because he was away. I missed him even when he was here. I missed the way it used to be. I know it was silly of me, but I felt he didn't love me if he didn't want to live with me.

"I should be back in Dublin in the morning. I'm dying to see you. What are you up to tonight. In with Julia? Or out somewhere nice?"

"Just out with an old friend I bumped into out of the blue. We said we'd meet up for a bit of a chat."

"That sounds nice. You can tell her all about me."

"It's nothing much, just a drink and a chat."

"Will you meet me for lunch tomorrow?" He sounded far away even though he was only in Cork.

"That'd be great. It seems like you've been away for ages."

"I know. I missed you, I want to talk to you. I have something I want to tell you, but not on the phone and not in a hurry. We can go out and have a slap-up lunch. Will you book somewhere? I have to run now. I'll talk to you tomorrow."

"I have a better idea. Come here for lunch and I'll make us something tasty – you must be sick of hotel food."

"That'd be great. Love you. Bye."

"Love you too."

I wondered what he wanted to talk about. I was afraid he wanted to call it all off. Who could blame him? I'd been distant lately.

"I notice you didn't tell him you were having dinner with Danny in about half an hour."

"No, I forgot. I'll tell him tomorrow."

"Yeah! Right!"

"He'll be OK about it."

"Right – well, you better jump in the shower or Danny will be here and you won't be ready."

"I'd better dash."

It was a quick shower. I cut chunks out of my legs, shaving them in haste – I thought I'd bleed to death. I put on too much perfume and too little make-up. Julia was right about the blue dress, it was perfect. I didn't look drop-down-dead gorgeous, but then again I didn't look too bad either. I heard the doorbell and ran down to get to it before Julia.

"Wow, you look great!" I was charmed that he noticed.

"Thanks, you don't look too bad yourself." He looked drop-down-dead gorgeous. Black, shaped jacket. Blue jeans. White shirt.

"Come in, I'm just ready."

"Hi, Danny. Remember me?" Julia appeared out of nowhere. I had half expected her not to show her face. I was hoping she wasn't going to eat the face off him. But the minute she saw him she relaxed and smiled.

He smiled over at her. "Julia! Wow, Julia!"

"It's good to see you, Danny. Done any good party tricks lately?"

They both laughed.

"It's great to see you too, Julia. No, I gave up the party tricks. The last one I did didn't go down too well. What have you been up to since I saw you?"

"Nothing much. Keeping Ma out of trouble mostly. What have you been up to yourself? Anything exciting?"

"I've branched out on my own since I saw you last. I set up my own photography business twelve months ago. It's going well. It's what I've always wanted. Listen, I'm sorry, I should have kept in touch with you. I'm a bastard for not doing that. You've grown up a lot. You look beautiful."

"I see you're still a charmer." She giggled.

"No, I mean it, you are beautiful. I mean it too about not keeping in touch."

"That's OK. It would have been awkward – I understand. So you followed your dream then. Became master of your own destiny."

He winked over at me. "You've done good here, Emma."

"Hey, I know I've done good. We don't need you popping back into our lives to tell us."

"Right, consider me reprimanded."

The doorbell rang again.

"That'll be Colin. I'm off. Nice seeing you again, Danny, even though I told her she was mad to go out to dinner with you." She turned to me, "Don't forget I won't be back until tomorrow so lock up when you get back in, won't you? And don't forget to put the cat out."

"Cat? I didn't know you had a cat? When did you get one?"

"No. We didn't. That's code. What she meant was: 'Don't forget to send Danny home.'"

"Ah. So it's role reversal now, is it? The daughter advising the mother. Cute."

"I am always open to a bit of advice."

"So, Julia, there's a boyfriend, is there? I hope he treats you well."

"Well enough. Could try harder."

"Well, that's not good enough. You don't want to be going out with a bastard like me now, do you?"

Julia just laughed.

She came over and gave me a peck on the cheek and to my utter amazement she then went over to Danny and gave him a friendly punch in the arm. I had forgotten that the two of them got on really well when he was in my life. I had forgotten that one of his greatest fears was that he'd marry me and, through no fault of his own, would be a bad father to Julia.

"I did miss you, you know!" she shouted back to him as she left.

"She is truly amazing, Emma. I really missed her too. You don't know how many times I went to ring just to see how you were both doing. I suppose I wanted to know you were both all right so I'd feel better about it. Then thought I was being selfish so I didn't make the call. I'm sorry now I didn't."

I just shrugged my shoulders. His sweet talk wouldn't work on me. It was more the way Julia was with him that was haunting me.

"I really missed you too," he started. "I –" I jumped up. "Want a glass of wine? Have we time?"

"All the time in the world." He took off his jacket. I wished he'd left it on. I could see the broadness of his chest and shoulders and I was getting a bit hot and bothered.

"Hey! When did you get this? It's amazing." He was standing in front of my new painting.

"I just got it in Paris." I filled him in on my finding it

as I handed him a glass of wine.

"Cheers!" He clinked my glass and took a sip of the drink. "Wow, this is terrific wine!" He took another sip. "Do you remember when we bought the other painting?" He went to sit down. He didn't sit on the armchair he had been sitting in earlier. He came over and sat right beside me on the couch. He was right up beside me. I could feel the heat of him. I could feel his strong arms. I wanted him to put them around me. I jumped up again to stop myself having such thoughts.

"I'll put on a bit of music, will I?" I took a large gulp of wine. It was amazingly good.

"Only if it will help you relax. You're like a hen on a hot griddle. Will you relax for God's sake? It's only me."

There was a CD in the machine so I just pushed the start button and sat down beside him again. This time I kept a bit of a distance between us.

'Love Is All Around' came on.

I jumped up and turned it off. I didn't need those song lyrics. I didn't want to feel it in my fingers feel it in my toes or feel anything anywhere for that matter. I didn't want him to feel anything anywhere either. I didn't want him to remember that it was our song. The one we always sang after we'd had a few drinks. The one we always had to dance to at a party.

"Here, leave that on. Isn't that our song? God, do you remember it? Remember the way we used to sing it whenever we got a bit pissed?"

I pushed the start button again.

"Oh," I said as nonchalantly as I could. "Was that the one?"

He just looked at me. He knew I knew.

Everything was conspiring against me. Julia, the CD, and I had to admit the wine was having a bit of an affect on me too. I suppose it was because I kept gulping it down and topping it up, just to be doing something. My body was letting me down a little bit too. I was starting to feel a bit of a tingle every time Danny spoke. I sat down beside him. I sat a bit too close to him.

Right, Emma, this is silly. It was time to give myself a good talking to. *You are being stupid. You are just having a drink with an old friend who means nothing to you any more. There is no need to be nervous. You are in a relationship with another man. You cannot possibly have any feelings for this man.* My tummy was all butterflies and they were all going mad. Flying in a frenzy. Some of them had reached my legs and my head. Some of the cheeky buggers had even reached my nether regions – I was not happy about that, but my nether regions were delighted.

I turned to Danny. "We'd better go, if we're going." Then it happened. We kissed. Well, he kissed me. But I didn't stop him. I let him kiss me and I think I kissed him back. I certainly didn't shove him off.

It was as simple as that. That's how it started. With a big juicy, lovely, toe-tingling kiss. Then he pulled my cardigan off. I helped him strip off his shirt. He took his shoes off and pulled his jeans and boxers off in one move. His body looked great. He was happy to be with me. I could see he was pleased. There was no hiding it. I moved my hands all over his body and felt just how pleased he was. I was tingling all over. I thought he had electrocuted me. I thought the bastard had a cunning plan to stun me with electricity and then take advantage of me. Well, no one was going to take advantage of me. Not if I got to him first.

He pulled off my dress and his breathing got heavier. He devoured me with his mouth, his tongue.

He looked directly into my eyes. Deep into them.

"I've missed you. I love you. I never stopped loving you."

"What?"

I stopped dead in my tracks.

I climbed off him and sat on the floor.

I don't know where the tears came from. I only know there were loads of them. All down my face. All over me.

He sat on the floor beside me and put his arms around me as I sobbed for Ireland. For me.

And in that moment the moment was gone.

"Emma, Emma, I'm sorry."

"Don't be. It's too fucking late to be sorry."

I struggled to put my dress back on.

"Talk to me, will you?"

"Oh! You have such a bloody nerve! Do you know

how many times I wanted to talk to you after you up and left? Do you know how many times I wanted to hear that you never stopped loving me? How often I wanted to tell you that I never stopped loving you? To tell you that I was missing you? But I couldn't, could I? Because I thought you had stopped loving me. How dare you leave me when you still loved me? How dare you hurt anyone you still loved the way you hurt me."

"But it was you who told me to bugger off, remember?"

"Well, that was the first thing you ever did that I told you to do."

"Emma, we can sort this out."

"How?"

"Well, if you still feel anything for me we could try again. Would you want to do that?"

"Oh right. It's that simple, is it? If we hadn't met on the plane I would never have heard from you."

"I think you would. I think the timing wasn't right before."

"The timing sure is crap now."

"Why? We're both footloose and fancy free. We're still free agents. We can do what we want. Please, Emma, I know it will work this time. I love you."

"Well, I have news for you, buddy! We're not both free agents. Nor are we both fancy free. I am in a relationship. A very good relationship. Ronan is good to me, he's kind and he won't run out on me. No matter what, he'd stay and battle it out. He wouldn't just fuck off into mid-air."

If he was gobsmacked, he covered it well. "If your relationship with this guy, Ronan, is so good then why did you kiss me?"

"I don't know. It was a mistake."

Now he was gobsmacked. If I had slapped him across the face he couldn't have been more stunned. He was shocked. He kept staring at me.

I put my hands to my mouth and started crying again. There was nothing else to do only cry.

He got up and dressed himself. He left his shirt open.

"I'll see myself out."

And that was it. He was gone. Again.

I was left sitting there half naked.

All alone.

I bundled up the rest of my clothes into my cardigan and hugged them. I heard the key in the door.

"That shagging bastard!" I heard Julia shout as she banged the hall door.

"What did he say to you? What did he tell you? He had no right to say anything. It was between him and me."

She stopped dead when she saw me. She must've got a fright when she saw me huddled on the floor.

"Oh, Ma, what's happened?"

"Didn't Danny tell you?"

"No, I haven't seen him since I was here with you."

"Then what did you mean when you said, 'the shag-ging bastard'?"

"I was talking about my bastard, Colin."

"Oh, Julia, what happened?"

"You first, what did that bastard do to you?"

"It wasn't him, Julia. It was me. What did your bastard do to you?" I asked as I hugged her.

"It really wasn't him, Ma. It was me."

"You can't keep making excuses for him, Julia."

Neither of us took comfort from the other.

That's the thing about broken hearts – no two broken hearts break the same way.

In silence I set a tray with two cups of tea. I took out our secret store of treats from the back of the press.

Silently, Julia put on the DVD, an old black and white film, our favourite: *Madam* X. Tonight, we'd have a good cry and a chocolate binge.

Tomorrow, we'd talk about bastards and what they are capable of.

Tonight we'd just sit and make each other feel just a little bit better. At least we knew how to do that. At this moment just a little bit better was better than nothing.

CHAPTER EIGHT

Abigail was like a bull. I think she was raging she had missed all the excitement with me and Danny and the excitement with Julia and Colin.

"Why didn't you ring me? Both of you. One of you. You know you could have rung me at any time of the night. How the two of you could get mixed up with a bastard each is beyond me. I suppose I'm in no better situation. Who would have thought it was possible to score a hat trick with men? Three big bastards!"

"I bet Geoff isn't a bastard. He only appears to be one. Danny isn't a bastard either. He was lovely."

"Well, lucky you! Colin is a bastard."

"At last someone's talking sense. Facing the facts. Emma, you are such a fool. Good on you, Julia, you've got more sense than your mother. So where's your lovely man now, Emma? He bolted, didn't he? And you're still calling him lovely. Honestly, Emma, sometimes I think there is no hope for you."

"Ah, Abigail, he only bolted when I told him I was with Ronan."

"Are you mad? What did you tell him that for?"

"Because she just couldn't help herself. She just can't help telling it like it is, can you, Ma? She can't help herself."

"Did you bring me over the newspaper and a few tea bags like I asked you to?"

"Of course, you were able to ring me for those, but no one rang me to tell me all the gory details of last night. I bet you put on an old weepy film and sat stuffing your faces. You could have asked me to come over. A good weep was just what I needed last night."

I wasn't listening to her. I was busy with the newspaper:

Madame Celeste
Scorpio
October 23 – November 22

Today you have everything just within your grasp. You have to reach out and grab it. Then it's up to you to keep a tight hold.

"We thought you'd be asleep, didn't we, Ma?"

"Yes, I just didn't think to phone you, I'm sorry."

Julia plodded into the kitchen with the tea bags. She looked like a big child in her big blue fluffy slippers and her Mickey Mouse pyjamas. I wanted to give her a big hug. To cuddle her the way I did when she was a baby. Keep a tight hold of her. Protect her from bastards like Colin.

"You OK?" I asked her. I bet she'd got as much sleep as I had. None.

"No."

"Oh, Julia," said Abby. "Come on, tell us what happened. We can all console each other." Poor Abby was in fix-it mode.

"Julia, you don't have to tell us if you don't want to."

"It was so awful. I made a complete fool of myself. I will never be able to go anywhere again. I can't show my face in public."

"It can't be that bad." I was hoping it wasn't that bad.

"I'm telling you, it was awful. We were at the party and it was good. The whole gang of us were there and Angela, that's the girl who's going away and whose party it was, gave a bit of a speech. Then her dad made a bit of a speech and it was so soppy and pukey. Anyway, I said to Colin that it was a pukey speech. He said he thought it was good. He thinks everything Angela does is good. Then the dancing started and I said I wanted to dance. He said he was happy sitting talking to the lads. So I got thick and sat beside him in a huff."

"Well, who can blame you? He should have danced

with you." I was nothing if not a loyal mother.

"Go on." Abigail didn't want the flow interrupted.

"Well, then Angela came over and said to Colin that as it was her going-away party she was going to have one last dance with everyone. He was first as she was going alphabetically and can you believe there is no one called Adam, Alan or Brad in our lot. All Freddies, Grahams, Johns and even a Victor. Anyway, up Colin gets and starts dancing with her. I thought I'd explode watching them gyrating all around the place making a show of me. Then it got all slow and romantic and I thought she had suctioned herself onto him. It was mortifying. Colin said it was only a bit of fun. Yeah, right, as if, fun like hell. For everyone else, except me. I had to pretend I thought it was a laugh. When she was finished with Colin she just strolled over to the very handsome Dave and pulled him up to dance. She completely ignored the very boring Dan with the very bad breath which just goes to show she is either a lousy speller or a very clever woman. Needless to remark, I had a quiet go at Colin. He told me to stop being so childish and grow up. So I stormed off like a big child. And everyone saw me. I'm mortified and it's all Colin's fault."

"I bet no one even noticed."

"Thanks for trying, Ma, but I know they noticed. I could see them trying to pretend they didn't."

"So, was that it? Did you just storm out and come home? Did that git let you come home on your own?"

"No, he ran out after me. He came in the taxi with me and then I guess he went back to the party."

"Did the two of you make up or are you still fighting?"

"Too bloody right we're still fighting. I told him to consider himself well and truly dumped. They were my last words to him."

"Oh! Julia. All you and Colin do is dump one another. It'll be back on by tonight."

"Not this time."

"Well, whatever you think. I just can't keep up with the two of you."

I really hoped that this time it was over with Julia and Colin for good. I was wondering would a little word in his ear do any good. Like, 'Bugger off and leave Julia alone, you big bastard'. Maybe that would be a bit too strong. Maybe 'Fuck off' would be even stronger and work better. Alternatively, I could reach out and grab hold of his weedy neck and keep a tight hold of it until he begged for mercy. I felt better, now that I had a plan. I work better if I have a plan of action.

I heard a key in the door and remembered that Ronan was coming in for lunch. I jumped up and ran to the fridge. Checked its contents. Empty. Then back to the hall to greet him.

"Hi!" He was carrying a huge big bunch of flowers.

"Oh! They're gorgeous. Thanks." I hugged him and I kissed him on the cheek. I felt like Judas. I knew I looked guilty. I got a visual image of Danny last night. I tried to clear it from my head by thinking of what I was going to magic up for Ronan for his lunch.

"I'll just get a vase in the kitchen."

"Hi, Julia. How's it going? Any news? Hi, Abigail."

"Hi, Ronan, I'm glad you're back. We need a bit of normality around here."

"Hi, Ronan. Did you have a good trip?"

"Thanks. Yeah, it was a great trip actually. Do I take it something has happened here? Come on, what is it?"

I held my breath. She couldn't land me in trouble, could she? Not her own mother?

"Nothing much. I dumped Colin, that's all. He deserved it. Abby thinks Geoff is having an affair and Ma –"

"Julia!" Abby let out a shout. I don't know if she was shouting because she was disgusted at Julia for letting it out about Geoff or because she thought Julia was going to let it out about me and Danny.

"Julia!" I knew exactly why I was shouting at Julia.

"Well, Ronan, as I was saying – Ma is being her usual jolly self and trying to make it all better. So tell us, how did Cork go? I could do with a conversation that doesn't end in tears."

Poor Julia was feeling guilty, she was babbling.

What had I done? I should never have put her in this position.

"I promise I won't cry, Julia. Cork was great. A total success."

"Way to go, Ronan!" She was happy for him.

"I'm thrilled for you." I gave him another Judas kiss on the cheek.

"Now tell me all about Paris."

"It was brilliant. I wished you were with me though."

"We'll go in the spring. Paris is at it's best in the spring. Wow, I see you got another painting. It's amazing."

"Isn't it? I'm just going to check on lunch. You sit there and relax."

"I could get used to you spoiling me."

I looked in the freezer. Not one instant meal in it. I seriously will have to get more organised for emergency situations. I stood there with the flowers in my arms.

I was hoping for divine inspiration.

It came in the form of Abigail.

"Emma, I'm sorry – I have to go," she said out loud. Then whispered to me, I'll be back in two minutes with quiche and salad. Leave the back door open."

"You're an angel, Abigail. A real angel."

When I went back into the sitting-room, Julia was sitting on the floor chatting away to Ronan. The way she always did. I was a bitch for putting her in such an awkward position with him. I had made her feel totally uncomfortable. There was nothing I could do. It's such a horrible feeling – knowing you know something you know another person should know but in order to protect an entirely different person you just say nothing. It was very complicated. She was trying to protect me. I was betting it was making her feel horrible. I would seriously have to get this mothering thing right.

It was easy when Julia was a little girl. I just did everything for her and kept her sheltered from the big bad world. As she got older I encouraged her to make decisions and stand on her own two feet. To face the big bad world. Now that she was all grown up I relied on her too much. I valued her opinion and I respected her judgement. But it wasn't fair on her. I was her mother. Mothers are supposed to be able to stand on their own two feet. Mothers are supposed to be level-headed and secure in themselves. I was such a terrible role model. You'd wonder how Julia had turned out so great.

"Julia, you'll get your death of cold sitting on that cold floor. Are you going to get dressed at all today?"

Sometimes I was a typical mother.

Julia got up off the cold floor. "I'm just going up now to have a shower."

Sometimes Julia was an exemplary young adult.

I was charmed that I had resisted the temptation to hang around the house in my dressing-gown and slippers. I felt good in my jeans and a pink Gap T-shirt. My make-up was covering a multitude. I looked normal. I felt totally abnormal.

"Are you having lunch with us?" I asked Julia.

"No, Abigail said Dylan is over at the house. I'm going to get dressed and go over to talk to my favourite famous person."

She plodded up the stairs and made a huge commotion getting ready. I set the table in the dining-room to make the lunch look special. I was praying that Abigail wouldn't be too long.

"I'm starving. It's great you cooking lunch for me. What are we having then?" He came into the dining-room and was heading into the kitchen.

"Oh, no you don't! The kitchen is off limits. It's a surprise."

"I don't smell anything."

"Well, that's good, then you won't guess what little delicacy I have prepared for you will you."

"It better be ready quick because I could eat everything in sight."

He grabbed me around the waist and started nibbling at my ear and neck.

"Put me down, you big glutton."

"Come on, give me kiss. I've missed you. Did you miss me?"

"Of course I did." I gave him a light kiss on the lips and pulled away. He wouldn't let me go. I didn't want him to. I wanted to kiss him all over. I wanted to make love to him. I couldn't. I might never be able to touch him again. Guilt is a terrible thing. A guilty conscience is a terrible thing. I wanted my clear conscience back so I could kiss this lovely man and take pleasure in it.

"Call that a kiss? Come here!" He gave me a long lingering kiss.

"Put me down. I have to check on our lunch. You open a bottle of wine and I'll be back in a minute."

Julia came in. All dressed up and glamorous-looking.

"Why don't you stay and have a bit of lunch with us before you go?" Ronan just couldn't help being nice.

"I might choke on it," Julia replied.

"What? You might what?" He couldn't believe what he had heard.

"I might joke about it."

"Oh, joke."

"Yeah. I might joke with Dylan about it. You know, tell him that my ma is cooking up a storm. Preparing the most romantic meal ever and that the two of you love-birds are going to tuck into her fabulous cooking." She glanced at me. I had the good grace to blush. She shouted over to Ronan. "Enjoy it! I'll see you later."

I could barely look at her. She was pissed off with me, big time.

"See you, Julia!" Ronan shouted after her. "Oh! Wait. I nearly forgot. Remember that CD you asked me to keep a look out for. Well, I got it. I saw it in a music shop in Cork. The guy told me I'd good taste. It's in the car. I'll walk out with you and give it to you. Back in a minute, Emma."

"Great. Thanks, Ronan. I've been trying to get it for ages. Thanks for remembering." She gave him a hug and they left.

I ran into the kitchen. Nothing. I opened the back

door and looked out for Abbey. I heard her talking to Ronan and Julia.

"Hi, Julia."

"Hi again, Abigail. Ma's in the kitchen. Go around the back. I'm on my way over to see Dylan. Is he still there?"

"Yeah, Julia, he's over there. Be gentle with him – he just told me him and Roz have split up. I have to hurry, Bye."

She ran up the side passage and handed me the bags.

"I was nearly caught, Emma. I'm getting too old for this."

"You and me both."

I sent her packing back to her own house before Ronan came back and invited her to join us for lunch.

There was a warm quiche wrapped in tin foil. A bowl of mixed salad and a bottle of Paul Newman's salad dressing. God bless the man. God bless Abigail. I knew exactly how the shoemaker felt each morning when he woke up to find the elves had mended all the shoes in his shop. It was a fairytale.

"God bless them every one!"

"What?"

Ronan was behind me. He handed me a glass of wine. "I was going to open that nice wine we put away for a special occasion, but I can't find it."

"Oh! I wonder what happened to it."

"Not to worry." He took a sip from his glass. "This is

quite good actually."

He gathered up the red-stained cork and the foil paper. He threw them in the overflowing bin. He pulled out an empty wine bottle from the bin.

"Well, would you look at this! Here's that bottle I was looking for. You drank it! You polished it off." He was teasing me and laughing. But it wasn't funny. It was the bottle of wine I had opened last night and drunk with Danny.

"So, you little alco, did you polish it off all on your own? Or did Abigail help you?"

"I'm sorry I didn't realise that was the one you were keeping for special. I'm so sorry, really sorry. I'm a terrible person." I felt an overwhelming sense of guilt. How could I?

"Don't be silly Emma, it's only a bottle of wine."

"But I shouldn't have drunk it with someone else. It should have been with you. The two of us cuddled up on the couch. Listening to music and drinking wine. I'm sorry. Can you ever forgive me? I am such a terrible person. You deserve better than me. You are such a nice person."

"Will you stop? What are you going on about? It's only a bottle of wine. It doesn't matter. You shouldn't be getting so upset over a bottle of wine. I'm sorry, this is all my fault – I shouldn't have said anything about the stupid wine in the fist place. It was there to be drunk. Who better to drink it with than a very good friend? I bet you and Abigail demolished it. Now come on, forget it. I can't believe you're getting so worked up over a bottle of wine!"

"You're too good to me. Do you forgive me?"

"There is nothing to forgive you for. God, but you're a silly woman sometimes. You drank a bottle of wine, so what?"

"But do you forgive me for everything? Everything I have ever done to you?"

"What's this? Are you looking for general absolution? What's wrong with you today? You're acting really strange."

"You're right. I'm sorry. Let's sit down and I'll get the food from the oven."

It smelt delicious. It looked delicious.

"Mmm. Looks and smells delicious. What's in it?"

"Fish."

"What sort of fish?"

"Fish fish. Cod and whiting and a bit of smoked cod."

"Lovely. Fair play to you."

He was delighted with all the trouble I had gone to for him. I was only sorry I hadn't gone to any trouble at all.

He served me up some salad and I gulped the wine back.

I cut the quiche and put some on his plate. He broke a piece off with his fork. I was toying with mine. It was the guilt. I was feeling sick. I honestly thought I'd choke if I ate anything. I couldn't look at Ronan. I was staring at my plate, toying with my food.

"Ahhhh!"

Ronan was enjoying it, but I couldn't look up. I was hanging my head in shame. Toying with the salad now.

"Aaaahhhhh!"

I lifted my glass and my head at the same time. And at exactly the same time Ronan stood up from the table grabbing at his neck. Pulling at his collar and tie. Trying to loosen them. He was marching up the room sweating. He was gasping for air, but looked like he couldn't get any.

"Ronan! Ronan! What's happening? Ronan! What is it?"

He slumped on the armchair. He was shaking and sweating. He was turning a very bright shade of red.

"Jesus, what's wrong with you?" I loosened his collar and tie for him. Immediately he gasped again for air and this time it seemed to fill his lungs. The red colour seemed to fade a bit.

"It's OK, I'm OK now." He said huskily. Very huskily. started crying.

"I'm OK, Emma."

"I'm phoning for an ambulance. You might have had a heart attack. I am such a bitch."

"No, don't, I'll be fine. Just give me a minute. I only had a tiny bit of the quiche. But I can't believe you made a quiche and put shellfish into it. I even asked you what you put into it. You never mentioned shellfish."

"Oh my God, Ronan. Your allergy. I'm sorry. How could I have forgotten your allergy to shellfish? What is wrong with me?"

I ran out to the hall and rang an ambulance. So what if he didn't want one. If he didn't go in the shaggin' ambulance I could always go in it myself. I could feel myself going into panic mode. I think I was on the verge of having a major heart attack. My heart was beating like a big base drum in my chest, it was deafening. Jesus, I could have killed him. Abigail could have killed him. I never would have given him shellfish. Abigail didn't know not to.

I poured myself another glass of wine and drank it down in one mouthful. The big base drum in my chest seemed to like the drink and it calmed down for a while.

I poured another and drank it the same way. It tasted good. The big base drum seemed to stop altogether. My left arm was a bit numb though. Then again so was my right arm. Actually, I was a bit numb all over. I started to forget about what I had done with Danny. I started to forget about what I had done to Ronan. I started to forget what a bitch I was. What a total bitch I had been.

I opened another bottle of wine. Gulped back another glass and forgot who Danny was.

I went over to Ronan, handed him a glass of wine and sat on his knee. I kissed his forehead and his cheeks.

"Can you forgive me?"

"Of course. I should have guessed about the fish. I just

thought you'd remember." He kissed me on the lips. Full on.

"I do remember."

I opened all the buttons on his shirt. He was tanned and smooth. I put my hand in to feel his chest.

"Do you want to come upstairs?"

"To see your etchings?"

"And a lot more besides."

I gave him the bottle of wine, I carried the glasses and he followed me up the stairs.

He put his arms around me and held on to me. I hugged and squeezed him. He kissed me lovingly then kissed me some more, more passionately. I started pulling his shirt out of his jeans. I was pulling and chucking. It seemed an endless shirt. I put my hands up under his shirt onto his bare back. So strong, so familiar. I opened the buttons of his shirt and ran my hands over his chest. He pulled my T-shirt off and opened my bra. My boobs fell gently into his hands. He kissed and sucked me all over. I pushed myself onto him wanting more. I pulled at the belt of his jeans, but couldn't manage to open it.

"Jesus, give me a bit of help here, will you?"

He obliged and sat up and opened his belt. He started on the buttons of his jeans and I stopped him. That was a treat I was reserving for myself. I opened his fly and pushed my hand in to feel him. God, it felt so good! Such a buzz that I made him this excited. I pulled his clothes off him like a woman let loose.

His hands were all over me and he pulled my thong off. I pushed him back onto the bed and got on top of him.

"Oh, Ronan! I love you. I'm mad about you."

"Emma! I love you."

The doorbell rang.

"Jesus! Is that Julia?" He pushed me off him. He jumped up off the bed and ran to the window.

"No, Julia has a key. Leave it. Whoever it is will come back later. You come back here to bed." I lay seductively on the bed. Legs akimbo, arms open wide. Doing my best at a sexy smile.

"Oh, no. Oh no. For fuck sake."

"What is it?"

I jumped out of bed and ran to the window.

"Did you ring an ambulance?" he asked.

"Yes, when I thought you were going to die. When I thought I was going to die. Well, I thought one of us was going to die."

The doorbell rang again. This time they kept their finger on the bell. Any minute now they'd break the door down to find whoever was in need of them. We ran around the room like naked idiots looking for something. Neither of us knew what we were looking for. I found my dressing-gown so I put it on. Ronan found a big white bathrobe so he put that on. We went down to answer the door.

"Did you phone for an ambulance? What's the problem?"

"Well, actually there is none. There was one, but we sorted it out." I tried to comb my hair with my fingers. To make it less tossed-looking.

"I had an allergic reaction and she thought I needed an ambulance, but as you can see I don't. I'm perfectly fine now. Sorry we didn't ring to cancel. We were just so delighted that I was all right that we forgot. Sorry to have called you unnecessarily"

"You see I gave him shellfish and he can't eat it. I nearly killed him. He could die if he eats too much shellfish. Thank God he only ate a small bit. I know it could have killed him so I rang an ambulance which would be you. Which would be why you're here. You see, I nearly killed him. It was a close thing. Then I thought I was going to have a heart attack. I had a pain in my chest and then my arm went numb. I thought it was going to fall off. Then I realised that I was only having a panic attack so I wasn't going to die after all." I was babbling and I was confessing to attempted murder which I was sure was a jailable offence. I looked beyond him to see if the police were with him. They weren't.

"Thank you for coming, but there is no need. We should have rung to cancel the call. I'm terribly sorry." Ronan was able to make perfect sense even though I was probably going to be arrested.

"Actually, I didn't nearly kill him at all. It wasn't me. It was my friend. My best friend Abby. She did it. She made the quiche. But he is OK now. I saved him."

"Abigail didn't nearly kill me. You did. Abigail wasn't even here."

I couldn't believe Ronan said this in front of the man. A witness.

"I should have told you earlier, but I didn't want to spoil your day. Abigail made the quiche and salad. The whole lunch. But I did supply the wine and the company. Are you mad at me?"

He was laughing.

"No, I'm not mad at you. I could never be mad at you. I'm so glad it wasn't you. To tell you the truth I was a bit hurt that you had forgotten I couldn't eat shellfish. I love that it was Abigail. I love you."

He gave me a wonderful kiss. I kissed him back. I love kissing.

"Em, em. When the two of you are quite finished. I am sorry to interrupt. You two just carry on doing whatever it is you want to do. We'll just hang around here in case one of you tries to kill the other or one of you decides to have a heart attack or even a little old panic attack. We have nothing better to do, so we'll just hang around here for the day."

"We are really sorry."

"Sorry. We should have rung you to cancel, we know that now."

"That's all right then." He looked us up and down. I had sex written all over me. Ronan had sex written all over him. I guessed by the smile that the ambulance man could read people very well.

We closed the door and barely made it back up the stairs. I ran into my bedroom. Threw off my robe and jumped on the bed.

Ronan walked in slowly.

"I need to talk to you. I want to tell you something. It's serious. Are you listening?" He closed the door behind us.

Oh, shit. I bet he had slept with someone while I was away or was that me that had slept with someone when he was away? I shouldn't have had that last glass of wine. One of us had slept with someone. I couldn't remember which one of us it was. It was all very confusing.

"You slept with someone? How could you?" I accused him. I wanted to know who he had been with.

"What? Where did you get that idea from? I'd never do anything as low as that to you. What sort of a worm do you think I am?" Poor Ronan, he was indignant.

So if he didn't sleep with someone that left only me. I must have slept with someone. I wondered who I had slept with.

"Well, what serious thing do you want to tell me?"

"Well, I've been doing a lot of thinking lately. I was very lonely without you when I was away and when you were away. I missed you more than I thought I ever could. So I got to thinking about the two of us and about what you were saying about us living together. I realise that it would be better for Julia to stay here where her friends are. So, if you still want me to, I'd like to move in. It's silly you being here and me being in my place. I'm over here so much of the time that I think I should just pack up and move in. The sooner the better. What do you think? It's a big step, but I think it's the right step, for both of us."

I noticed he was babbling a little. I hoped he didn't mean he was going to move in right now. I had wardrobe space to sacrifice to him and I needed advance warning before that ritual could take place.

"I think it's the best idea you have ever come up with."

"Well, try this other one on for size then. I got two ideas for the price of one. You know that I have made all the money I could ever want to make. I have been lucky. I was in the right place at the right time and was able to design the right thing for the right time."

Jesus, he was making no sense to me and the room was starting to spin a bit. I rolled over on the bed.

"Well, I have decided that I might retire." He was sitting on the bed and it was all really intense.

"But you're so young. What would you do?"

"I'll still design what I want, but only when I want to and only for whoever I want to. Only do work I'd enjoy. We could travel. Live a little. What do you think?"

I didn't know what to think. He was making all my dreams come true. Did he want me to retire too? I wasn't ready to give up my independence after only finding it. I was in the lucky position where I could mix travel and my job.

"I love you, Ronan. I'd love you to move in. I'd love to travel with you and live a little. Pour me another drink, will you? Are you not having one yourself?"

"It's a bit early in the day to be knocking them back, don't you think?"

"No, I don't. Anyway, it's a bit late to be telling me that. I think this is a special occasion. You are going to move in with me. You didn't die. I didn't have a heart attack. You want to retire. You want to come and live with me. I want you to come and live with me. That's loads to celebrate."

I was very seriously drunk and he was very seriously making a commitment to me. Which was what I wanted. It was exactly what I wanted.

It was what I had wished for, what I had hoped for. I loved the bones of him. He was so safe and so kind. He was gentle and thoughtful. He had a passion about life that was contagious. Most importantly of all he loved me and he loved Julia. He was good at doing the little things for us.

"Well? Is it a bad sign that you're having to think about it? I thought you'd be delighted." He looked so disappointed.

"I am. I am delighted. I love you, Ronan."

"Oh, Emma. I was so stupid before. I should have jumped at the chance to live with you. I want to be with

170

you forever. I was just being daft. I thought we were going too fast, but we're not. I want to be with you through all the good times and the bad times. Through the little things and the big things. I especially want all the little things. I want to be there for you all the time."

"Oh, I love you so much, Ronan."

"Will you marry me, Emma?"

This was supposed to be the most wonderful moment of my life. I had wanted him to ask. I had hoped he would. He just chose the wrong moment to ask. The day after I had been as unfaithful to him as if I had slept with an army of men.

"Will you marry me? Will you?"

"What?"

"Let's not just live together, let's get married. I've thought about nothing else for the past few weeks. We are perfect together. I know I got cold feet when you asked me to move in and now I'm going for an even bigger commitment. I just want to be with you and I think you want to be with me. We love each other. Why just move in? Why not make a real commitment?"

"Well, why the fuck didn't you say that when I needed it? When I asked you. Why didn't you ask me last week, or even yesterday?"

"Because you were in Paris and I was in Cork. What difference does it matter when I say it? If it's what we both want the timing doesn't matter."

"Timing is everything," I said and I went out to the

bathroom. I started to cry.

"You OK?" he shouted after me.

"Yeah," I managed. "I just have to use the bathroom."

When I got back he was under the duvet. He pulled it back and I climbed in under it with him. He put his arm around me and I snuggled up to him. Right into the soft place between his shoulder and arm.

He started rubbing my nipples.

The bloody waterworks started again.

"You're crying." He was so good at stating the obvious. "I hope it's because you're happy. You still haven't answered me." He was so bad at spotting the obvious.

"I wish it was. I should be happy. I should be deleriously happy, but I have to tell you something. I have to be honest with you if we're going to do this and I really do want to do this."

"I'm all ears." He gave me a squeeze.

"First, the answer is yes, I will marry you and I will always love you. But I did a terrible thing on you last night and I have to be honest with you and tell you or else I will be starting out on the best part of my life with a lie between us and I don't want that. I really do love you, but last night I did a foolish thing. I kissed Danny and I nearly had sex with him."

Ronan sat bolt upright. Maybe I shouldn't have blurted it out all together.

I continued talking as quickly as possible, not wanting

him to get a word in or have all my words sink in.

I was feeling very sober now.

"We didn't have sex, we just kissed and nearly did and I'm so sorry now. I really am. I'd never do anything to hurt you and I thought we had drifted apart. I thought I had pushed you away. That you didn't love me because you wouldn't move in with me."

"For fuck sake! Are you serious? You can't have. I thought Danny was out of your life. I thought all that was finished. How long has this been going on?"

"I'm sorry. I'm so sorry. Danny is out of my life. It is finished. It hasn't been going on at all. I met him on the plane from Paris and agreed to meet him. If you were here, you could have come with us." I tried to kiss him, but he was distraught.

"To watch you *nearly* have sex with your ex-lover? You were just about to have sex with me and tell me none of this. The only reason you're telling me now is because I asked you to marry me. You wouldn't have told me otherwise, would you? What sort of a slapper does that? What sort are you? I don't understand you. You are not who I thought you were. What happened?"

I don't know why I felt the need to tell him every little detail. I just knew I had to. I had to tell him everything. Show him I was sorry. Show him no mercy. I think I told him too much. I don't think he was able to hear any of it. Pity there was no Show and Tell in school when I was young – I'd have been great at it.

He got up out of the bed and in a dazed sort of way he got dressed. He was moving in slow motion. He rubbed the tiny scar above his eyebrow. His old war wound, as he called it. It was where someone had kicked him in the head in a game of rugby when he was a young fella. He always rubbed it when he was worried, hurt or agitated. He was all three. He pulled on his boxers, his jeans, the belt. He left them gaping open in the old familiar way I loved until he put on his shirt. When he tucked it in he buttoned his jeans up and did the belt. Again in slow motion he put on his jacket. He looked pathetic. He looked at me and his eyes were so heavy and sad. The blueness was all gone out of them. They were grey and lifeless. I couldn't believe I had done this to him. I would never forgive myself. He would never forgive me.

He tried to leave, but I pulled out of him.

He shrugged me off.

"Please! Listen to me! I said I'm sorry. Will you please listen to me? I didn't mean it to happen, it just did. Tell me you forgive me."

"It's too late," he said as he looked directly at me. He gently put his hand along the side of my face and then kissed me softly on the lips. "Good-bye, I love you."

I knew he was going for good.

He was hurt. I never meant to hurt him. He was a good man. What sort of a bitch was I?

"Please talk to me – we can work this out – I know we can!" I shouted after him.

He said nothing. He just left. He walked out on me. Something he would never have done unless I forced him. I had certainly forced him. I was such a tart.

I was sick of crying, but I cried again. I thought I might never stop. I thought I heard my heart breaking. A loud cracking noise in my chest. I could feel that it was broken. Badly broken.

"Ma! Ma!" I heard Julia running up the stairs. "What's wrong with Ronan, he's in bits." She burst into the bedroom.

"What happened? The man is shattered. He told me he had to go and that he'd always keep in touch with me. Where's he going? What's wrong?"

"He's gone for good, Julia. What am I going to do?"

"No, he's not. He'll be back. What happened?"

"I had to tell him what happened with Danny."

"What? Don't worry – he'll understand. He'll be OK." I noticed she didn't say he'd be back once she knew what really happened.

She knew Ronan nearly as well as I did. If I had wanted to kill him I couldn't have chosen a better way. Even an overdose of prawns couldn't have killed him off any better. He would never forgive me for being with someone else. Especially for being with Danny. Ronan was a one-woman man and whatever lucky woman he found to marry instead of me would be a very lucky woman indeed. I just wished I was a lucky woman.

CHAPTER NINE

"I can't believe I missed all the excitement again. I'm seriously thinking of moving in here myself for a while. I keep missing everything. Although, there's enough excitement going on over at my place to satisfy all my needs. Why am I coming over here looking for more? Geoff is acting all suspicious. He's being overly nice to me. I am always suspicious when he's overly nice. There is a fine line between nice and overly nice. I know the difference.

He's gutted about Roz and Dylan breaking up. He keeps saying she was a lovely girl and that Dylan must be mad to let her go. All of a sudden last night just as we were getting into bed he told me that I was the most beautiful woman he had ever met and that he thanked God every day that I was his wife. I nearly melted. Only for the fact that I know he has a hotel room booked for a dirty weekend with someone else I'd have bonked him from here to next week."

"I still think your imagination is running riot, Abby."

"Poor Emma, are you all right? Was it terrible? Did Ronan ring you today?"

"No, he phoned Julia to see if she was all right and to tell her to ring him if she wanted anything. He told her he'd keep in touch with her. He didn't want to talk to me. He told her he was busy. He's gone for good, Abby. It was awful. I'll never forget his face. He's not coming back, Abby."

"I know, Julia told me earlier. I hope it was nothing to do with my quiche. I had no idea about his allergy. I'm sorry."

"It's not your fault. I should have come clean with him earlier."

"Well, we're in a right mess both of us."

"Excuse me, would you like to include me in that too please? You needn't leave me out of it. I want my fair share of sympathy. Anyway, Ma, you brought this on yourself. I warned you. I knew that Ronan would be pissed off with you for even meeting up with Danny after all the history there is between the two of you. It would have been one thing if you had told him. But you had to go off sneaking behind his back. I don't understand you sometimes."

"Well if you keep going on at me like that you'll get

no sympathy from me. I know I fucked up. You don't have to keep telling me. Anyway, you're too young to get sympathy. Only aged has-beens like Abby and me deserve sympathy. Bucketfuls of it."

"Here, less of the aged and has-been remarks about me, please!"

"Sorry, Abby, but face it we are aged has-beens."

"Well, I don't know what's got into you, but whatever it is you'd better snap out of it. It would be very difficult for me to stay best friends with someone who thinks of herself, and more importantly, of me as aged."

I was feeling sorry for myself and I felt I was entitled. If only I hadn't been so fickle. So stupid. If only I hadn't been on that plane. If only Danny hadn't been on that plane none of this would have happened. If only I hadn't let my body make all my decisions. It has a habit of making the wrong ones. I felt worn out. My poor body was worn out – thank God it was incapable of making any decisions.

I have lived a life beyond my years. No one of my age should have had all the hurt I have had. I wished I had lived my life like everyone else. A nice ordinary life. Been born, grown up, met a man, got married and had babies. In that order. There was no order to my life.

Maybe my need for commitment stemmed from my past. From Alex walking out on me. Maybe I was wrong to want a man to make a commitment to me. Maybe I should be making a commitment to myself always to be true to myself. Maybe that would be enough.

Why did I always want a man to prove his love for me by moving in with me or proposing to me? Was it just to have someone? Anyone? Did I need someone that badly? No. Did I want someone that badly? Yes.

So I had two men within arms' reach and even closer, both professing their love for me, and I had spoiled it. Maybe the truth of the matter is that I was frightened to live with anyone any more. Had I learnt how to protect myself from them walking out on me when we were living together by making them walk out on me before we even got that far?

The greatest protection of all. Force them out. Maybe I didn't want to lose control over my life. I was used to only thinking about me and Julia so maybe I didn't want to have to include someone else. Did I only want the smooth bits and none of the rough bits of life? If you saw where I was twenty years ago you'd understand. It was all rough bits. I was a single parent. I was broke. I had turned my life around. I had learned to play safe. I played within the rules – my rules.

So, did I subconsciously force them away?

"Well, I, for one, am not going to mope around." Julia had all the enthusiasm she should have at her age. I wondered what sort of an example I was for her. What chance had she got with a role model like me? I hoped she was strong.

"The more I think about Colin the more I think I

was right to stand up for myself," Julia announced. "He was in the wrong. Lately, he has been in the wrong a lot. I know I handled it very badly, but we'll excuse me on the grounds that I'm only learning. Well, if I learnt anything, I learnt that I'm not going to take any crap any more. The next guy I go out with will be one who does the little things for me and I do them for him. He will want to dance with me any chance he gets. I've decided I'm going to become a heartbreaker. Treat 'em mean, keep 'em keen."

"Well, I'm going to give blokes a chance," I joined in. "I'm too eager for them to do the 'til death us do part' routine once I know I'm madly in love with them. The next time I'm with a bloke, if there is a next time, I'm not going to give them any indication of how I feel. Keep them guessing. Let them bend over backwards trying to get me to commit for a change. I'm going to become a back-breaker. Treat 'em mean, then treat 'em meaner."

"Well, shag that! The two of you are right. It's time I stood up for myself. I really love Geoff and it's time I made up my mind once and for all if he ever did have an affair and if he is having one now. I owe him that much. That will be my mission. But if I find out that he is having an affair then I'll cut the balls off him. I've decided, I'm going to become a ball-breaker. Treat 'em mean, then treat 'em to fuck all! At least that way you get to keep them. That's what I should have been with

181

Geoff, a ball-breaker. I'm too nice."

"Yeah, but we love you being nice," said Julia. "I'm going over to your house to see Dylan. I'll be back in a while."

It was great for Julia that Dylan was around. They had always been great pals. Nothing romantic – better than that, friends. I'd say Dylan knew more about Julia than anyone else. I didn't like thinking about it too often – I liked to think I knew everything about her. I was wise enough to know that I didn't. I was wise enough to know that I didn't want to know the things I didn't already know. Some things a mother is better off not knowing.

"You better make the most of him, Julia," said his mother. "He's off to sunnier climes in a couple of days. He's doing a swimwear photo shoot."

"He was telling me. It sounds dead exciting. I'll miss him though."

"You and me both." Abigail would really miss him this time when he went off again.

After Julia had left, Abigail said: "I told Dylan about his dad booking the hotel room. I asked him if he thought Geoff had a fancy woman. He says I'm being stupid. He just fell around the place laughing. He thought I was crazy. He told me to just tell Geoff the hotel rang and see what he says."

"He could have a point. Why don't you?"

"I think I might."

"I think you owe it to him."

"Well then, that's me sorted. What about you?"

"I have made a decision. I'm going to go away for a couple of days. Get away from Ronan and Danny and all the mess. Go somewhere that I can be on my own for a while. Mull things over. I'm going to talk to Julia and see will she come with me. If she won't I'll have to have a rethink. What with the hassle between her and Colin I don't think I can leave her."

"I'll take good care of her for you."

"How can you when you'll be with me?"

"What? I can't just up and go off on a holiday!"

"It's not a holiday, it's a cure. It'll only be for a few days. You're the one with the three months holidays. You're not going away with Geoff until the end of the summer. Come on, take advantage of the teacher's holidays you're always getting slagged over. Come with me."

"Do you know, I think I might. What harm would it be?"

"No harm at all."

"Where would we go?"

"I don't know. We could go and get some brochures and see if Paradise is in any of them. Failing that we can pick somewhere else."

"Right now?"

"No time like the present."

Julia came running back in the door just as myself and Abigail were heading out. She nearly knocked me over.

"Ma, you'll never guess what? Go on, guess! You never will though. I'm so excited."

"Colin wants you to go back with him." I rolled my eyes up to heaven.

"No, something far better."

"Tell me. I give up. What is it?"

"Dylan wants me to go away with him. He's going on that photo shoot and he wants me to go with him. Please tell me I can go. He says I can work at the shoot. You've been at me for ages to get a summer job – well now I have one. Isn't it great?"

Abigail and I followed her back into the house. I put the kettle on. This was a bit of a bolt out of the blue. I hate bolts out of the blue or out of any other colour for that matter. A bolt out of the black would have been just as bad.

"Where is this place? I suppose it's some place I've never heard of where they've no electricity or running water and no means of communication?"

"It's a little island off the coast of Italy. I forget the name. He told me, but it doesn't matter. It's hot and exciting that's all that matters. I've never been to Italy before. Remember that time when you went to Florence and you said you thought you were really Italian you felt so much at home? Remember you wanted to trace your family tree because you were so sure there was Italian blood in the family. Since then I've always wanted to go. I've always wanted to see for myself if I could feel that

184

too. Imagine it. Me going off to Italy. Bruschette. Panini. Crostini. Pasta. Ice cream. The home of all my favourite foods. Yippee! This is the best thing that ever happened to me!"

"Well, thanks for that! I'd like to think I had something to do with the best thing that ever happened to you. I'd like to think I featured in that sort of an event. I had thought it might have been the day I saved every shilling I had, scrimped and scraped to buy you that shiny red bike."

"That was a great day too, but I thought Santa gave me that."

"Well, what about the time you needed the costume for the school play and I sat up all night, sweating and bleeding all over the material and turned you into the best pumpkin Cinderella ever had."

"That was a great day too, but I always wanted to be Cinders herself."

"Well, what about the day I surprised you with the violin and got you music lessons. That was a great day. You were thrilled when I gave that to you."

"That was a great day too, but it was the piano I really wanted to learn."

"Jesus, did I do nothing right? Is there not one day in your miserable life with me that you can say was the best thing ever happened to you? If I'd known that top of your list of great things that could possibly happen to you was a week in Italy, I'd have done it years ago.

Fulfilled your dream before now. Wouldn't you wonder how stupid I was all the same not to spot it? Jesus, who'd have kids? Thanks be to God I stopped after one."

"Ah, Ma, don't be so touchy. If you really want to know what's top of my list of greatest things that happened to me, well, it was a long time ago. It was when I was crying one night in bed and you came in and asked me why. I told you all the girls in school were bringing their dads on the camping trip the school was going on and I had none to bring and you told me I was being foolish and that you were a dad and a mam for me. Remember? You struggled through every miserable moment of that trip. Hiking in cow dung, eating badly burnt half-raw meat, cooked over a fire. You gave the best rendition of 'Ging Gang Goole Goole Goole Goole Wash Wash' anyone ever heard. That was one of the best. There are lots more. The envelope with Grandad's wishes for me to soar and fly that you gave me. That was special. There are loads. They are all in one huge big pile of memories. They are in the very special pile. I have other piles. Ordinary piles. This trip to Italy will be top of one of my ordinary piles."

"Oh Julia! I'm a silly woman and a lucky woman. You are top of my pile." I didn't mention to her that my pile was a very big and very messy one.

"So come on, tell us more about this trip." Abby who had been standing around like an extra at a Steven Spielberg film finally got a few lines to speak.

"It's brilliant. A photo shoot on a fantastic island. It's amazing. He told me all about it. Ma, it looks like paradise."

I think it was when she said the word 'paradise' that Abby and I both looked at each other, knowingly.

"Please, please say I can go. I'm old enough to go anyway. I'm only being nice asking you and I guess you'll have to lend me some money upfront, but as I'll be working I can pay you back. All my accommodation will be paid for."

"Right, you can go."

"That was quick. I told Dylan it'd take me hours to break you down."

She jumped up and wrapped her arms around me. "Thanks. I'll send you a postcard and bring you back a pressie."

"Wait! There's a condition."

"With you there is always a condition. What is it this time? I have to ring you everyday? Wear complete sun block? Anything, whatever you say."

"I'll lend you the money if you let me come too."

"Are you joking? You are joking, aren't you?"

"No, me and Abby were just off to get brochures for a holiday to Paradise, but if you're telling me that this place you're going to is Paradise then that's where we should go."

Abigail butted in. "It'd be great to see Dylan working and Geoff and the rest of them can manage without me.

It'll be good for them."

"Both of you?" said Julia, amazed.

"Well, if both of us go we won't be hanging around with you all the time. We'll be off doing our own thing. You won't have to mind either of us. We can look after each other." I laughed.

"I give in. I just give in. I'm going to tell Dylan." She ran off again.

"Looks like we're all off to … wherever it is we're going to." Abigail was delighted.

"You don't think there is anything going on between her and Dylan, do you? Remember we always thought they'd get together eventually?"

"No. I don't think so. They're both just a bit raw and taking comfort from each other. Sure, isn't that what they always did? If one of them was ever in trouble they always ended up crying on each other's shoulders."

I was hoping Julia was only crying on Dylan's shoulder and not snuggling into it. It would be all very complicated if they were with one another in the biblical sense. It only crossed my mind now that maybe they had already slept with one another years ago. Maybe that was one of the little secrets they didn't share with their respective mothers. I was so pleased they never thought to share it with us. Anyway, time would tell. If there was something between them I'd see what it was when I was away with them. I'd handle it then. For the moment I was thankful enough that I was going away with them. I could be their chaperone.

I consulted Madame Celeste. I hadn't had time to read my horoscope earlier. I was wondering if she would know about my plans.

Madame Celeste
Scorpio
October 23 – November 22

This is the time for making plans. Where there is no plan there is no destination. Where there is no destination there is no reason.

It was perfect.

"This is just what I needed, Abby. To get away from all the aggravation in my life. After all, what possible aggravation could we have in Paradise?"

"Absolutely none, we'll be leaving all that behind."

CHAPTER TEN

The last few days had been a total madness. I looked and felt liked a plucked chicken. There wasn't a spare bit of hair anywhere to be seen. Not on me, not on Abigail and not on Julia. Between the three of us we had left the makings of several toupees behind us in the beauty parlour.

Julia had decided to get a spray tan so she'd look well in her bikini and out of it.

Abigail had a body wrap to make sure she was all toned up.

I walked the legs off myself looking for a swimsuit that would make me look nearly as good as the two of them.

I needed one that made me about two stone lighter, six inches thinner all around and about a foot taller. I was very disappointed when I didn't find one.

However, I found the next best thing. I found a tankini. A strappy tight T-shirt with matching bikini bottoms, for big bottoms. It was in bathing-suit material.

I got a black one with white trimmings and a multi-coloured one. Pinks, blues and greens. I bought a black sarong and a pink one. Black flip-flops with big white flowers on the toe and plain pink flip-flops. I was set.

Ronan still hadn't been in touch. Neither had Danny. Both of them were well and truly pissed off with me. Who could blame them? Ronan had kept his word and had rung Julia again. She said he sounded more hurt than pissed off. I think she rang him once, but she didn't tell me, I overheard her. She was acting a bit suspiciously and to be honest when she said she was using the phone I thought she might be ringing the toe-rag Colin so I stood outside her door listening.

"Hi, Ronan."

Blank.

"She's OK, I think she misses you."

Blank.

"I wanted to talk to you because … hang on a minute, will you, Ronan?"

I made a run for it and hid in the bathroom.

She barged in the door.

I was sitting on the loo.

"You might want to pull the seat up and your trousers down," was all she said. She said it very smugly.

So even without having to fill in all the blanks, I guessed she had rung Ronan. I was glad she was still in touch with him.

I actually enjoyed the flight. I hardly even noticed we were flying. I sat in the middle of Abby and Julia and they looked after me. We sat in first class. Dylan arranged it. Flying first class is like not flying at all. There is legroom and there are little treats heaped upon you. No sooner was I in my seat when the air hostess arrived with a newspaper which I put to good use.

Madame Celeste
Scorpio
October 23 – November 22

It's good to try out new exciting things even if it is with old familiar friends.

No sooner was I finished reading my horoscope when she returned with more treats.

Luxury is great for making you relax.

As soon as I stepped off the plane I felt at home again. Had I been met with a pile of ironing and a big basket full of washing I couldn't have felt more at home. I loved the atmosphere in Italy. Even though we were in a fairly big airport the magical Italian temperament was evident. People were shouting at each other and crying and hugging one another. Some were leaving, some were arriving. All of human life was there. All with their own sad or happy stories to tell. I felt wonderful being in on it all. Having my own story, being different and in a different place. There is a freedom about being away from your own patch.

Julia was on a cloud. She was flying high and taking everything in.

"It's exactly like you said." She put her arm into mine.

"I know what you mean about loving it. I feel it too."

We collected our baggage. Mine was the biggest case. I'd brought tons of clothes with me. I also had an empty case inside my case. Sort of like the Russian Doll of suitcases. I was planning to fill it for the return journey. I knew I'd be paying for excess baggage on the way back. There is always a price to be paid for excess baggage.

The ferry to take us to Aronna wasn't going to sail until later and the dock was only half an hour away by taxi. We had three hours to kill. I knew exactly where to kill them.

"Let's leave our bags in the left-luggage department for a couple of hours and get a taxi into the town. Explore a bit."

"Great idea." Abigail was all on for it.

"Brilliant." Julia was in her element.

"As long as there are no shops involved." Poor Dylan was still young and innocent enough to think that Julia, his mother and me could be in place like this and not shop. He didn't know any of us very well. I was thinking that if he had slept with Julia he would know this little detail. I took it as an indication that they had never slept together. I took it as a very good indication. We all piled into the first taxi in the rank.

"How do we ask him to take us to the market?" I asked Julia.

I don't know why I thought she might know. She hadn't done Italian in school, but I imagined, given the all-round, overly expensive education she had that she would know that important sentence in Italian and indeed in every other language.

"How would I know?" Julia was no help. What a waste of an education!

You'd wonder what they are teaching our children in school these days. They should be teaching them something useful.

I looked at Dylan. Surely a superstar like him would know?

"Don't look at me like that. I am not a market person." He looked back at me blankly.

Abby just shrugged her shoulders.

I could see I was carrying a lot of dead wood on this trip.

"You want me take you to market?" The little darling Italiano driving the taxi like a madman spoke. He spoke English. I nearly kissed him only I was sitting in the back and he was in the front. Julia was sitting in the front. I was going to tell Julia to kiss him only she didn't look like she would and he wouldn't understand why she didn't want to and then he certainly wouldn't bring us to the market.

"Yes, yes, you darling man! To the market!" I stretched out my arm in between Julia and him. I pointed my finger straight ahead at the windscreen.

"To the market!" I said as I pointed.

"To the market!" Abigail said.

"To the market!" Me, Abigail and the driver said as he swung around another corner and put his hand on the horn.

Julia slid down in her seat.

Dylan slid down in his.

Kids nowadays get embarrassed too easily.

The market was exactly as I knew it would be. The Italians know how to do a market. Stall after stall stuck out like a frill at the base of the tall, ornate, old brick buildings. Endless stalls straining with vast amounts of the best quality of everything lined the cobbled streets. The smell of coffee, fresh bread and fine Italian leather filled the air.

"I have died and gone to heaven," Julia said.

"Thank God, I'm with you," Abigail added.

I just swooned.

Even Dylan, who like all men, hated shopping, loved this. This was more than shopping. This was an experience.

Soft leather bags in every colour of the rainbow hung from the stalls. Gloves to match each bag were laid out. Flat and in pairs. Turquoise, pink, red, purple. Any colour. Purses and wallets of every shape and size.

Prints of Florence, The Duomo, Michelangelo's David, the Ponte Vecchio. Watercolours of the leaning tower of Pisa. Notebooks with covers of Rome, the Eternal City. Mouse pads of Fontana di Trevi. Cherubs everywhere on everything.

We soaked it all in.

"Euro?" I asked a weatherbeaten lady as I tried on a chocolate-coloured leather coat. It was fitted, single-breasted and came down to my calves. It was magnificent. The softest leather.

She took out a pen and a notebook from a big pocket hanging around her waist.

She wrote three hundred euro.

She handed the pen to me. I took it. Crossed out the three hundred euro and wrote two hundred. I handed her back the pen and the game began. She wrote two seventy five. I wrote two twenty five. She wrote two sixty. I wrote two forty. She wrote two fifty-five. I wrote two fifty. I put the pen into her pocket and held out my hand. Game over. She took my hand and shook it. I gave her the money. She gave me the coat.

Julia wanted to play the game too. She wanted a full-length black coat which looked amazing on her. The game began again and they shook hands on three hundred and fifty. Then everyone wanted to play. Dylan bought a jacket, a very butch, tan jacket for two hundred and fifty. And Abigail bought a short box jacket for one hundred and fifty.

The lady spoke a load of Italian at us waving her hands high and low, smiling and pointing at all four of us. Then she took out a fifty euro note and gave it back to Julia. It was our bit of discount.

"Thank you." Julia was charmed with her luck money.

"*Ciao*," I said using the bit of Italian I had picked up somewhere.

"*Ciao*," Abigail and Dylan said together.

"*Ciao, bella!*" Julia got that little bit carried away. Then again Julia was the one with the fifty euro in her pocket and I was the one who had paid for her coat.

We had just enough time to grab a taxi to the airport, collect our bags and head for the port to catch the ferry. But, if I had gone home there and then I would have been able to say I had a wonderful holiday. Watching Julia's excitement was fully satisfying.

We boarded the ferry minutes before it pulled out.

Although it was a hot day and the sky was clear blue, there was a gentle breeze coming up off the sea. Lovely lounging chairs were scattered around the deck.

"This is fantastic. Look at the colour of the sea. Have you ever seen anything as blue?" I was completely smitten by the scenery.

"I'm dying for a coffee, to be honest," said Abby. "Anyone else want one?"

"I'd love one too, Ma," said Dylan. "I'll come with you."

"Me too, Abby," said Julia.

198

"Do you mind if I don't come with you? I'll just stretch out here on one of these loungers and relax. I love it up here. It'll only be sticky and hot inside."

"OK, see you in a few minutes. We won't be too long."

I pulled a sun lounger out a bit so I could see everything that was going on. It only took a couple of minutes for me to go into a semi-coma. I was mesmerised, watching all the people on the deck.

A little girl with a mop of the curliest, darkest hair I had ever seen was sitting in one of the chairs singing in Italian. Her eyes were chocolatey brown and she had long eyelashes that any woman would envy. She was angelic in a pretty white dress that showed off her bronzed skin. She stood up and started to dance while she was singing. Twirling around, her dress flouncing out from her chubby bare legs. This was the stuff dreams are made of. It was idyllic.

The little girl ran over to me. I smiled at her.

"*Ciao.*" I thought she might not understand me if I spoke in English.

She stopped dead in her tracks, took one look at me and started to cry. Cry is an understatement. She started to bawl. I wanted to tell her to go away.

"Shoo!" I whispered.

She screamed. She roared. Idyllic doesn't ever last very long. She opened her mouth and wouldn't stop. You'd think I'd given her a wallop.

A man ran forward, gave me daggers looks and swept the little girl up into his arms. He smothered her in kisses and she stopped crying. She started blathering to him in Italian. He put her up against his shoulder and started walking away. She could see me over his shoulder. She pointed at me and started to cry again. She was an obnoxious young one all the same. I had done nothing to upset her.

She pointed at me again. I made a face back at her. Her father turned around. I put my hand to my face and let on I was just scratching my nose. I wasn't able for all this relaxing. It was killing me.

Two boys were trying to climb the railings at the edge of the ferry. The mother tried to get them down. I couldn't watch. I was afraid they'd fall overboard and drown. Every now and again I took a sneaky look. She was animated as she tried to explain what would happen to them if they fell. I guess she must've mentioned the rescue helicopter or something that made it sound exciting because they kept climbing. She gave them a soft slap on the bum and did a bit more shouting. I wanted to go over and tell her that bribery would work better. If she bought them an ice cream their hands would be full and they wouldn't be able to climb. She was a young mother. Her boys were only small. I was experienced. I decided not to go over. She wouldn't understand me. Even if she spoke English.

We could see L'isola Di Aronna in the distance. It

looked very small. As we got nearer, it looked even smaller. We had been told it was a very remote part of Italy and that it hadn't been touched by tourism. It was, by all accounts, an untouched part of Italy with all the authentic Italian traditions and ways.

A small crowd gathered around as we all got off the ferry. They wanted autographs from Dylan. Word had got out that he was arriving. Abby was delighted with all the attention he was getting. I was delighted myself. Dylan was great. He signed everything and posed for photographs. Abigail was bursting with pride. Me and Julia were chuffed too.

There was a car waiting to bring us to the hotel.

He must've gone to the same driving school as the taxi driver. He was just as reckless.

"This is fantastic. Look at the countryside." I was hanging out of the window of the car. I was soaking in the atmosphere and ambience. The driver went at break-neck speed through a large puddle in the road. I was soaking.

"Who'd have thought there'd be a puddle there?" I asked my fellow-travellers who were falling around the place laughing at my wet face and hair.

The landscape was a mix of rock, trees and sand. Dry sandy soil and tall, top-heavy trees. Every now and again we came across a puddle of water where a hose had been let run through a row of vines.

The houses were dotted along the roadway and back

from the roadway tiered up high against the rising landscape. They were coloured in muted yellow, creams and
a terracotta colour. Most of them had a balcony. Each
house had shutters on the windows. Shutters painted in
green or sometimes in brown, others in natural wood.
There was a rustic quality about them all. The terracotta, rich cream and warm grey slates on the roof gave
the houses a timeless charm. I was charmed by it all.
There is something about Italy that is like no other place
in the world. The history is seeping from everywhere.
They respect the past and the old. They embrace the
new and the young. They have acquired a perfect
balance of times past and times present. They don't pull
down the old to make way for the new. They put the
new beside the old and the history seeps from one to the
other.

"Look, that must be our hotel. Isn't it beautiful? It's so
remote and old-world looking." Julia was pointing out
the window at a large building painted in a rich yellow
ochre with rust-coloured shutters on the windows.
Ornate balconies filled with flowers were dotted all over
the building. It was full of charm. It was magnificent.

"Right, this is it. Out you get." Dylan was in his
element.

The driver got out of the car and opened the door for
us. I felt like a film star. He went to the boot to get our
luggage. Dylan stepped forward to help him lift out all
the bags. Even with Dylan's help, the poor guy had to

make several trips. I had lost the run of myself in the market. If I ever needed purple, yellow or turquoise gloves I now had them and the shoes to match them and the bag to match the shoes.

A wonderfully flamboyant man came out of the hotel to greet us. He was handsome and suave. He started talking Italian to the driver. They were waving their arms around at each other like they were swatting flies. The driver reversed the car out and was gone in a blaze of dust.

The owner of the hotel started winking at me and Abby. Poor Abby started winking back at him. We had been warned that no one spoke English. I guess this was his way of being friendly, but it was a bit silly Abby responding. She looked ridiculous.

"Will you stop with the winking," I whispered to her.

"Winking? Winking? I'm not the one winking – he is." She winked at me.

"Jesus, Abby, you're winking in sympathy with him. Will you stop!" I winked at her. The hotel owner saw me winking and winked back. Abby saw him winking at me and she winked. He winked right back at her.

Julia just stood looking from one of us to the other to the other. Then instead of winking she rolled her eyes up to heaven.

Abby was gobsmacked.

"He's a ride, don't you think? And what a ride. Look at the colour of him? I wonder is it an all over tan?"

"God, Abby, you're the pits."

"So you don't think he's a ride, then?"

"Of course I think he's a ride. Look at his hair. It looks pure white against the tan. He looks rich too. What a wonderful combination – rich, good-looking and only speaks Italian. I'd want to be blind, deaf and frigid not to think he was a ride. Even my loins are crying out for him."

"Well, get in the queue. I winked at him first."

"Will the two of you ever think about something else other than sex for five minutes so we can sign in and get sorted out? Even if he can't understand you he will know bloody well what you're talking about. The two of you are drooling." Dylan, being a typical Irish Neanderthal couldn't possibly appreciate the magnificence of this fine example of Italian manhood. If he did appreciate it he wouldn't verbalise it.

"Spoilsport!"

"Jesus, the youth of today are no fun at all!"

The hotel owner stepped forward. He had stopped winking and was now smiling.

He was wearing beautifully tailored clothes. Cream trousers and a black shirt. His shoes were black leather. He had a ring on the little finger of his right hand.

"Hallo to you all. I am Marco. I am very happy to greet you." He had the good grace to turn to Dylan and explain. "I speak English very well and I understand it even better."

Abby and I had the good grace to blush.

"I'm Dylan and this is Abigail my mother and her friend Emma and her daughter Julia."

Marco took our hands. He didn't shake them the way you'd expect him to. He just held on to them. I was mortified. Abby was delighted. I could see she was delighted. She was all smiles.

"You two ladies look far too young to be mothers of these big children."

Abby and I beamed.

"I bet he says that to all the ol' ones," Julia whispered.

Marco shook hands with everyone.

"Come in and I will show you around."

He was bursting with pride in the apart-hotel as he showed us around. Big stone steps led into a big spacious lobby with spotlessly clean white tiles on the floor. I wondered if they put anything on them to keep them that clean. Apart from a mop and a bucket of course.

The walls were painted a wonderful shade of terracotta. Wonderful big picture windows framed magnificent views of the sea. There were easy chairs in white and couches in terracotta. Huge terracotta tubs with wild exotic plants took the spartan look off the place. From the lobby through glass doors we went into the bar. The white tiles continued, still spotless. The walls in here were all white except for one wall. That was picked out in terracotta. There were more plants in the bar. And more windows with more amazing views.

205

"Oh, it's beautiful, Marco, really beautiful." I knew what I was talking about and it was magnificent.

"Marco. You – have – magnificent – place. Magnificent – hotel."

Julia and I started to giggle. Abigail was talking pidgin English to Marco. She was raising her voice, shouting at him, as if he were deaf.

"Thank you. You are most kind. Now I will get you to sign in and I will show you to your apartments. We have ten apartments and the rest are all double rooms. If you are not happy with the apartments, I can show you a room if you wish."

"Any chance of him showing me a double room and his etchings at the same time? I wonder is he married?" Abby whispered to me. "What do you think?"

"I don't know, but I do know that you are."

"Not while I'm here I'm not. What's sauce for the goose is sauce for the gander."

"Maybe, but gooses and ganders don't get hurt by each other."

"It's geese and how do you know? They could be bitterly hurt each time one of them tries a bit of sauce. From their beaks to their webbed toes they could be gutted. How do we know?"

Dylan came to the rescue.

"Julia and I will share an apartment and you and Emma can share another one. What do you think? It makes sense. Julia and I will be heading out early in the mornings to work. You can take your leisure getting up and getting out without us disturbing you."

"That suits me."

"Me too."

He went over to confirm the arrangements with Marco. Julia went with him.

"What's going on with the two of them?"

"Well, I'm only Julia's mother, I don't know why you're asking me. I'll be the last to know. You'll be the second last to know, you being the boy's mother. They must've had it all arranged all the same. Julia doesn't look a bit surprised. Pleased, but not surprised."

"Isn't this great?" Julia came back over to us she was looking a bit too pleased with herself.

Not one of us spoke in the lift. It was just as well we were only going to the first floor. Our apartments were next door to each other. They were identical in every way.

There were two doors on the right hand-side and one on the left as we entered the apartment and a huge living-room just ahead of us. The door on the left led into a small kitchen with old scrubbed pine presses, a two-ring hob, a small circular pine table and two chairs with woven seats. It was very rustic and charming.

"Isn't it great? Not that we'll be using it much. I don't know about you, but I don't intend to do any cooking."

"We should get some milk though. I brought tea bags. Just in case we want a cup of tea."

207

"Let's see what the rest of the place is like."

The first of the other two doors led into a bathroom. It was surprisingly big. Really big. Everything in it was white and gold. The big old-fashioned bath had a shower in it. A toilet and a hand-basin completed the room. There were plenty of clean towels.

The second door opened onto a huge big bedroom. The tiles in here were cream and the walls painted terracotta. There were two big beds with scrubbed pine headboards. The quilt was cream with terracotta-coloured flowers trimming the edges. Two wardrobes and a dressing-table, all of scrubbed pine, added to the wonderful charm of the room. Check curtains in terracotta and cream hung on either side of a big glass door that led out onto a balcony. The view was magnificent. Narrow cobbled streets up to one side and on the other side steps down to a glorious beach.

The living-room was spacious. The walls were painted a deep rich cream. Terracotta slate tiles on the floor. A big soft sofa in cream and terracotta check and an ornate stained-glass-topped coffee table. There was one armchair that matched the couch and a TV on a stand. There was a large balcony with the same views as from the bedroom.

"Wow, isn't this wonderful!" Abigail took a deep breath. "I'm glad you made me come, Emma. I'm going to make the most of it."

"This calls for a drink." I pulled my case into the

bedroom. In my hand luggage I had a bottle of Bacardi from the duty-free shop at Dublin Airport. Although there was no savings on price it was handy to be able to pick up a bottle in the airport to bring with me. We had each brought a small carton of pineapple juice from home. I got glasses out of the kitchen and mixed up the drinks.

I handed one to Abigail and noticed she had taken her wedding and engagement rings off. Even though it was a warm balmy evening a shiver came all over me. Abby would have to be watched. She was a very sexy women let loose in a very romantic country. She looked like she was on the look out for a gander with plenty of sauce. She could create havoc among the saucy ganders over here.

We took our drinks out onto the balcony off the sitting-room. Two lovely deck-chairs and a small table were all the furnishings on it. There were pots full of every colour of flower, all heavily scented. We sipped our drinks. Abby looked at her ring-less finger. I was wondering what she was thinking.

I was thinking that I could stay here forever. Grow grapes and make wine. Go for long walks and mix with the natives. Plant olive trees. But there is more to making wine than growing grapes and a few days somewhere does not a native make.

CHAPTER ELEVEN

Madame Celeste
Scorpio
October 23 – November 22

This is a day for playing a supporting role. Let someone who knows what they are doing take the leading role. Learn from them.

I was charmed to see that the hotel had English papers – one with Madame Celeste's horoscopes. I had my fix before breakfast.

"Good morning to the two beautiful young ladies, this morning!"

Marco came over to the table as we were being served breakfast. There was an amazingly beautiful woman with him. She had the same colouring as Abby, but her face was more defined and square. She was wearing white trousers and a white strappy top. Her hair and her eyes were pitch black.

"Good morning, Marco." Abigail wasn't overly friendly.

"Good morning, Marco. We had a lovely night, last night. The apartment is so lovely and we had a few drinks on the balcony before we went to bed. We were more exhausted than we knew."

"I am pleased that you like everything. What are you going to do today?"

"We'll have a little explore around the island. Maybe go down and see how the photo shoot is going – it's supposed to be starting today. I'd like to have a swim too. And we have to taste some of the local wine. We have so much to do, Marco, it's a pity we're only here for a few days."

I laughed and Marco and his ladyfriend laughed. Abby forced a little laugh.

"But you can always come back to finish anything you start here on Aronna." He winked at me – a full-on wink.

The cheeky beggar, I thought. I also thought I must look half decent for him to be winking at me all the time. It's amazing the little things that make you feel good.

"I must tell you that this is Maria. If you want

anything she will help you."

I put my hand out to Maria and she shook it.

"I'm Emma, this is Abigail, Abby for short."

"It's lovely to meet both of you." She was very gentle, very soft-spoken.

"You have a beautiful place here, Maria."

"Yes. I love it. We are very busy now because of the photo shoot. It's very exciting."

"Yes, it's the first time I have ever been with Dylan when he's been working.

I'm looking forward to seeing it."

"He's a terrific man – you must be very, very proud of him. He's so friendly and charming." Maria knew how to win Abby over.

"Thank you, yes, I am very proud of him. I have three other boys I'm proud of them all."

"It must be wonderful for you. And I have met Julia this morning, she is a lovely girl. They make a lovely couple. They look lovely together."

"But they aren't a couple," I said. "They are just friends. Best friends."

"No, they aren't dating or anything like that," added Abby.

"Oh, I thought they were. There is a spark between them, isn't there? I will see you later."

We watched as she went to each table and talked to the guests. Making everyone feel important.

"Did you notice it?"

"What?" said Abby.

"The spark, did you notice it?"

"I suppose I did, but I think it's only that they are such close friends. What do you think?"

"That's what I was thinking," I said. "It'd be an awful mess for you and me if they got together. We'd end up taking sides in rows and everything."

"Yeah. When they were babies it seemed like a good idea. But now that they are big adults it seems like a horrible idea. There'd be the sleeping together bit and all that. No, it's best that they are just good friends."

"Best friends," I agreed.

"Here, what do you think of Maria? She's amazing, really beautiful, isn't she?" Abby was very taken with Maria.

"Stunning." I was a bit taken with her myself.

"So he's married."

"Yes, you can cross him off your list."

"That's a pity, he was the only one on it," she said wryly. "What do you make of her?"

"I thought she was nice. She sounds friendly. I wonder if they have any children?"

"Probably a big brood of them." Abby sounded a bit begrudging to say the least.

"Yeah, I'd say Marco enjoys making babies. They have a nice set-up here all the same. I could get used to this."

"How come they all talk English?" she wanted to know.

"Yeah, and better than us. You can't say anything but they understand it."

"Who told us they didn't speak English anyway?"

"That'd be your son, Dylan. Remember?"

"Oh, yeah."

"Come on, let's go for a walk into the village. Have an explore. We can go to the beach later."

The streets were all cobbled and narrow. If I stretched out really hard I could reach right across to the houses on either side. It was steep at first and I found myself struggling, but then around a bend it got better. It levelled out. Then the narrow street opened up to a little piazza.

It was bustling with people. Tourists and locals. I suspected some of the crew from the photo shoot were mixed in with the crowd.

The square was full of shops with local produce. The smell of freshly baked bread filled the air. Displays of wine, honey, fresh bread and cheese were mouth-watering. We explored all the little shops. They were laden with local art and craft. Hand-painted tiles, hand-woven rugs and beautiful jewellery. Wonderful rings and earrings made from amber.

"Aren't these beautiful?" Abby was holding a hand-painted glass. It was in turquoise and gold. There was a set of six. Each one a little bit different.

"Yes, I think I will be needing my extra case on the way home."

A stall in the middle of the square sold ice cream. There was a café with tables and chairs outside.

"Will we sit down and get something to drink?" Abby said. "It'd be nice to sit and soak in a bit of the atmosphere."

There was a middle-aged couple sitting opposite us. They were holding hands. They were smiling and talking and only had eyes for each other. It was hot where they were sitting right out in the sun. Abby and I were in the shade. The man reached into his pocket and pulled out a white handkerchief – as he opened it out to wipe the sweat off his face some confetti fell out of it onto the ground. The woman started to laugh and pointed it out to him. He laughed and then turned and kissed her. She pointed to another table. It was in the shade. He held her hand as he led her over to the table. For a moment they restored my faith in love. Not young love. I never lost my faith in young love. Julia was young and I knew she would find love. Young love is easy to find. Perfect bodies find perfect lovers. Young lovers only risk a broken heart. Middle-aged love is harder to find. Stretchmarks and wrinkles tend to put potential lovers off. Only when you have had love can you miss being in love, miss being loved. I missed being loved. I missed being held.

I turned to tell Abby how much I missed being loved.

"Did you see the couple over there?" I said. "I wish I was her."

216

"No, you don't."

"I do, Abby, she's in love. The guy she's with loves her loads. She's so happy. He's so happy to be with her."

"You could have been her if you hadn't gone rocking the boat, or the bed as the case may be. Anyway, you don't want to be her. She's too perfect and … she has a pimple on her fanny. You'd hate that."

"Jesus, that's amazing! How can you tell that she has a pimple on her fanny from here?"

"Because she's so bloody perfect that her having a pimple on her fanny is the only thing that's making me feel any way good!"

"Here, I know what'll make you feel really good. I'll treat you to some ice cream. There is nothing as orgasmic as Italian ice cream. It's toe-tingling good."

I perched my Nike hat on my head and headed over to the ice-cream kiosk. There was every flavour and colour of ice cream. I am very fussy about my ice cream. I like only vanilla. I don't like any sprinkles or chocolate flakes or silly dips. I adore plain, good, old-fashioned, wonderful vanilla.

"Can I have two ice creams, please?"

I pointed at the tubs and tubs of mouthwatering, delicious ice cream. I was hoping the weatherbeaten ice-cream guy understood English. I was in luck. He understood me perfectly. He knew what I wanted.

"In dish? In biscuit?"

"In cone." I pointed at the wafer cones.

"Flavour?" He pointed at all the flavours.

"Vanilla." I pointed directly at the creamy white one.

"Chocolate?"

"No. Vanilla."

"Yes, vanilla. Chocolate top?" He pointed to a chocolate dip.

"No."

"Nuts?"

"No."

"Syrup?"

"No."

"Fruit?"

"No."

Dear God, could a person not even get a plain vanilla ice-cream cone? I was worn out.

"Two. Vanilla cones. Nothing else. Nothing more. Plain and simple."

He got on with the job in hand. Fair play to him he knew what he was doing. The finished cones were absolutely huge. All creamy and smooth. I walked back carefully to Abby and handed her one.

"Wow, they're big!"

I licked all around the dripping edge of my own.

"Did they not have any chocolate dip?"

"I didn't think you wanted any. You never said."

"A few nuts?"

"I didn't think you'd eat them."

"Bit of syrup or fruit?"

"No. The bastard had nothing just plain old-fashioned ice cream. I don't know why you didn't get up off your arse and get it yourself if you're so fussy. I had no idea you were a connoisseur."

"Well, I like it dripping in toppings if you must know." She took a long lick around the cone.

"Now you've got some on your nose." I pointed out to her.

And just as I pointed – *plop*! My ice cream fell out of its cone. It landed with a '*plop*' directly on my foot. I was wearing flip-flops. My toes were bare. My toes were covered in ice cream and freezing. I kicked my foot out to get the ice cream off.

Abby pulled out a wad of tissues from her bag. "Here, use these."

I bent down and tried to wipe it all away. It was between my toes and under my foot. This was one of those times I could have done with a lover. He could have taken pleasure in sucking my toes. He could have licked each one clean. I could have taken pleasure in it myself. Just for fear I might be thinking about any sort of pleasure, never mind indulging in it, Abby interrupted me.

"Here, use this." She handed me a small bottle of water.

Was there no end to the equipment this woman had in her possession?

"You don't happen to have a lover anywhere about

your person, do you? One that's into licking toes."

"Sorry, I'm all out of toe-sucking lovers."

She bent over me. I was on my hunkers washing my foot.

'Plop!'

"Jesus! Oh, no! Get it off! *Ahhhh!* It's freezing."

The plop I felt was the ice cream out of Abby's cone landing on my back.

"Oh, God, Emma, I'm sorry. Here, let me wipe it. Here, open your dress – the ice-cream is running down your back."

"Ahhhh! Ohhhhh! Would that be the icy cold river of ice I feel flowing down my back, Abby? Would that be what that would be, would it? Would it? I know bloody well what it is! Get it off, will you!"

I shook myself and my cap fell off my head onto the ground.

I moved my shoulders and wriggled my body up and down. I tried to reach down my back with my arms. The ice cream was all over my back. I jumped around as the freezing cold ice reached the top of my bottom. My flip-flop was all wet and slippy. I lost my balance and faltered. The old Italian with the guitar stood up and came nearer. He played a tune to match my actions. I was only short of putting my right leg in and shaking it all about. Doing the hokey-cokey and twirling around. A small crowd gathered and started to clap. They thought I was doing some sort of a dance or other. That I was the street entertainment. They started whistling and cheering. Maybe because Abby had opened the back of my dress and my boobs were all but hanging out of the front of it. God alone knows what was keeping them under wraps. An old man threw a coin into my cap. More coins followed. I was blushing now. Bright red. The ice cream was gone from my back and my toes. I was a bit sticky, but that was all. The situation I was in was very sticky. I kept moving because I was afraid to stop. I looked to Abigail for assistance. She was clapping her hands and stomping her feet and cheering me on. She was gone mental. I guess it was fear. She was as afraid as I was. I was afraid if I stopped I'd be lynched by the crowd of onlookers for false pretences. There was quite a lot of money in the cap now. The more the crowd cheered the more I got into it. I started to enjoy myself.

"Jesus! Ma! What are you doing."

"That's the electric slide. Good, isn't she?" I could hear Abby shouting.

That was all the encouragement I needed. I gave it all I had.

I felt Julia's hand on my arm. "You're making a right show of yourself! For God's sake, will you sit down!" She was smiling out to the crowd. Bowing, trying to get me to bow out gracefully. "If not for God's sake, will you stop for my sake? You're making a right show of me!"

That was it. My bubble was burst. I hate making a show of Julia. That's the thing about kids, they're really easy to make a show of.

I took a final bow and picked up my cap. The crowd cheered.

I looked at all the coins in the cap. I had made a very lucrative show of myself.

"Well done, Emma! That was great!" Abby was delighted.

"Will you stop encouraging her!" Julia was not amused.

"I'm her friend – I'm supposed to encourage her."

"Yeah. Encourage her with normal things, like getting her hair cut or what to wear. I think the two of you have lost the plot."

"Lighten up, Julia, will you? I was only getting some ice cream off my back."

Abby and I started to laugh. It was lost on Julia. She was too busy looking around to see who exactly I had made a show of her in front of.

I only noticed then that Julia had a glass of wine in her hand and it was obvious that she had already had a couple of glasses. Maybe even a couple of glasses too many.

"Isn't this just the best?" Abby was in great form.

"It's great, but I wonder what the locals make of the invasion."

"Well, they seemed to enjoy you're little outburst, Ma. Actually, they're really nice about it. A few of us have been chatting to them, getting the low-down. You see that guy over there? The old guy sitting on the stone seat. He was born over there …" She pointed to a house that was immaculately kept. Pots and pots of flowers of every colour were all around it. "He was born in that house, got married in the church down the road and he still lives in that house. He's eighty-two years old and he has never left this island. Not even for a day. Can you believe that? This is his world. Just what you see here. Can you imagine it? He says, why would he leave such a beautiful place even for one day? That would be one day he'd miss being here. He says he'd be leaving his heart behind."

"Hey, that's powerful stuff, Julia."

"He must've had a very happy life here." Abby was going all dreamy on us.

"Yeah, imagine feeling that passionate about a place and the people in your life." I was going a bit dreamy myself.

"I think it's mad. To be stuck on an island for eighty-two years is daft."

"Obviously he found everything he ever needed here. He sounds happy. Sometimes, Julia, you can be a pain in the ass."

"You want some coffee? Something to eat?"

A dish of a guy was asking.

I was hoping he was on the menu. Dish of the day.

Abby and I were staring.

"Can I have some wine, please?" Julia had just

knocked back the last drop of her glass of wine.

"Thanks," she said as Dish brought out a jug of wine and three glasses. He poured the wine then left the jug on the table.

"Do you want to get some lunch?" I asked Julia, thinking she needed it.

"No. I'm fine with this." She poured herself some more wine.

I decided to order something for myself, hoping she'd eat some.

"Can I have some bruschetta, please?"

"The same for me, thanks," Abby said.

Julia didn't say anything. I was tempted to make her eat something to soak the wine up, but she was a big girl now and I couldn't make her do anything she didn't want to.

"Where's Dylan?" Abby was looking around for him.

"I think he must have gone back to the apartment. I've been looking for him and I can't find him. I came up here with the others to see if he was here. Our paths must've crossed somewhere and we missed each other. There was some trouble between the director and the photographer. They had a blazing row. I'm not sure what happened as I did a disappearing act before blood was shed."

"I hope it won't have an affect on Dylan. He won't like it if there's any trouble. You know Dylan. The eternal peacemaker."

"Oh, I think he'll be all right. He has found someone to hold his hand. I met the model that's working with him. She's stunning-looking. She's all bosom and bum and just ribs in between. Talk about accentuate the positive! Everyone thinks she's lovely. Although, I can see right through her. She'd eat him up and spit him out if she got the chance. By the looks of her and the looks she was giving him she intends to get plenty of chances. I think she's a bit of a slapper myself."

"Julia! I'm sure she's lovely."

"Only lovely-looking. She's not so nice a person though. She really excluded me. She was hanging out of Dylan all day. I thought I'd puke. I never even got a look-in. She says she's only new to this game and would Dylan mind minding her and look out for her, just for a day or two?"

"She's probably just nervous."

"Conniving more like. I'm only new to this game too, nobody is minding me! She did the 'poor helpless me routine' so brilliantly, she should be an actress. Funny thing is it worked – she had Dylan eating out of her hands before you could say spaghetti bolognese. He was putty in the aforementioned hands. Yuck! I hate it when women do the 'poor me, I'm only a woman' bit. It makes the rest of us look like half-jacks. Can you believe Dylan falling for it?"

"I don't think Dylan is that easily fooled. He was probably just being nice."

"Yeah, he's always nice." I was glad Julia had given the right reply. After all, Abby was Dylan's mother.

The Dish came back with our food. It was as melt-in-the-mouth delicious as he was.

"Here, try this," I said to Julia as I cut a piece off my delicious bruschetta. I really wanted her to eat something. The wine was strong and she was drinking too much and too early.

"I have to go to the loo." Abby was looking around. "I wonder where it is?"

"It's right over there, Abby. At the back of the café. Want me to come with you?"

"No, you stay with your mam, I'll find it."

"Will I go with her?" Julia asked as Abby was halfway across the square.

"No, she'll be fine, honestly." I was glad to have a few minutes with Julia on my own. "Listen, Julia, don't drink too much. The wine is stronger than you think and in the heat it'll go straight to your head."

"Too late, I think it's already gone there." She giggled.

"Will you be careful with Dylan? Both of you have just finished relationships. It would be easy to fall into each other's arms for consolation. Someone is going to get hurt. I don't want it to be you. Neither do I want you to mess him around."

"I won't, I promise. I don't feel so broken-hearted when I'm with him. I barely think of Colin. Anyway, Dylan is all set to fall into someone's arms, but they ain't mine. He's looking for consolation from his new ladyfriend."

"Well, don't go thinking the best way to cure your broken heart is to break a few yourself. It doesn't work like that."

"We're only friends. Dylan looks on me as a kid sister. I know that for sure. He doesn't even see me as a woman."

"Well, he must be blind then." I looked at the low-cut strappy pink dress she was wearing. It was short and cute. She looked all woman in it.

Abby came back. Dylan was with her. There was another girl with him.

"Hi, I've been looking everywhere for you," he said to Julia.

"Well, I've been here all the time so you mustn't have looked very well for me."

I was cringing at Julia's bitchy tone.

"This is Jane. She's working with me and Julia. This is my mother, Abigail, and her friend, Emma. Emma is Julia's mother."

"It's lovely to meet you." She was a sweet young girl. A very dawny, sickly-looking girl – stick-thin except for her boobs and her bum, which were very shapely. She looked pale and out of place in the sunshine. I loved her flowing pale-blue dress. It was so sexy on her. On anyone else it would have been just an ordinary everyday dress.

"You want to mind you don't get sunburn. Have you

put on some sun cream?" Abigail couldn't help mothering the girl.

I have to admit I had been looking at her pale skin and thinking the same thing myself.

"Jesus, she has everyone minding her now!" Julia had whispered, but I was sure Jane heard her.

"Total sunblock is what I have to use. I'd love to be all brown and healthy-looking, like Julia. She's fantastic, and those eyes! I see she got them from you. She's the image of you."

I was bursting with pride. She was trying to win Julia over.

We all turned around to look at Julia.

Julia was slumped in the chair. Her two knees pointing in different directions. Her two arms just hanging loosely by her side. Her head was tilting to one side. Her mouth hanging open. She neither looked fantastic or healthy. She looked almost dead. She was dead drunk. She was fast asleep. The wine had knocked her out. I was mortified.

"Poor Julia! I told her not to drink too much wine." Dylan tried to straighten her out. He pushed her two knees together. They opened out again. He pushed them together again and they stayed together. We all held our breath. We relaxed when we saw that he had been successful. As we relaxed so did Julia and her knees. Slowly they opened again.

"Me too. I told her to stop drinking ages ago. Years

ago, in fact, but she didn't listen to me then so why should she listen to me now?" I could see his efforts with Julia's knees were useless so I didn't even bother to get up and help him. Maybe no one would notice she was with me if I ignored her. Abby was kinder to my daughter than I. She pulled a light wrap out of her bag and handed it to Dylan.

"Here, try this. I brought it to keep the sun off my shoulders, but as we're in the shade I don't need it. Julia's need is greater."

Dylan spread the wrap over Julia's legs. She let out an unmerciful snort by way of appreciation. Dylan laughed. Abby laughed. Julia started laughing. I didn't laugh. I just went red. Who was making a show of who now?

"Oh, I nearly forgot!" said Dylan. "Marco wants us all to have dinner with him and Maria tonight. He seems very taken with the two of you."

"Isn't that really nice of him?" I said. "He's a nice man. He's very friendly. Maria is lovely too."

"I don't know if I'll bother," said Abby. "I was hoping to find a little hideaway to have dinner tonight. I thought the four of us might eat together."

"Well, we could do that tomorrow night," suggested Dylan. "Come on, Ma, just for tonight. Will you come?"

"Come on, Abby! It'll be good and we'll all be there."

"Right, right, whatever you say."

"Mammy! Mammy! I think I'm going to be sick." There was no denying Julia now. I had to go over and sort her out.

"I'd better go. See you all later." Jane ran off at the mention of sick.

"Look, we'd better get Julia back to the hotel. I don't want her making a show of herself getting sick here." And making a show of me.

"How are we going to get her back?" Abby was looking at Julia who had gone back asleep again. She looked like a rag-doll.

"That's easy." Dylan hauled at Julia and lifted her over his shoulder like a sack of potatoes. He started to walk off down the road carrying her. The crowd started cheering.

"Give it a rest, you lot!" Dylan shouted back at them – which only made them worse.

"You're no officer and certainly no gentleman!" one of the tourists shouted out.

"You got yourself a little souvenir then, Dylan?" That was one of the crew.

"Are you going to declare her at customs?" That was another.

The smart remarks and loud guffaws were endless, but all in good fun.

Then in one loud chorus they all started singing, 'Love Lifts Us Up Where We Belong'.

I was dreading having to relate it all to Julia when she woke up, but she slept all the way back to the hotel.

"I'll dump her on her bed for a while and she'll sleep it

off. See you both later."

Abby and I went into our room.

Abby crashed down onto her big bed.

"I'm going to have forty winks and then get ready. What do you think?"

"Good idea. I might have forty myself or at least twenty."

I felt all hot and bothered so I took off my clothes and pulled on a long flowing, white nightdress that I had brought with me because it's so cool and light. It's lovely for plodding around in in the heat. I lay up on top of the covers of my bed.

I could hear voices.

"Shhh! Abby, do you hear that?"

We listened.

"How the hell did I get here?"

"By magic."

It was Dylan and Julia. Their balcony doors were open. Ours were open too. There was a lovely breeze blowing.

Abby stopped listening and was dozing off.

I started to drift off myself.

"Come here to me, big boy!" Julia's voice was all sultry. I jumped up when I heard her.

Abby stayed sleeping. I guessed she couldn't hear them. My bed was right beside the balcony. I could hear everything.

"And why would I do that?"

"Because I asked you nicely and I fancy the arse off you."

"Julia, you're drunk. You don't know what you're saying."

Everything went quiet.

"Oh, Dylan!"

I didn't want to hear Julia, but I could.

"Just get some sleep, Julia. You'll be all right in a while." Dylan was being kind. I didn't want to hear my daughter make a show of herself. I was debating whether to go in there, march over to her, give her a slap, tell her to shut up and then make my escape. I could leave before they ever realised I was in the apartment.

I got up to close our balcony doors. I resisted all temptation to close theirs.

I didn't resist the temptation to lean over the little dividing wall to peep in at what was going on. Dylan was pacing up and down holding a wastepaper basket. As far as I could make out Julia was sprawled out on her bed. Either that or there was a third person in there with exactly the same flip-flops as Julia. I didn't even want to consider a threesome so I just took it to be Julia. If she'd only get up I might have been able to make eye contact with her and tell her to shut up.

I leaned over the wall a little bit more, but still I couldn't see anything much. Before I knew what I was doing I was hiking my flowing nightie up in the air and getting over the wall. I was standing on their balcony, like a peeping Tom. I hid tight in against the wall. Dylan's back was to the doors. Then, I was delighted to see Julia about to stand up. She faltered and sat down again. She was like Bambi. I was deflated. Then she made a second attempt. She managed it this time. Well done, Julia! I felt like Bambi's mother, bursting with pride when her little deer took his first steps. Julia hung her arms and, I suspect, her full body weight around Dylan's shoulders. The man had the patience of a saint. Ronan was a bit like that. I wished he was here now. He'd know what to do in a situation like this. Suddenly, Julia lifted her head up off Dylan's shoulder. Now was my chance.

I stepped out and shook my head at her and gave her my special 'stop making a show of me' stare. It was the one I used in the supermarket when she was a child and would scream the place down if I didn't buy her hundreds of bars of chocolate and barrels of ice cream. I was hoping she'd still recognise it. It was a long time since I had to use it. Although, maybe I should bring it out of retirement when we're in the supermarket these days. It might stop her putting the hundred bottles of shampoo and the barrel-load of conditioner into my trolley.

I stood on the balcony and stared my evil stare at her. I waved my arms and shook my head – all negative gestures. All saying 'stop what you are doing, you gobshite!'.

"*Ahhhhhh! Ahhhhhh!*" Julia was screaming and

pointing at me. "It's Mammy! It's my mammy! She's a ghost! Do you see her? There, on the balcony!"

I ducked back against the wall.

"There's no one there, Julia."

I came out of hiding and again gave her the evil eye. This time I wagged my finger at her too for maximum effect.

"Mammy! Mammy! I'm coming!"

"Julia! Stop, will you! There is no one out there. Look!" Dylan came out onto the balcony, but not before I had time to jump back over the wall onto my own balcony and make a dash into my room.

"Julia! There is no one there. You're imagining things. Lie down. Try to get some sleep."

"Only if you get in beside me."

I lay in the safety of my own bed for ages. I was trying not to think about what was going on next door. Trying not to think that my daughter was making a gobshite of herself. I thought she said she knew what she was doing.

I strained my ears to see if I could hear anything.

There was a thumping sound. Then another one. Then a muffled sound and Dylan shouting.

"*Julia!*"

She had probably jumped on him. Thrown herself at him. I really didn't want to hear any more. There is only so much humiliation I can stand. I was way over limit. I put my pillow over my ears. It was great. I could hear nothing.

Except a loud knock at the door.

"*Emma! Emma!*"

I jumped up off the bed and let Dylan in. I was delighted to see he was fully dressed and fresh-looking. There were no visible marks on his body. Well, none that I could see from where I was standing.

"Can you come in next door, Emma? Julia is looking for you. She's vomiting all over the place!"

I ran in as quickly as I could.

"Julia!"

"Oh! Mammy, I feel awful." I was delighted to see she was fully clothed even though she was awful-looking.

"Don't worry, you'll be fine. You just had too much to drink."

"You warned me, didn't you? You told me not to drink too much and what did I do? What did I go and do? I didn't listen to you. I ignored you, Mammy, I kept drinking. Then a horrible thing happened – I saw an image of you. You were on the balcony. It was the worst thing I ever saw. You looked awful. You were wearing a shroud and shaking your head and your hands at me. It was a vision. You looked so old!"

I could have spit. I looked old.

"She swears she saw a vision of you out there." Dylan was pointing onto the balcony.

"Poor pet, that's ridiculous. Why would I be on the balcony?" I felt guilty not telling her the truth, but it was enough that half the family had made a show of the whole family. There was no need for the whole family to make a show of the whole family.

She got sick again, into the wastepaper basket that Dylan had strategically placed on the floor. Her aim was good. I'll say that much for her. That is all I will say for her. There was nothing else good about her at the moment.

I thought once she had been sick she would sober up quick enough. I was wrong. She must have been very drunk. She only calls me Mammy when she's very drunk, which I'm glad to say isn't that often. Well, not in front of me anyway. She probably calls me Mammy when she's out with her friends every Friday and Saturday night getting tanked up.

"You warned me about a lot of things, Mammy, and I totally, totally ignored you. Do you hear me? I totally ignored you. Well, I have to tell you as I sit here on the edge of this beautiful bed in this beautiful place with my head in this beautiful wastepaper basket that you were right on all counts. You warned me about men. Did I listen? Did I hell?"

I held my hand on her forehead and put my other arm around her shoulders. Poor Julia. She looked wrecked. Dylan was great and handed me a cool, damp, face-cloth.

"I don't think I warned you about men, Julia. I think it was advice I was giving you." I was mortified in case Dylan thought I was anti-male.

"No, Mammy, fair play to you – you warned me – big time. That toe-rag Colin was a toe-rag, do you know that? A total toe-rag. Remember the night of Angela's going-away party? After he brought me home he went back to the party and gave her one."

"Gave her one what?" I thought I knew where this was going, but I wanted to be wrong. I wanted him to have given her one drink, one cigarette, one lethal injection, anything but what I thought.

"One, you know, *one*. Something to remember him by. Much more than a farewell kiss. Do I have to spell it out for you?"

"No, thanks, I get the picture."

Dylan was pacing up and down coughing in all the appropriate places.

"Sex, a ride, a bonk, whatever you're having yourself …"

"Now, I definitely get the picture, thanks."

"Anyway, he said that I had finished with him that night and he was a free agent. He asked me to go back with him, but I told him that my mammy had warned me about toe-rags like him."

"You didn't!"

"Well, not in so many words. I told him toe-rags were not on my list of datable species. Bastards, bums and bollocks were all on it, but toe-rags weren't. He didn't like being the lowest form of species."

"Colin wasn't right for you," Dylan piped up. "Sure

you've been saying it yourself for ages. You told me several times that you didn't know what you were doing with him. Remember, you said it was lust and that one day you'd be in love and you'd know the difference."

I was impressed. His mother had reared him well! He was very obviously a better friend to my daughter than even I knew.

"You're good at this, Dylan." At least I appreciated what he was trying to do. Julia was just grunting at him.

"Come on! This is very hard on you." He was so gentle. "I'll get you a cup of coffee."

"Ah thanks, Dylan, that's really kind of you. I am in trauma – you have no idea how hard it is to watch your only daughter making a show of herself, but I won't have a coffee if you don't mind. I'm not feeling great at the moment." My stomach was sick looking at Julia.

"Sorry, Emma. I meant Julia. Julia, will I get you some coffee? Of course I was going to ask you too, Emma. Are you sure you don't want one?"

"No. Don't mind me. I'm fine." I couldn't believe Julia had put me in this hellhole of a situation.

"Julia. Will you drink some coffee? Come on, Julia. Sit up. I'll get the coffee and you drink it. It'll do you good." He was being a bit firm now. A bit more assertive. Maybe his true colours were coming to the fore.

"Jesus, no, are you barking mad? Shag off with the coffee, will you!" The assertive bit was contagious. Julia had got a dose of it now.

"Well, what about tea? Or water?"

"Just water."

Dylan got the water from the fridge. It was lovely and cold. Julia sipped it gently.

"Dylan, what are you doing here?" She turned to him and on him.

"What do you mean? You really are losing it now, Julia."

"No, I know what you're doing here, but what are you doing, being here?"

He looked at me. I shrugged my shoulders.

"I don't know what you're talking about, Julia. Maybe you should try to get some sleep."

"I'll go and get two tablets for her, it'll settle her stomach." I really wanted something to settle her mouth, but I couldn't think of anything short of a gag.

I went back into my own apartment. I put the tablets in my pocket and went into the bedroom to ask Abigail if she knew anything that would shut up a mouth that was letting itself down. She was fast asleep. I left her to it.

I went back in to suffer more humiliation next door. I'm such a glutton for punishment.

"What are you on about, Julia? Tell me!" There was a very tetchy edge to Dylan's voice.

Dylan was sitting beside her on the bed now.

Then he started wiping her face with the damp cloth and for a moment I felt like an intruder. What would be so wrong with these two getting together? I'd have to have a word with Abby and tell her I thought it might be good for both of them. I'm sure between the two of us we could convince Dylan how good it would be for him. Julia seemed to be convinced already.

I stood looking at the two of them. Yes, they were good together. Her show of jealousy at anything-but-plain Jane this afternoon spoke volumes.

He dabbed her two hands with the cloth. "Go on, Julia, tell me what you mean. You know I'm here for the photo shoot." Dylan was soft spoken.

"I know that. But you shouldn't be here, should you? I promised Roz I wouldn't tell you. I promised her. I don't think it's fair that she made me promise. You're my friend longer than her or should that be she? Anyway, it's you I should be most loyal to. Right?"

"Right! So come on. Out with it. Spill your guts." That was the wrong thing for Dylan to say in the circumstances. I nearly ran forward with the wastepaper basket again. I was hoping she wouldn't take him literally.

"Roz told me that she loved you but that you didn't feel the same way about her. She said if you did love her you would have asked her to stay, not to go to Africa. She thought that the only reason you wouldn't ask her was because you didn't want her. She said you were very eager for her to go. She'd have gone anyway, but she would have liked you to have wanted her to stay. She wanted the two of you to talk about it. She wanted some sort of a commitment. She thought you could make a commitment to each other. A ring, a promise or even a shared wish to be together. She thought your relationship was going to be able to stand up to her being away, but you just cut her off. She's madly in love with you, Dylan. She thinks you did the dirt on her. She kept saying you were in love with someone else. I told her she was crazy, but she wouldn't listen to me."

I couldn't make head or tail of what she was saying. Then again that didn't matter. No one even noticed I was in the room. Dylan seemed to understand every word Julia was saying.

"I had no idea," he said softly. "I thought she wanted to go out there with a clean slate. I thought she didn't want me. I only encouraged her the way I did because I thought that was what she wanted. I know it was what she wanted. I didn't know how she felt. I never did the dirt on her. I can't believe she thinks that. She should know me better than to think I'd do something like that on her. I didn't ask her to stay because I didn't want to come between her and her dream. What a gobshite I've been!"

"Well, you'd better do something about it."

"What? I have no phone number for her. She was to ring me in a couple of weeks when she got sorted."

"Didn't she give you an e-mail address? She's still in London, in the hospital getting extra training. She'll probably check her mail there. Mail her."

"Yes, yes, she's there for three weeks. She's meeting the doctors and the rest of the team going out and getting up-to-date training, seeing videos on what to expect over there and anything else she might need. Remember she said she could back out of it if she felt that it was too harrowing for her."

"Yes. But don't go thinking she'll back out of it. I don't think she will."

"I have to get in touch with her. I didn't know I'd hurt her. I didn't mean to. I have to fix it. Thanks, Julia."

He kissed her on the forehead.

She closed her eyes.

CHAPTER TWELVE

Abigail looked absolutely fantastic. A show-stopper. For someone that didn't want to go to the meal in the first place she certainly went to town on getting ready. Her hair was shining and not one of them was out of place. Her make-up was done perfectly. Her legs looked really long in tight black trousers and her boobs were just bursting out of a black strapless fitted top. A black lace wrap across her shoulders gave her an elegant look. I'd have to do a lot of catching up not to look like the dowdy friend.

I needed to relax first. I was all on edge. Between climbing the walls with worry about Julia and climbing balcony walls I was worn out.

If I never saw another drink again it would be too soon.

I slumped onto a sun lounger on the balcony. Abby

opened a bottle of wine and poured me a glass. Automatically I took it. It hit exactly where it was supposed to hit. I had decided that it would be silly never to drink again, but I sure as hell was never getting drunk again.

"It was awful, Abby, I don't know how she got herself into such a state."

"It's easy on this stuff." She held up her glass.

"I feel sorry for her. Dylan has definitely made an impact. You'd want to see the way she was looking at him. She's smitten. He hasn't a clue. He's going to e-mail Roz. I suppose you can ask someone to marry you by e-mail these days. They'll get engaged by e-mail and don't get me wrong, Abby, I hope it works out for them and I hope he's blissfully happy. It's just that I'll be like sticky tape again trying to fix poor Julia's broken heart. I don't think I can go through all that again."

"It's hard to keep up with all the comings and goings. I'm nearly afraid to go asleep these days. Every time I close my eyes something happens."

"All the same, I think she's great for telling him to get in touch with Roz, don't you? Fair play to Dylan, I really don't think he has a clue that Julia is mad about him. Even though she did say it all very bluntly to him. He just thought she was babbling again. I hope she's all right now. I hope she'll be all right tomorrow and the next day and so on and so on."

"Dylan just knocked on the door while I was in the

kitchen. He said Julia's finally fallen asleep. He was going downstairs to see if Marco knew where he could send an e-mail. He told me he was a bit confused that Roz had said nothing to him about how she felt before she left. I told him most women don't tell their true feelings. He said he thought we were all barking mad. He said he can't understand why we can't just say what we feel. Must be the hormones he said. I gave him a clip on the ear and said I didn't see him wanting to be a monk all the same. The dawny little one, what's her name again?"

"Jane. Jane, that's her name. Anything-but-plain Jane."

"Oh, yes. Well, she came along the corridor asking him to show her where the lobby was. She was lost apparently. She said she's a bit nervous. I think Julia is right. I think she has her claws into him. Anyway, the big idiot said he was going down that direction and he'd bring her down and show her. I ask you? How can you get lost in this place? She's really striking though, isn't she? She was wearing or nearly wearing a bikini and a sarong."

"Speaking of clothes, what the hell am I going to wear to this dinner tonight? I'd better make some sort of an effort. You look stunning, by the way. Geoff is lucky to have you."

"He might not have me for long."

"Oh! Don't say that. Sort it out when you go home.

In the meantime let's have a good time."

I went into the bathroom to have a shower. I couldn't hear very well through the sound of the water, but I swear I heard Abigail say: "Oh, I intend to. I most certainly intend to."

More than what she said was the way she said it. She meant business. I pretended not to hear her at all. It was better that way. Well, she was a grown adult. I really wasn't in the mood to be minding her and Julia. I needed some minding myself.

I decided to wear a very nice white boob-tube that was covered in blue beading. Every colour of blue. White linen trousers and blue strappy sandals really showed it off. The sapphire and diamond earrings Danny had given me so long ago were terrific with it. I could already see the start of a tan – so what if it was out of a bottle. My make-up and hair looked as good as a non-professional could get them.

"Wow!" Abby, knew how to buck me up.

Julia was still asleep, so we left her alone.

Dylan wasn't ready yet so we left him alone too.

The two of us went down in the lift together. 'Sisters Are Doin' It For Themselves' we sang.

Then braced ourselves and made an entrance.

Marco and his wife appreciated it.

There was no one else around to appreciate it.

"Where is everyone?" Abby asked. The place was deserted. I could see she was disappointed. She was all dressed to pull and there was nothing to pull.

"All out for dinner," Marco replied. "They will be back to the bar later on for the drinks."

"Are we all set then?" Maria asked.

"We were going to wait on Dylan, if that's all right." Abby was nothing if not loyal.

"Oh, yes, of course, we can have a drink then while waiting." Maria led us into a lovely room. Two of the walls were all glass. The view out over the sea was breathtaking.

"What a beautiful room!"

"Wonderful!"

The floor was white marble with green and copper rugs scattered around. There were two long, comfortable soft Italian leather couches facing out to the sea. They were a beautiful shade of tan. I sank down into one of them and kept sinking. I was wondering how I would ever get out of it. I'd have to get everyone to pull me out. The leather had a tight grip on me. Maria sat down, but she didn't sink. Neither did Abby. Then with no effort at all Maria got up to pour the drinks. No limbs flailing all over the place to get her balance. She was very elegant as she stood up and poured us all a drink.

It was hard to take my eyes off the view, but the rest of the room was competing for my attention. I could pick up a few tips here. I was raging I hadn't brought my camera down with me. I could have taken photos of everyone. More importantly I could have taken lots of shots of the stunning interior and used them for work. There were huge earthen pots filled with tall, tall plants with exotic-coloured flowers. There were two solid walls in the room painted a light tan. One wall was full of photographs. Black and white and colour. Some old and some new. I wanted to get up and look, but it would have been too much of an effort to get out of the seat.

I turned to see if the photographs continued onto the last wall, the one behind me. I leapt up out of my seat. Well, at least I tried to. My legs and arms were flailing all over the place. I seemed to have more of them than the standard two of each. I felt like an octopus. I thought about aborting the effort. Pretending I didn't want to get up. I assumed a nonchalant position half in and half out of the seat. My head was nearly where my arse should be and my legs were wide open across the floor. I don't think I fooled anyone. I don't think I looked my most attractive, but there was nothing I could do about it.

"Do you want a hand?" Marco thought he was being a gentleman. Any gentleman worth his salt would have seen my situation and completely ignored it.

"No, I'm fine. I was just admiring the painting." I rolled my eyes towards it and lifted my arm up to point. It was like a periscope arising from the back of my seat.

"Magnificent." He went over and stood in front of it. He obviously wanted me to follow.

I was no idiot. I was happy slumped where I was even if my neck was killing me. I had no intentions of trying to escape from the chair again.

"Beautiful." Abby had no difficulty getting out of her chair.

"Wonderful." Maria joined them. I felt so left out. It was so unfair. I must've been stuck with the only chair in the place that kept its occupant captive. I was having none of it. With a very undignified final effort I managed to stand up. I stood gazing at the painting. I was breathless. The final effort had nearly killed me.

In the middle of the wall, in pride of place, was a huge canvass. Greens, blues and vibrant reds, a blue dot in the bottom right-hand corner.

"Amazing!" I said. I noticed that we were all reduced to one-word sentences. I tried to make a longer one: "Don't you just love it? It's one of mine."

"One of yours?" Maria asked.

"Oh, not one I painted. It's just that I have two of this artist's paintings on my own wall at home."

"Don't you just love his work?" Maria was as enthusiastic as I.

"I wish I had more. I could fill the house with them. Where did you get it?"

"From the artist, himself."

"You don't know him, do you? I know nothing about him. He keeps a very low profile."

"I don't know him all that well. You're right, he's a bit of a recluse, but he has a little studio at the far end of the beach."

"Here? This beach? Do you hear that, Abby?"

"Does he live here then, Maria?"

"Yes. For most of the year. He travels a little bit too. I don't know him well. He seems like a nice man. He's very quiet, keeps himself to himself and we respect that. He arrived here in Aronna about five years ago. No one knows where he was before that. They say he's a bit of a lost soul."

I liked the sound of him, me being a bit of a lost soul myself.

"We'd love to see his studio. Would he let us call up there, do you think?"

"It would be great to see it and talk to him." Abby was almost as eager as I to see more.

"I'm not sure. Sometimes he comes walking along the beach. I usually just wave and leave him alone, but if I see him I can ask him."

"That'd be wonderful." I was bursting with excitement.

"Does he live alone? Has he a family?" Abby was good at asking the questions I wanted to hear the answers to.

"No, he has no family."

"So this is where you're all hiding!" came Dylan's voice. "I hope you don't mind, but I brought Jane with me. She's at a bit of a loose end. The rest of the gang thought she was eating with me tonight and they've already gone on. We don't know where they are."

"That's no problem, there is enough for everyone,"

said Maria. "I believe Julia isn't too well and not able to come. You are very welcome."

Julia was a fool. Here she was letting a golden opportunity of having dinner with Dylan slip through her hands. Not alone was she missing an opportunity, she was giving Jane the very opportunity she was missing. How could she let Jane take her place so easily? Jane, on the other hand, for all her gormless talk, was a very clever woman. Her frilly little top was ultra-feminine if just a little bit see-through. Just enough of a tease. Every time she bent forward, which was very frequently, you couldn't help wondering if she was or wasn't wearing a bra. The skirt was less frilly but tighter. The sandals were high. She was perfectly made-up. She had the poor-me-femme-fatale routine off to a treat.

"I am so sorry to intrude. If it's any problem I can eat in my room." Pause for everyone to insist she stay. And they did. Ad infinitum and ad nauseam. She lapped up all the infinitums and nauseums.

"No, you can't eat alone in your room! That would be silly."

"That would be dreadful!"

"Don't be so silly!"

"Well, you're here now, you may as well stay." I even joined in myself.

"Yes, indeed." Abby sounded as if she had just worked out Jane's plan.

"Dylan is so kind. He insisted I come along with him.

It's so embarrassing." She batted her super, duper, longer-than-anyone-else's eyelashes at us all as she sat down beside Dylan. I noticed her lightweight body didn't even make a dent in the leather. She didn't sink down at all, but her skirt somehow managed to go up.

I was sitting on the arm of the chair now. Balancing my arse on it. I was no fool. There was no way I was getting myself suctioned into the seat again.

"Come, have a drink. You are very welcome here." Marco, being the gentleman that he was, handed her a glass.

"This is lovely of you all, cheers." She smiled and the whole room lit up. I noticed Dylan's arm was resting along the back of the couch. I noticed Jane resting her head against his arm. I noticed Abigail giving her daggers looks.

"Did you manage to make contact with Roz?" she asked Dylan.

"Yeah. Marco has all mod cons here. I sent her an e-mail. I'll check later to see if there is any reply."

"Roz is Dylan's girlfriend," Abby announced.

Jane looked very disappointed.

"Ex-girlfriend," Dylan corrected.

Jane looked very pleased.

"Shall we have dinner?" Maria stood up.

"You really do have a beautiful home. Have you and Marco lived here all your married life?" Abby asked Maria as we walked down a row of steps.

"What?" She started to laugh.

"What's so funny?"

"Marco and I are not married. He is my brother. I thought you knew! He will laugh when I tell him what you thought." She linked Abby down the last two steps and whispered to her. "Marco never married. He says he never had time to look for only one woman to love when there are so many to make love to. I tell him the right one will find him when the time is right. He says he's too old to settle and that I am a romantic. Maybe he's right, but it would be nice for him to have a special woman in his life."

"And what about you, Maria, have you a special man?"

"Not now – I was very lucky though. I was married to a lovely man. He was from Florence. We had a wonderful marriage. He died seven years ago. I loved him very much. I was devastated when I first found out he was sick. Even more devastated when he died. Marco was a great help. He helped me to realise how lucky I was to have to have loved and been loved."

"That's so sad. Do you have children?"

"We would have liked to have children, but it wasn't to be."

"I'm sorry."

"And what about you, Abby? Your husband is not with you."

"I'm separated from my husband." I nearly dropped

down dead when I heard her blatantly lying. I looked around to see if Dylan had heard her. She was safe – he was busy talking to Jane.

Maria went on talking to Abby, not knowing what a big liar she was.

"Oh, I'm sorry. Are you separated long?"

"Just a while. But I'm fine about it."

"And you have four boys. That must be hard without their father around."

"I'm well able for it."

She was such a liar, I couldn't get over her.

"So, you have no girls then?"

"No, Julia, Emma's daughter is the nearest I have to a daughter. We're very close, aren't we Emma?"

"Abby is a stand-in mother. Julia is lucky."

"And what about you, Emma?" Maria stopped and turned to me. "What's your husband like?"

"I haven't a clue. He left before Julia was born."

"Oh. I seem to be saying all the wrong things tonight. I'm sorry."

The poor woman was so mortified.

"Don't worry."

"It must have been hard on you too, rearing Julia on your own."

"Not so much now as it used to be."

"Does Julia's father have a good relationship with her? Does he see her?"

"Never. He never wanted to see her. Imagine he's out

there somewhere and he knows he has a child and he isn't even curious about her. I think that's weird. I think that only someone who has had their heart removed could be like that."

"Yes. You could be right."

The poor woman, she was sorry she asked.

"And have you a new man in your life now?"

I'm not sure if it was the gentle way she asked or the fact that she was willing to risk putting her feet in it again by asking an awkward question or a combination of both or maybe because she was such a genuinely lovely woman that I didn't mind her asking. Then again maybe it was plain old-fashioned pride. I didn't want her feeling sorry for me. All on my own in the world with no one to care about me. For whatever reason I decided not to give my usual 'cut 'em down to size' reply.

Instead I found myself opening up to her.

"I messed up, big time, Maria. Not only with one man, but with two. Neither of them can forgive me now. They both marched off into the sunset. They will never forgive me. I think I hurt their pride. You know, when they say the best way to hurt a man is to kick him in the balls, well, I think they're wrong. I think the way to totally shatter a man is to kick him in his pride. Like I did. That's one they don't forgive too easily. So, Maria, any hope I had of a special man in my life is gone. I have only myself to blame."

"The right one will find you, no matter where you are

or what you have done. He will be drawn to you. Timing, Emma, it's all about timing."

We walked under an archway full of heavy-scented blossoms. A table had been set in a small patio area that was directly on the seashore.

Maria showed us all to our places. I was sitting next to Marco. Abigail was on the other side of me then Dylan and Maria and Jane and back to Marco.

The food was melt-in-the-mouth delicious. The air was balmy. The moon was full. The company was wonderful with the exception of Jane who really got on my nerves. She was being so sickly nice to Dylan.

Maria was a wonderful cook.

Italian breads and dressings and fresh salads filled the table.

In the centre a huge dish of pan-fried fish and shell-fish done in olive oil smelt amazing.

The prawns, still in their shells, reminded me of Ronan. Not that the poor man looked in any way like a prawn. Although, as I looked at the cute little things lying there all forlorn and lost I could see a sort of resemblance. That was the same lost expression Ronan had on his face when I had done the dirt on him. He had forgiven me so easily for nearly killing him, but he couldn't forgive me at all for nearly sleeping with Danny. Now he didn't love me. I had spoiled it. I had spoiled it with Danny too. Nobody loved me. I felt really sorry. Really sorry for myself.

This was a place to be in love. I wished someone, somewhere was in love with me. I imagined what I would do if Ronan just strolled up here now and walked over to me and took me by the hand and led me off into the most romantic night I had ever seen.

I turned around and for a moment, just a fleeting one mind you, I thought I saw the shadow of a man walking along by the cliffs onto the beach. My heart gave a little jump. I'm not sure if it was a jump of excitement or fear.

My poor heart recognised the man. Why else would it be jumping? For a moment I thought I recognised the man myself. If both my heart and myself recognised him then it must have been someone we had both felt something for for sometime. As there was no one in my life at the moment who was being kind to my heart or myself, I had to assume it was someone who had broken my poor heart.

I strained to see if it was Ronan. I strained to see if it was Danny. Then he was gone. I couldn't see him any more. I got up off my seat to see if I could see where he had disappeared to. Imagine if it was someone looking for me? Imagine if he had followed me here? I went to the edge of the patio and leaned across the timber fence. He was gone.

Maybe it was someone I hadn't met yet. Maybe it was someone I was destined to meet soon and I was getting a little taste of what was to come. I am a huge fan of destiny. When reality is crap, destiny is all we've got.

Had I just seen the love of my life? Was there anyone there at all? It's amazing what you can imagine when you're desperate.

I turned again to go back to my seat, but Abby was sitting there now. She was animated, talking to Marco. I knew she fancied him. He fancied her. I should have reminded her again that she was married, but maybe she was as desperate as I was.

"Emma, what is it? Are you all right?" Maria was at my side.

"Yes, I'm fine. I just thought I saw ... Nothing. It doesn't matter."

"You look lost. Are you sure you're all right."

"I was just thinking how easy it is to make mistakes and how hard it is to get someone to forgive you for them."

"A gentle soul will always forgive. A heart free from bitterness will always forgive. But you too have to free yourself first. Forgive yourself first. Then it will be easier for others to forgive you. If you carry the burden of guilt you have only yourself to blame. Guilt can destroy things."

Maria was right. I was eating myself up with guilt. Well, no more. I had had enough. I had been stupid. I admitted it. I owned up to it. Where did it get me? Nowhere. I wasn't going to feel guilty any more. The slate was clean.

"I'm so glad I came here, Maria. It's beautiful. It's so

raw and alive. I'm glad I came and I'm glad I met you."

She gave me a hug.

"Now tell me, Emma, is Abby all right with Marco? He is a bit of a ladies' man you know."

"I think they both just want a bit of fun. Will we assume they're old enough to know what they're doing and leave them to it?"

We could hear Abby laughing and Marco clapping his hands at some story she was telling him. I was hoping it was the one about the diamante thong – I thought Marco would enjoy it.

CHAPTER THIRTEEN

"Emma, Emma!"

I could hear someone calling my name in the far-off distance. I was standing in a flowing blue gown looking down a lush green, well-trodden pathway. There was a mist coming down. I headed off down the pathway. I was in my bare feet. The grass felt soft underfoot.

"Emma, for God's sake!" I heard him call again.

At the end of the pathway the mist was heavier. I couldn't see properly. Then, suddenly, it cleared. Out of the mist, handsome as could be in a tailored tuxedo, came the most handsome man I had ever seen. He looked lost. He was looking for someone. He was looking for me. I stretched my arms out to him. He stretched out to me. We ran slowly towards each other. We were inches away from embracing. From wrapping our arms and anything else we could manage around each other.

From him lifting me up in his arms and laying me down on the sand and devouring me. Just inches away.

"You came looking for me!" I cried out to him.

I was shaking. Waiting. Wanting.

"Wake up, Emma! Please wake up!" Abigail was shaking me, a bit to violently.

"Go away. I'm about to be carried off into the sunset and shagged on the beach."

"Emma, I need you!"

"I know, my darling, I need you too! I'm coming! I'm coming!"

"Emma, stop messing and listen to me. Wake up!"

I was shaking harder now. So hard that the misty pathway disappeared. I tried to remember exactly what it was like. To get it all back again, but it was gone. The misty path and the handsome hunk too.

"This better be good," I said to Abby. "Stop shaking me. The damage is done. I'm awake."

"Well, open your eyes and listen."

I tried. God knows I tried to open my eyes, but they just wouldn't open.

I had stayed in the bar until all hours last night talking and dancing and having great fun with the film crew and Maria. Abby never came in from the patio. I don't know what time she got back. I must have been asleep at the time. I remember hoping she was having mad passionate sex just before I drifted off asleep. Mad and passionate enough for the both of us. I certainly wasn't getting any. I never heard her coming in.

"I am listening."

"Your eyes are closed."

"Can't a person be awake with her eyes closed?"

"Once you're sure you're really awake?"

"I am. Look." I waved my right arm at her. My left arm was still dead as were both my legs and the rest of my body. I was only delighted that my right arm was fully functioning.

"A terrible thing has happened. I'm going to have to get off the island. I think I'm going to die."

I sat bolt upright.

"If that was just to get me to wake up, it worked. If you have just found out you have something wrong with you and you are actually going to die it was a horrible way to waken me. Either way I hate you. I told you before never to use that expression lightly."

"Oh, shut up and listen will you, Emma!"

"All right, all right, what did you wake me up for, you bitch?"

"Wait till you hear. Remember last night when you left to go into the bar and I was sitting out on the patio with Marco. Well, it was lovely, we had some wine and we were getting on great. He asked me what was the story with my husband and I told him that I was separated from him and that he was having an affair."

"You said what?"

"You heard me. I'm not going to repeat it all over

again. Anyway, he said he was delighted to hear that I was separated as he didn't want any husband coming after him with a shotgun. I told him there was no danger of that. He said he couldn't believe any man that was married to me would even think of having an affair with another woman."

"Hey, I've just noticed you still have your clothes on from last night. How come? Are you only just back now? What time is it? Did you sleep with Marco? How come your cardigan is on inside out. Oh, my God. You didn't? You did? Did you?"

"That's what I'm getting to. Stop with all the questions, will you? Did you notice the glass doors at the side of the hotel down at the patio area."

"Yeah, I was wondering where they led to."

"Well, they led to a cosy little basement sitting-room. You can sit down there and look out directly at the sea. It's wonderful when the moon is full. So, anyway, I was a bit chilly sitting out on the patio so I put my cardigan over my shoulders and Marco asked me was I cold. I said I was a bit chilly, but I didn't want to go up to the crowded bar. He said he was delighted to hear that because he didn't want to go into the bar either. He said we could go into the beach room and continue our chat."

"I hope it was only your chat he was after."

"Will you stop! So in we went to the beach room. He left the doors open and we sat down and had more wine.

There is another little room in there. It's the wine cellar. Once we were inside he asked me was I warm enough. And I said to him: 'If you want you could put your arms around me and we could cuddle up to keep warm. You never know what might happen.'

"You cheeky bitch! I bet it wasn't even cold."

"That's beside the point. Sure what was the harm in a cuddle? We cuddled up together and it was just glorious. I felt like a real woman. A sexy, desirable woman. The moon was shining across the water and I could hear the waves making gently clapping noises as they hit off one another and rolled up the beach. There was a very soft breeze that swayed through the tops of the plants on the patio. There was a balmy smell of sweet, scented flowers."

Abigail was walking around the room, her hands swaying to her words. She was getting a bit carried away.

"Spare me the wind blowing through the leaves shit and get on with what happened, will you?"

"But it was so romantic, Emma, like something you'd only see in a film or read about in a book. It was special. So romantic. A perfect setting."

"OK, I get the picture, there you were cooped up in a beach house that stank of wine. The sea and the wind competing with one another to get your attention and most importantly of all the randy Marco sitting beside you all ready to pounce."

"Well, I just want to set the scene for you."

"Well, you have set it in great detail so now get on with it."

"God, you're awful. Have you no romance left in you?"

"No, and you woke me up just when it looked like I was going to get some."

"So, anyway, there I was in a perfect setting. The next thing I knew Marco gave me a peck on the cheek and on the lips. He told me I was 'a beautiful sexy, woman'. I was lapping it up. He had a little grope of my tits and we had a big snog. Then, just as we were sitting there, mouths open, hormones flowing, all set for the next instalment I heard someone out on the patio. I turned around quickly to see where the noise was coming from. Just as I turned Marco went to kiss me and he missed. He hit his mouth off the side of my head. I was mortified. Then I heard the noise again and this time we both looked. We could see everything from where we were sitting in the dark. The soft light was still lit on the patio. Everything was as clear as it is now. You will never guess who was out on the patio."

"Who?"

"Guess, go on! You never will."

"Will you just get on with it! I'm hanging on your every word!"

"Now you're making fun of me. Do you want to hear or not?"

"I'm sorry. Go on."

"Well, it was that Jane person. She must have left her bag behind earlier and had come back for it because she reached in under the table and picked it up. She sprayed some perfume on her wrists and her neck and then one last squirt on her boobs. Then put on a bit of lipstick."

You could hear a pin drop in the room. If anyone was silly enough to drop a pin while Abby was talking.

"Go on. I feel you're going to tell me you witnessed a Mafia hit. Or that Jane is really an undercover agent or a mass murderer."

"Well, it's better than that. Marco was all set to call out to her and ask if she was all right. I told him not to. I didn't want her coming in, seeing what was going on. I didn't want her knowing any of my business."

"Dead right too. If you're going to commit adultery it's best to have as few people as possible in on the act. A plain Jane that is after your son would definitely be the wrong person to tell your affairs to."

"It wasn't adultery or an affair, it was only a bit of fun. So, I thought, now that she had done her beauty routine she'd leave. But she didn't. She sat down on one of the seats on the patio and poured herself a drink. I didn't know what she was up to, but I could see her arranging herself. Pulling her neckline down and her hemline up. Then I heard someone else on the patio. It was Dylan. My Dylan."

"Well, who else's? How many Dylan's are there on this island?"

"You're not taking this at all seriously, Emma."

"I am, honest." I decided to shut up.

"I nearly died, you know. Oh, sorry – OK, so I didn't nearly die, but I was very, very uncomfortable and it was nothing to do with the fact that I was sprawled out on a cane couch. There was plenty of padding. Marco felt very uncomfortable too. He thought there was going to be a bit of humping and bumping going on between Jane and Dylan and I'm sure he didn't want to watch what he wasn't getting himself. I swear, I was going to get up and go out to them and let them know they weren't alone, but I couldn't. I was frozen to the spot. I couldn't move. Anyway, what could I have said? Me and Marco were just inspecting the wine for tomorrow's dinner. Me and Marco were lost and wandered into a dark room and fell onto the couch. Me and Marco were wanting a bonk and could he and Jane vacate the patio as it was already taken. No matter what I would have said the visuals would have spoken for themselves. If we had gone out it would have looked awful. Dylan would have been really embarrassed, not to mention my embarrassment. His mother coming out of a dark room on a romantic night with a randy Italian. The child wouldn't even need an imagination."

"Oh, Abby, what did you do?" I nearly started giggling, but I knew it wouldn't go down well. She would have clamped up and I would never have heard the whole story. It was too good to miss.

"What could I do? I sat like a Muppet and held my breath. Marco thought I was having a fit. I had my hand over his mouth and my other arm holding him down into the seat to make him sit still. It was awful, Emma. Then I heard Dylan sit down beside Jane and pour himself a drink. Next thing I heard Dylan saying to Jane: *'So this is where you got to. I didn't know where you were. I thought you were lost. You said you were only coming back to get your bag. I thought I should follow you. I hope you don't mind.'*

'Not at all. I'm delighted. It was so nice here I just sat down for a while. It's nice to be sharing it.'

'It is lovely. Bit chilly though.'

'Well, you could always put your arms around me and we could cuddle up together and keep warm. You never know what might happen.'

"Can you believe the nerve of her? Only I was frozen to the spot I'd have gone out and hit her with her own bag."

"But wasn't that exactly what you had said to Marco?"

"Yes, but that's different. She set Dylan up. She sat there and blatantly set my son up. The cheap hussy offered it to him on platter. I couldn't believe my ears. But I still did nothing about it. If I had gone out I would have wrung her cheap little swan-like neck."

"What did he do? Will you stick to telling me what actually happened and stop telling me what you wanted to happen!"

269

"Well, then it got all embarrassing. Dylan stood up and I thought he was going to give her a big snog. He didn't. He just stood there with his hands on his hips and shrugged.

'I'm sorry, Jane, I don't think about you like that. I was just trying to help you because you said you felt so out of it. I'm sorry if I led you on or if you got the wrong impression. I already have a girl in my life. I'm working my way up to doing the right thing for her. I'm trying to think what the right thing is. All I know is that as long as I'm with her I'll be happy. I just can't stop wanting her. Do you understand?'

'Yeah. She's a lucky girl. So, will you introduce me to the handsome director on the shoot then? I hear he's single.'

"Can you believe that? She didn't even put up a fight for him. She just moved on to the next poor sucker. Then the two of them started laughing at some in-joke about the director and the air was cleared."

"That's unbelievable. She's some mover, isn't she? A narrow escape for Dylan, I'm thinking. He must be mad about Roz all the same. Poor Julia. I knew she hadn't got a chance."

"Yeah. But wait till you hear the rest. That's not the end of it."

"Go on, I'm all ears."

"Well they just sat for a few minutes and then Jane said: *'It's probably just as well because neither your mother or her friend like me very much.'*"

"Oh, she never said that! Did she?"

"Yeah, she landed us right in the shit, we were like the evil stepmothers. She's a princess at getting the sympathy vote."

"What did Dylan say? I hope he didn't believe her, even though I have to admit she was right. I think I felt she was a threat, but to what I don't exactly know."

"Me too. I think I knew that she was going to make a move on Dylan. Well, she certainly had you and me sorted."

"Go on, will you! I'm going to die myself if you don't get on with the rest of it."

"Well, Dylan said: 'Go away out of that! They do like you. The two of them are great. My ma is going through a bit of a silly patch at the moment though so maybe that's why she doesn't appear so friendly. That's why I'm glad she's here, having a good time.'"

"Good job he didn't know how good a time you were about to have!" I laughed. Abby completely ignored me.

"Well, I couldn't get over him saying I was going through a silly patch, then he elaborated: 'It's funny though because my poor ma is going through agony at the moment and I could very easily put her out of her misery, but because of a promise I made I can't. She thinks my dad is having an affair and bringing someone to a hotel for a dirty weekend. Her imagination is running riot. If she knew the whole story she'd see how funny it is.'

'It can't be that funny if she's going through agony.'

'Well, it'll only be a temporary agony. She's in for the

271

nicest surprise of her life and she hasn't a clue. My dad is bringing her away for a weekend to a very plush hotel in Ireland and she doesn't know. It's all a surprise. He has a suite booked. He has a beautiful ring for her and he has arranged for me and my brothers all to be sitting at a table in the dining-room when she walks in for the evening meal. It'll be brilliant. She'll love the whole lot of us being there. It'll be the best buzz ever. So, you see, even if I did want to put her out of her misery I can't spoil the huge surprise for her. This'll be the best thing ever. Dad is going to tell Emma nearer the time and have her and Julia come to the dinner with us. He's afraid if he tells Emma too soon she might spill the beans.'"

"Me? Spill the beans? I'd never do that. Hey, isn't that really lovely of Geoff. Now there's romance for you."

"I know. Isn't it amazing? He's a dote, isn't he?"

"So is that it? Did they go back inside or did you declare yourself?"

"After all that there was no way I could declare myself. Anyway, there's more. So they got chatting and they kept drinking she asked him if he wanted to fool around a bit and 'no one need ever know'. Just a one-night stand, she said. I couldn't believe anyone could be such a tart."

"What did he say? Get on with it, will you?"

"He was wonderful, Emma. I was so proud of him. Only I couldn't I'd have given him a round of applause. I was chuffed."

"For the love of God will you tell me what he said!"

"Well, what he said was: '*I don't do one-night stands.*'"

"Wow."

"Wasn't that something for a mother to be proud of?"

"But what did she say. I bet she wasn't as chuffed as you."

"Well, he softened the blow for her by adding: '*But if I were to do them, I'd certainly do it with you.*'"

"Then she said: '*I bet you've had loads of offers. This girl must be something special.*'

'*She is.*'

'*I bet you've left a trail of broken hearts behind you?*'

"*Not that many. There was this one girl I really thought was it. I thought we'd be married and have kids by now. I was mad about her. I'm ashamed to admit this but I even slept with her in my parents' bed. They still don't know. I really cringe whenever I think about that. She was a mature student and did some cleaning in our house as a part-time job. We had a great thing going. I guess she went home to Croatia. She just disappeared one day and I never saw her again. I don't know what happened. One minute we were all over each other in bed. Then I had to go to a photo shoot and I was getting ready. She kissed me and went into the shower. I left and that was the end of it. It was the last time I set eyes on her. From that day to this I have never seen her again. She didn't even come back to do the house. I asked my mother why and she said that she had to leave. My ma was a bit upset that she left. I could tell by the way she told me.*'

'*So she broke your heart then, did she?*'

'She certainly did. I'd love to know what I did wrong.'"

"Ah, ha! The lovely Martina. Her of the diamante thong. So it was Dylan giving her loads, not Geoff! Didn't I always tell you Geoff didn't do anything. You better be good at eating humble pie when you get home because you have a ton-load of it to eat!"

"Imagine Geoff arranging that weekend for me? I'll have to let on I know nothing about it and so will you."

"Too bloody right I will. So what happened then?"

"Well, I was so delighted that I had solved the weekend away, CIKB and the landing incident and all at the one time that I started crying. Then, Jane and Dylan started to walk back to the hotel.

"Do you hear something?' Dylan said. They both stood and listened. I held my breath and my tears. *'Now you're imagining things,'* Jane said back to him. Then they went back up to the bar.

"I relaxed a bit and let go of Marco. He gulped for air and said I was a crazy bitch, only the way he said it with the accent and his sweet face looking down on me, it sounded lovely. Nearly like a compliment."

"What? You don't mean to say you had your hand clamped over his mouth the whole time? The poor man!. So, did he get his jollys?"

"After all that? What do you take me for? I ran out as fast as my legs would carry me but not before I swore him to secrecy.

'I assure you, my dearest Abigail, I will not be telling

anyone about this mad night of passion I nearly had,' were his exact words. Actually, I think the mood was gone off him. Imagine, I was only seconds from getting my knickers off for him to get my own back on poor Geoff – who was telling the truth all along and I wouldn't believe him. Oh, Emma, I am such a bitch! I swear I am going to be so good to Geoff from now on. I am always going to give him the benefit of the doubt in every situation."

"I'll believe that when I see it. Didn't Dylan tell you all along that Geoff wasn't bringing a woman away for the weekend?"

"I know, but I thought he was only saying it so I wouldn't leave Geoff. I thought he was only trying to make everything all right. I believe him now though."

"Good. It's about time."

I hugged her and I could feel she was holding back the tears. I let her. Sometimes it's important not to cry. To keep the energy for something more important.

"Hey, I feel sorry for Marco." I started to laugh and was delighted that Abigail started laughing with me.

I pulled off my nightdress on the way into the shower.

"Oh, yes, poor Marco. He's gone home so deflated. I was all set to lie down and paint a big WELCOME all over my body in bright red print one minute and the next minute I was jumping up and running back here. He must be so frustrated."

"To say the least." I really felt sorry for poor Marco.

Maybe I could give him a bit of tender loving care later.

"It's such a mess, Emma. I won't be able to look Marco in the face again. What am I going to do?"

"Nothing!" I shouted from the bathroom. Checking to see if I needed to shave my legs. "You won't have to do a thing. I think Marco has got the message and I don't think he'll come near enough to you again for you to look him in the face. Imagine, I slept through it all! I'm delighted for you, all the same, about Geoff. I knew he was one of the good ones."

"Me too."

I raised my eyebrows and laughed in the safety of the bathroom. Knowing Abby couldn't see me. I said nothing.

"Let's get out of here. We're wasting precious time. Come on, you've been in there long enough."

"OK, OK. Looks like we've missed breakfast and nearly lunch. Let's get something to eat downstairs and then go down to see Dylan and Julia at the photo shoot. What do you think? I'd love to see what's happening."

"Me too. I'll be ready in a second."

I lathered the sun-cream all over my body and waited for it to dry. That's the only bit I hate about holidays. Having to dose with sun-cream every day and then with after-sun every night. I wouldn't mind so much if I had someone to rub it in for me. To rub it all over me. Rub it in places that would never see the light of day never mind the blazing sun. Someone who would delight in it.

Cover every little bit of me. Make sure there would be no danger of me getting sunburn. Someone, who loved me enough to do it just because he wanted to. The thought of it was making me ache.

I got dressed quickly before I had to have another shower. A very cold one.

CHAPTER FOURTEEN

I bought a paper and some postcards on the way down to the beach. I was planning on sprawling out on the beach in the glorious sunshine later on and I was going to write them then. *Glad you're not here* to Danny and *Where are you?* to Ronan. Wouldn't you imagine one of the bastards would have followed me by now? I know it was a bit farfetched that they'd get on a plane and come all the way over there. If the two of them came they could have a duel on the beach. Draw pistols at dawn. But neither of the bastards thought enough of me to follow me. OK, so neither of them knew where I was, but they could have asked Geoff. Geoff would have told him. They could have found me if they really wanted to. It was blatantly obvious they didn't want to. I know I was only gone for a few days, but you'd imagine they'd miss me. It's terrible to have two people who could miss you and neither of them bother their ass. I'd like to have been missed.

The beach was a hive of activity. People swarming around everywhere. It wasn't as glamorous as I thought it would be. Nothing looked organised. There were a lot of people shouting. One man in particular was waving his hands in the air and giving out yards.

"That must be the director," Abigail whispered and pointed to him.

"Yes, he certainly looks as if he's in charge and they all seem to be running around after him."

"Well, it's the fact that Jane is sticking so close to him and making all those gooey faces that made me think he was the director." We laughed

"Seems to be working. He's purple in the face and obviously trying to impress. Aren't we the right pair of bitches, all the same?"

"Look, over there. It's Julia."

I called out to her and waved.

"Hi." She was out of breath. She had been running along the beach when Abby spotted her.

"Hi, Julia, where are you running to?"

"How's the tummy today, pet?" I gave her a hug. She looked lovely and none the worse for her ordeal yesterday.

"It's grand. Dylan tells me I missed nothing much last

night. I felt so bad not turning up for dinner though. He said Jane stood in for me – that was nice of her, wasn't it? I'm sure she took pleasure in it. She seems to have backed off Dylan. Dropped him like a hot potato and gone on to bigger and better things."

"We noticed," said Abby. "Last night was very nice and you were missed."

"You missed nothing, Julia." I felt sorry for her.

"I was just on my way to find you both. See what you were up to."

"Why? Aren't you supposed to be working?"

"Oh, I forgot to tell you the photographer walked off. He had a huge row with the director and stormed off. The director is going ape. I'm trying to avoid him. So who better to avoid him with than the two of you?"

"We were going to lie out on the beach. But looking at all this lot I'm not sure if I want to. I'd feel I had to cover up with all the perfect bodies flaunting themselves. It's the pits not having a perfect body on a day like today. If I ever eat again I want you to remind me of this."

"Ma, you're not that bad. If you come back up with me while I get my bikini, I'll come with you. May as well, there's nothing doing around here."

I was glad Julia was coming with us.

"There you all are. How are you today, Julia?" Maria was sorting through post and had a handful of papers in her hands.

"Fine today, thanks, Maria," said Julia. "Sorry I missed the meal last night. I heard it was delicious."

"It was a pity you couldn't come."

"You're busy today, Maria," I said.

"This place doesn't run itself, unfortunately, and Marco is nowhere to be seen today. I think he hightailed it off to the village early this morning. Avoiding all the work, no doubt."

Or avoiding Abby.

Abby had the good grace to blush.

"I saw him this morning. He seemed to be in a hurry to get out all right," Julia said in all innocence.

"Will you be seeing Dylan soon, Abby?" Maria was all flustered without Marco to give her a hand.

"Actually, he's up in the room," Julia cut in. "Marco is not the only one avoiding things today. Dylan is avoiding Tommy, the director. I'm going up there now to get my swimming gear – do you want me to tell him you're looking for him?"

"No, not at all. He left these beside the computer earlier and I just wanted to give them to him. Will you do that for me?"

"No problem."

As luck would have it Dylan was just coming out of the apartment as we came off the lift.

"I was just coming to look for you, Julia." He was all smiles.

"Ma, why don't you and Abby come in and sit on the

balcony and have a drink while I get ready. Then we can all have a drink together before we go. Who knows, we might even persuade Dylan to come with us."

I knew Abby was dying to say yes.

I thought Dylan was dying for us to say no.

"We were just going to go to the beach, Dylan. We just came back to get Julia's things. It'd be nice to have a drink while we're waiting on her," Abby said, delighted with herself.

"If you want us to go ahead, we can always meet up with Julia on the beach," I said to Dylan giving him a way out.

"No. This is great. I have to be back down to the beach myself in an hour to see what's going on or Tommy will have my guts for garters so I won't be able to go with you. It seems to be a right mess." For someone talking about a mess he was looking very relieved. I suppose a mess is better to face than three women sunbathing on a beach.

"Pour me a drink, will you?" Julia said.

She threw her bag and all the notes about who was to wear what make-up onto the table. She packed a little beach bag and then joined us out on the balcony. She grabbed up all her bits of paper. "I'd better bring these with me. I can read them while I'm sunning myself." She sorted through the papers. "I have to know who's to wear what make-up. It's mad really – I'm only an assistant. All I'll be doing is holding the make-up boxes. How hard can it be anyway? It's not as if I'd give Dylan scarlet lips and Jane none. I really don't see why I have to know all this."

"But it's knowing which box to hold for which model that's the trick."

"I suppose."

We sat out on the balcony. We sipped our drinks and each one of us in turn let out a very pleasurable "*Ahhhhh!*" sound. One of sheer pleasure. There are certain times when "*Ahhhh!*" is sufficient. When there is no need for anything else to be said. This was one of those times. Everything seemed perfect up on the balcony with the sun shining.

Then Jane spoiled it all.

"What the hell is this?" she shouted, waving two pieces of paper in front of us.

"What?"

"What?"

"What the hell is what?" said Dylan.

"This. It's a printout of your e-mail to Roz. You left it beside the computer. Maria handed it to me to give you."

"And you read it?" Dylan was incensed.

"Julia, you didn't?" I said.

"I didn't read it. I just saw it. It was mixed up here with all my other papers. I couldn't help but read it."

"What does it say? Here, show me." Abigail reached over to take it from Julia who was still waving it like a big white surrender flag.

"Let's have a look." I was getting a bit curious myself.

"Are you both mad? Give it here to me, it's mine. You should never have read it, Julia! I was going to tell you about it but I didn't get a chance."

"Well, now's your chance. I told you Roz wanted you and you send her this?"

"That is private. It's between Roz and me. No one else was supposed to see it. I can't believe you read it, Julia."

"Well, I have now, so why did you send it to her? Has Jane turned your head so much? Is that why you wrote this to Roz? Well, there's no need to ask where your brains are, Dylan. Jane is a fly-by-night. She'll be here today and gone tomorrow."

"What did he write?"

"What did he write?"

"He wrote her a good-bye note. A 'farewell to Roz' letter. A 'I have met Jane' note." Julia was raging. She threw the paper on the floor.

Abby picked it up. Dylan tried to grab it. The paper tore. Dylan crumpled up his bit. Abby read her bit. I read her bit over her shoulder. I pretended I wasn't reading it. She pretended the same. She just left it resting on her knee with her hand firmly in the corner holding the paper in place. Dylan was so busy arguing with Julia that he didn't notice Abby and me pretending not to read it.

"As soon as you saw 'Hi, Roz' you should have stopped reading it."

"Oh, right and I am a robot. That's what a robot would do, Dylan."

"No, Julia, that's what a decent person would do. No decent person would read another person's letters."

"So I'm not a decent person now, is that it?"

Abby and I weren't decent either – we read the letter.

"*Hi Roz,*

I hope all the training is going well and that you are looking forward to your grand adventure. I hope you remember to keep in touch with me and let me know how it's all going."

Julia and Dylan continued to argue as Abby and I read.

"No, that's not it. I just can't believe you did it. It's so unlike you. You are normally a decent person."

"I can't believe you didn't tell me."

Abby and I continued to read. I nearly asked Dylan and Julia to shut up until I'd finished. It was hard to concentrate with all the shouting going on.

"*I'm sorry I didn't ask you to stay, but I really want you to follow your dream. I am sorry if you wanted me to make some sort of a grand gesture. Some sort of a commitment to you. I am sorry too that I didn't say I'd go out and see you whenever I could. I think if we had been really serious about each other we would have done that when we said goodbye.*"

"I was going to. I was going to tell you."

"That you fell for the femme fatale bit!"

"Will the two of you please be quiet! I can't –"

Abby gave me daggers looks and a dig in the ribs.

"Sorry. Don't let me interrupt," I said.

Abby smiled and we both put our heads down to read on.

"I know now that you needed a commitment from me. I'm sorry I couldn't give it to you. I didn't know at the time why I couldn't give it to you, but now I know. I want to clear the air with you and not have you on the brink of a dream and unhappy. I think what we had was wonderful, but it was only supposed to last as long as it did. This is very hard to say or write. I really liked you, Roz – I had a wonderful time while we were together, but I don't think we were supposed to be together forever. If you think about it I think you feel the same.

The truth is, I am in love with someone else. I hope you understand. I hope you know that I never meant to hurt you. I hope you meet someone who is as special to you as she is to me.

All my love for now, Dylan xxx"

"Ahhhh," I said as I finished reading.

"Ahhhh," Abby said just as she finished reading.

Julia and Dylan were still shouting.

"Don't be ridiculous, I've only just met Jane!"

"So you lied to Roz. That's low, Dylan. That's so low. I expected more from you. I'm sorry now I told you about Roz. Why did you send that to her? You should have just told her that you were in lust with her all along and not in love with her."

"Oh, and you're the big expert on love all of a sudden then? I just didn't want her being hurt. It wasn't fair! I had to tell her how I felt. She deserved that. It was the right thing to do. I didn't want her to have false hopes."

"For who? For you, that's who. Well, fuck you, Dylan!"

"Fuck you too, Julia!"

The two of them stayed silent.

"I think we should go, Abby. We're only in the way."

"Well, you can go if you want to, Emma, but I'm staying to hear the rest of this."

"There is no rest of this!" Julia shouted.

"That's all there is!" Dylan shouted.

I felt like I was in the front row of some great Broadway show.

"Don't lie to me, Dylan, I am your mother. There were two pieces of paper. Is the other the reply?"

"Abby, will you leave the chap alone?"

"Thank you, Emma." Dylan was very grateful to me.

I was raging with myself. I was dying to know what was on the other piece of paper.

"I'm curious too now. I didn't read the reply. What did Roz say?" Julia started grabbing for the page.

"Will you stop, Julia!" Dylan wasn't impressed.

"Oh, you know what? I just got a great idea. Let's get Jane in here. Let's get the prizewinner in here. Let's tell her how lucky she is. She's in for a bit of a treat. Love at first sight, was it? Come on, get her up here! Tell her she's hit the jackpot!" Julia was being a bit too sharp.

"Will you stop! Shut up, the lot of you! If you must know what Roz said, here. Here it is. Read it yourself. She's fine about it. But don't blame me if you don't like what you read."

Julia took the piece of paper. Abby strained to see it. It wasn't so much of a strain for me.

"*Dylan,*

Thanks for getting in touch. It really is amazing here and I haven't even left for Africa. The group I am working with are fantastic people, I hope I don't let them down. Of course I'll keep in touch. Friends forever.

I did want a commitment, but since we've been apart I realise that if I had wanted it badly enough I would have told you. I think we were in lust. But good lust (lol).

There is only one person who could have told you that I wanted some sort of commitment from you and that's Julia. She's lovely.

You two are supposed to be together. I'm glad you finally discovered it for yourself before it was too late and you lost her altogether.

All my love to you and to Julia, Roz xxxx

"Shit!" Julia was shocked.

Abby and I didn't know where to put ourselves. We were shocked, but not that shocked. We just gave each other knowing glances. We could have told them years ago. They could have cut out all the crap and come to us. But they'd never have listened. Who listens to their mother these days?

We decided to make ourselves scarce.

"I do love you, Julia," Dylan said.

"Me too! I'm sorry I read your e-mail!" Julia was charmed.

They moved closer together and we left them alone just in time.

We let ourselves into our own apartment.

"Do you want a Bacardi and pineapple?"

"Will it help calm my nerves?"

"Not unless you're going to drink the whole bottle."

"Maybe I'll just have the pineapple on its own."

"Coming right up."

"On second thoughts just give me the Bacardi. No pineapple."

We sat out on our own balcony with our Bacardi and pineapple.

"This chill out and rest in the sun holiday is proving to be a bit too chaotic for me, Emma." Abigail was laughing.

"Well, let's hope there is nothing else that can happen. At least all the things happening are all good things, aren't they, Abby? You finding out about Geoff was a great thing. Julia and Dylan being happy is a good thing."

"Even if they can't or don't want to stay with one another till death do them part they'll have a bit of fun together anyway. It won't interfere with our friendship, will it?"

"Never, even if they have a blazing row, we'll still be best friends. It'd be some fun arranging a wedding together though, wouldn't it? Poor Julia and Dylan wouldn't get a look in with the two of us."

"But it would be a beautiful wedding, the wedding of the year."

"I think I'll wear pink and definitely a hat."

"What about pale blue for me? Or maybe even silver grey. Yes, definitely hats."

"A big wedding, I think."

"I could make the cake. You could find beautiful material for Julia's dress."

"Who would I bring, Abby? I have no one in the world who would want to bring me to a wedding."

"Well, Marco's available." She looked at me and raised her eyebrows. I didn't like the way she looked at me.

We sat deep in thought.

I was thinking that I could always hire an escort.

"*Ahhh, ahh, ahhh, oh, Julia!*"

"*Dylan, aaaahhhhh, I love you!*"

"*I love you too, Julia!*"

They had left their patio doors open again.

It was time for Abigail and me to get out of our apartment.

If we knew about nothing else, we knew all about timing, Abby and me.

CHAPTER FIFTEEN

"Let's get up and out of here now as early as we can."

"Yeah, I don't fancy hanging around here. I know what's good for me."

"There is no way I am going to listen to all that racket again. Jesus, if I heard one more moan out of the two of them last night I was going to go in to them and tell them to shut up."

"If it was anyone else I would have at least banged the wall with my shoe. But it's so embarrassing. I didn't want them to know I'd heard anything at all. I don't like being in this situation, Abby. It's more than a body can take. I'm melting with the patio doors closed."

"It's ridiculous – I feel like I'm being steamed in my own sweat."

"That's not ridiculous, that's disgusting."

"I'm just telling it like it is."

"I hope Julia doesn't pass out. She's expending a lot of energy and in this heat. I might have to have a word with her later. What do you think?"

"Well, you can do what you like, but I am never having that conversation with Dylan. You know, the sex conversation. As far as I am concerned I heard nothing last night. I'm not hanging around to hear anything this morning. I don't believe he has sex ever and I don't want to him to confirm if he does. I am going to pretend I heard nothing. I am going to pretend that Dylan is a virgin and will remain one until I want grandchildren."

"Well, I think he's already admitted to having sex with your cleaner, Martina. But we can forget about that if you want us to. The pretend idea is a good one. I'll pretend too. I hope we don't hear what we're going to pretend we didn't hear last night again tonight."

"I wonder should we ask to move rooms. It seems silly though. We'll be leaving soon and surely they have to stop whatever we didn't hear last night at some time. They can't keep doing it."

"Well, she probably takes after her mother in every way!"

"And if he takes after his mother in the same way then they might never stop."

"If it wasn't for the fact that we were talking about our children I'd find it funny."

"Well, we are, so hurry up and let's get out of here before they wake up and we have to try not to hear anything."

"I'm ready when you are."

"That's it then, we're off."

Maria was in the breakfast room.

"Good morning, Maria."

"Good morning, ladies."

"Hi, Maria. No Marco again today then?"

"Oh, he's around all right. One day off is enough for anyone."

"There he is." Abby spotted him. She nearly buried her head in her chest. She clearly didn't want him to come over.

"You're both up very early this morning. Making the most of your last couple of days?" Maria asked.

"Yes. I'll hate leaving. I have a few postcards to post – where will I post them? In the village?"

"No, they will be collected from here. Have you got them with you now?"

"Well, I have to finish writing them."

"Just leave them in the sitting-room we were in the other night, over on the table and I'll collect them later."

"Thanks, Maria."

"Now let me guess what you want to eat. Tomato and warm bread for you, Emma, and eggs and bread for Abigail. I'll bring oil for the bread."

"Great."

"Thanks."

She headed off into the kitchen.

"Watch out. Here comes Marco." I barely had time to warn Abby.

"Good morning, ladies."

"Hi Marco."

"Hi. Eh … Marco … I really am sorry about eh … well eh … you know …"

"Don't worry about it, my dear Abigail. It was a misunderstanding. I understand. You are very happily married – you just forgot to mention it. I understand perfectly."

Ooops, that was a bit below the belt!

"Now, Marco. Abby was not happily married until after she was with you. When she was with you she was very unhappily married." I had to defend my friend.

"Oh! I thought she was separated, nearly divorced. My mistake."

"I'm sure you never make mistakes, Marco. I'm sure you have only ever slept with women who are free and available. Anyway, it happened. Shit happens. Get over it."

"Emma!" Abby finally found her voice.

"Ah, fuck it, Abby. I'm sick of pussyfooting around after men. They fuck up big-time and expect us to sit around like the Vestal Virgins waiting for them to make up their minds what they want."

"Emma! Marco isn't Danny or Ronan. I fucked him up, remember?"

"Oh yeah. Sorry, Marco. But I think you're taking all this too seriously. OK, so Abby bruised your ego. I'm sure there are plenty of woman around here who would love the chance to kiss your bruises better if you just let them."

"Well, Emma, thank you. I will keep that in mind. It would be delightful to have all my bruises kissed better. Who are Danny and Ronan, by the way? Don't tell me you have two husbands that you forgot to mention."

"No, Marco. I have no husband. Danny and Ronan are only has-beens."

"I'm delighted to hear it. Do you know you are very attractive when you get angry. I like a feisty woman. Have a good day, ladies."

"Jesus! What do you make of that? I'd say I just got my knuckles rapped."

"I'd say you got your arse kicked and you deserved it. You led him on and then dumped him just as he was revving up for the big finale."

"And this is coming from you, Miss Squeaky Clean. Give me a break, Emma."

"I know I'm not squeaky clean, but at least I'm a free agent."

"Look, Emma, if you had a problem with me and Marco you ought to take a look at yourself and see why. Maybe you fancy him yourself?"

"Don't be ridiculous."

"Is it all that ridiculous?"

"Too right it is."

"Now, here we are. Abby. Emma." Maria put plates down in front of each of us. We just looked at them. Then swapped them over. I don't eat eggs.

"Here, I got you this." Abby handed me the paper. The horoscope page was open.

"Abby, I'm sorry."

"Me too."

"I really don't fancy Marco."

"I believe you."

We sat in silence. We were both waiting for the air to clear. We rarely let fly at each other and when we did we usually regretted it. I was regretting it big-time. I think Abby was too.

I read my horoscope and took out my postcards and finished writing them. I'd be back home before the cards ever arrived in Ireland. I decided not to send one to Ronan or Danny – if they hadn't bothered their very nice arses to come looking for me why should I send them cards? Abigail had hers already written. The one to Geoff was in an envelope. I guessed it was x-rated. I noticed Abby had her engagement and wedding rings back on again.

On our way out, still in silence, we went into the magnificent sitting-room to leave the postcards for Maria.

"Abby. Are we OK now?"

"I am if you are. I'm sorry."

"You have nothing to be sorry for. You're a grown woman – you can do what you want. I shouldn't interfere. I don't mean to."

"It's nice that you do. We can have a good look at the painting now there is no one in here."

"It's massive, isn't it?" I stood staring at it.

Abby started looking at all the photographs.

"Here, Emma, look at this. Isn't that Robert Redford pictured with Maria and Marco? Here's Al Pacino, Paul Newman – there are loads of fabulous actors. This must be a haunt of the rich and famous."

"I'm not surprised. They couldn't do much better than here."

"These ones must be of locals and family. Maria's husband was stunning. Here, look at him. This must be their wedding. She looks beautiful, but my God he's so handsome! Emma, come here and look at him! They look so much in love. Poor Maria, she's had it tough, hasn't she?"

"Where? Show me? He is handsome, isn't he? It's a pity they had no children. They would have been beautiful. I think Maria would have made a great mother."

"I wonder will they ask to take our photographs? I'll be highly insulted if they don't."

"They are amazing photos, aren't they? Look, this must've been what the hotel was like originally. They've really done a great job on it. Adding the apartments really didn't take from the character and charm of the place. Come and look at it, Abby – it still has the character it always had."

The door opened.

Abby and I turned to see who had come in.

"Oh! Excuse me," he said.

"Danny!" Abby said.

"Danny?" I said.

I couldn't believe it. I was gobsmacked. It was amazing. I nearly had to pinch myself to make sure I wasn't having a lovely dream again. There in front of me stood my darling Danny. He had come to find me. Give that boy a prize, he certainly did find me. He had come chasing after me. Funny how I thought it would be Ronan that would come looking for me … but it was Danny. God, he looked great! I was beaming at Abby. She was thrilled for me. This was heady stuff. I would never again doubt his love for me, ever again. Women would kill to be in my shoes, or flip-flops, they would give anything for a man to follow them to a small romantic Italian island. Aronna was proving to be a magical place. I might never leave it.

He looked fantastic. Even if he had looked shite I would have thought he looked fantastic. Anyone who had flown here specially to see me was fantastic. His tight bum looked fantastic in his jeans. His big broad chest looked fantastic in the Polo T-shirt.

"Oh, my God! What are you two doing here?"

"As if you didn't know, you perfectly fantastic man!" I ran over to him and hugged him. I kept my arms around him. I wasn't going to let him go.

"Danny! What are you doing here?" Poor Abigail just didn't get it. She was probably as surprised as I was that Danny was such a romantic. To be honest I was thinking that a few flowers would have added to the whole romantic experience. But I was never one to nit-pick.

"Well, I had to come," he said.

That's right. That's exactly what he said. He had to come. I'd never heard the like of it before. I was so charmed I thought I was going to burst. It just doesn't get any better than this. I was beaming from ear to ear. I gave him a squeeze and a kiss on the cheek. I could see he was delighted with the surprise.

"You had to come?" Abigail asked again. Poor Abigail, she couldn't get her head around the romance of it all.

"Yeah, like I said. I had to. How come you're here?" He seemed puzzled that Abby was with me.

I was a bit confused. "Isn't it me should be asking you that little question, my pet? Isn't it me should be wondering who told you where I was? It has to be Geoff. Did you do a little bit of detective work and find me? You're a regular sleuth, do you know that?"

I linked his arm. My hero. My trophy.

"Emma, what are you on about?"

"I'm just so amazed at you coming after me, my pet! I

301

think you're great to have tracked me down. I think a little reward will be called for later on. Can you think of anything you'd fancy by way of a little reward, Danny?"

The right answer was a ride.

"What?" He looked at me as if I had two heads. "Finding you? What do you mean? I didn't follow you. When did you get here? What are you doing here?"

That was not the right answer.

"We've been here a couple of days. We're here with Dylan and Julia. He's working and she's working with him." Abigail gave him the low-down.

"So you've been here all along? Thank God for that. I thought the pair of you were stalking me." He burst out laughing and Abby joined in.

I started laughing hysterically, but I didn't know why. I was a bit confused and I was beginning to get a bit of an uneasy feeling. I decided to stop calling him darling or pet until I found out more.

"What are you doing here, Danny? Do you have a particular reason for coming to Aronna?" Abby asked what I was afraid to. She was looking from Danny to me. Urging him to give the right answer.

"Well, I have to earn a living." He was really bad today at answering questions.

I made up my mind not to ask him any more. I hoped Abby would follow suit.

"You're here to work?" Abby asked another question – she was hopeless at following suit.

"They called me in for a photo shoot. The other photographer stormed off yesterday. I'm replacing him."

"Did you not follow …" I was about to ask a question. Even though I had made my mind up not to ask any more questions I was just about to ask a silly one and get a silly answer. I am such a silly woman. Abby came to my rescue and took over as question-master. She was good at it. She never cried when the contestants got the answers wrong.

"Danny, did you know Emma and I were here?"

I held my breath.

Abby held her breath.

Danny let out a huge sigh.

"How could I have known?"

The wrong answer.

"Danny, did you know Emma was here?"

I held my breath again.

Abby held her breath again.

Again Danny let out a huge sigh.

"No. What's this all about?"

The wrong answer again.

He had gotten all his questions wrong. I wished I was Anne Robinson, I could have told him he was the weakest link and given him shit. But I was me. I started to cry. I was gutted. No one had followed me. The pipsqueak was only coming to work. The big bastard.

I had been fooled. I had been fooled by Danny. I remembered my horoscope. Madam Celeste had joined the conspiracy and fooled me too.

Madame Celeste
Scorpio
October 22 – November 23

Someone, somewhere follows their heart. It will bring you
closer to them. Don't give up on them. Just wait for them.

That's what she said this morning. She led me astray.

Danny didn't follow his heart or me. He just followed
his work.

"This is great, isn't it?" Danny was all enthusiastic.
"Us all meeting up like this. It's fate, that's what it is."

Ah, fate my arse, I thought.

"Will you be around later, Emma? I have to go now,
they're waiting for me and my genius. I have to take a lot
of photographs. Be around later for me, will you?"

I will in my arse!

"We'll be around all right. We'll see you later." Abby
was just too nice. There is something wrong with a
person that is so nice to a person that isn't so nice to me.
It's not natural.

"See you later, Emma? What was all that about earlier
about a reward?"

"Yeah. I was just saying you'll get your reward some
day." But it sure as hell won't be off me. You big bastard.

He hadn't a clue what I was on about. Let's face it, he

hadn't a clue about anything.

"Right. OK. See you later then. I have to get down onto the beach. Someone said there was a short cut down to the beach from this room."

We showed him the short cut.

Abby and I stood at the big window and watched him make his way down onto the beach.

"Well, I certainly made a fool of myself there."

"No, you didn't. OK, so he didn't follow you, but it's still nice that he's here. He was delighted to see you. And I think you were delighted to see him."

"That was when I thought he'd done the big romantic gesture."

"Why don't you give him a chance? He might surprise you. He might be building up to one."

"I just can't wait."

"Come on, let's go down to the beach with him and watch him at work."

"I suppose it'd be no harm."

She took off at the speed of light.

"Danny! Danny! Wait. We're coming with you. Hang on!"

He stopped and even I could see he was delighted.

I had no alternative but to run after her and, of course, him.

He made a point of walking beside me. Abigail made a point of walking behind us.

"It's great to see you, Emma. Really great."

"Great to see you too."

"Sorry about the last time. Are you still with that bloke?"

"No."

"What happened?"

"I blew it. I had a one-night stand with a total bastard of an old flame and blew it with a decent man."

"Well, he might be decent, but he's a fool if he let you go."

"You let me go too. Not once but twice."

"That was different. The first time I was being a coward. The second time I was being honourable. It won't happen again."

"You were never honourable. You might not get a third chance."

"That was the old me. The new me is a very honourable man. Now I know what I want and I wait until the coast is clear before I go after it. I do the honourable thing these days. So is your coast really clear, Emma?

Before I had a chance to tell him that my coast was so clear there wasn't even a sign of a horizon on it, the bubbly bimbo, Jane, popped up out of nowhere.

"Hi. I'm Jane. you're the photographer, aren't you?" She didn't even acknowledge my presence. She didn't even give me a sideward glance. Then again, how could she? She was concentrating so hard on batting her overly long unnatural eyelashes that she was acting as a very welcome fan for Danny.

"That'd be me, I'm Danny. Hi, Jane, it's nice to meet you."

"I'm thrilled to have the opportunity to work with such genius. I think you are the most gifted photographer in the world. I have always loved your work." She was obviously a big fan of Danny's. She was overdoing it, though. I knew Danny would see right through her little game. He was no eejit.

I looked at his face expecting him to be unimpressed by her. I was wrong. He was thrilled. Beaming from ear to ear.

"Well, let's get on with it then!"

"Where would you like me?" She shone sex.

I didn't want to hear his answer. His track record at giving the right answer had spoiled any interest I might have had.

I couldn't stand by and watch her doing her chat-up bit again. It was like watching a rerun of a sitcom that was bad originally. OK to watch on a rainy Sunday when you've nothing else to do.

"I'll see you later, Danny."

"Yeah, Emma." He was engrossed in Jane. He had his arm around her very thin waist. He was giving her instructions.

I went over to Abigail.

"Well?" I said.

"Well what?"

"Well, did you see her or what? Did you ever see anything like her, the way she came crawling over to him? Chatting him up. Throwing herself at him. Did you see him? Lapping it up. Hanging on her every word. Drooling at her."

"Will you stop! He is only being nice to the girl. He has to work with her. The drooling was probably sweat. Did you ever feel anything like the heat? I'm melting myself. Will you just give him a break? He's so into you. He so wants you. What did he say? What did you say?"

"Nothing much. I didn't get a chance, neither did he. Plain Jane interrupted us."

"You can't blame him for what she does."

"And, boy, does she do it well! Will you look at her?"

Jane was certainly giving Danny her undivided attention.

"I see she's got her claws into him all right, poor Danny," said Abby.

"Poor Danny, my arse. He's well able for her." I wasn't sure if he was. I was hoping we'd never find out.

We stood watching Danny taking endless photographs of Dylan. Dylan was terrific. Then endless photos of Jane. She was pathetic. Then lots of Dylan and Jane together.

Then Danny called it a day.

He thanked everyone and gave them a round of applause which I thought was a nice touch, if a bit silly.

"Would you look at that!" Abigail was doing a very

definite nod over in the direction of Danny. Jane was running over to him.

"What's she up to?"

"You know what she's up to."

"Yeah. He'll be like putty in her hands. She'll only have to smile and he'll melt into her arms."

"Will you stop!" said Abby. "She probably just wants to thank him and tell him how great he was at taking her photograph."

"Or set up a date for later on. She's standing very close to him."

"No, she's not. You're imagining things."

"She's wiggled up closer. Look, their sides are touching. Side by side, all cosy. Arms touching. I might be sick."

"He's no fool," said Abby. "He'll step back in a minute. Give him some credit."

"She's good. I'll give her that."

"Good God! What is she doing now?"

"Would you look at her! What did I tell you? What the hell is she doing? Why is her mouth against his ear?"

"She's probably only whispering into his ear," said Abby. "She probably doesn't want to shout whatever it is she wants to say to him. She'll be telling him how wonderful he is. She'll be stroking his male ego. She won't want him to be embarrassed when she strokes it so she's whispering."

"I hope that's all she strokes. I really don't think she

needed to go up on tippy-toes to do her stroking. She's nearly the same size as him. She's having a great nibble all the same."

"Will you stop. She's not nibbling his ear, she's just talking to him."

"Her tongue is probably making its way in and out and out and in," I groaned. "All around his ear, into all the little bends. I don't blame her wanting to nibble his ears. He has nice ears. They're not hairy like some blokes."

"That's disgusting."

"Are you looking? She's putting her arm around his waist."

"Looking? I'm glued to the scene. She probably feels she's losing her balance. Those high shoes and this soft sand don't go very well together. The heels have disappeared."

"Her losing her balance? She was never very balanced to begin with. This is like watching a master at work. I wish I had a camera. Maybe I should go over and ask Danny can I borrow one of his."

"You're staying right where you are. Safe with me."

"At least she has her tongue out of his ear. What are they laughing about? I bet she's telling him how pathetic I am. How together she is. How old I am. How young she is. How fat I am. How thin she is."

"You're not fat, pathetic or old. He's just being nice to her. Just because they're laughing doesn't mean they're laughing at you. He wouldn't do that."

"I wish he'd move. If he moved she'd have to remove her hand from his waist."

"He's probably afraid she'll fall over."

"Can you believe it? She waited until he was laughing and now she's slipping her hand down. Would you look at her! Little by little she's moving it down."

"He mustn't feel it."

"God, Abby, it must be a long time since anyone felt your bum. Of course he feels it."

"I can't believe it."

"Fair play to her she landed it exactly where she wanted to. Right on his right bum-cheek. He has terrific bum-cheeks all the same."

"Look! He's noticed. He's stopped laughing. He's just standing there looking at her."

"She's going in for the kill. She's having a feel of his other bum-cheek. She's certainly an equal-opportunities woman. If she feels one cheek she feels it only fair to feel the other one. Not to make it feel left out of the feeling."

"He's gobsmacked. The poor fella."

"Poor fella my arse. Wow, she's kissing him on the cheek."

"Thank God it's not his bum-cheek."

"If he kisses her back I am going over there. I am going to tell him to bugger off again."

"He's pulling way. He's mortified. Scarlet. I feel sorry for him."

Abby was right. Danny had pulled away – he was striding across the beach.

"Dylan! Dylan! Come here, Dylan, I want a word with you! Well done. Terrific. Really great. Brilliant."

"He's going for safety. Safety in numbers."

"He looks like he's going to start running. He can't get far enough away from her. "

"I almost feel sorry for Plain."

"Well, I don't. She deserves it. Coming on to Danny like that."

"Not that you don't fancy the knickers off him yourself."

"That's entirely besides the point."

"I wish you two would make up your minds what you want. It's not fair to the rest of the world, you know. It's not fair to Ronan either."

"Ronan finished with me, remember. I'm a free agent."

"Poor Plain Jane hasn't moved. She must be in shock, her mouth is still hanging open. Will I go down and help her? Just tell her to close her mouth. The flies will be in there in no time."

"You'll go nowhere. I'd say she knows all about flies, maybe not the flying kind though. She'd never come to our rescue. A bird could nest in my mouth and she'd say nothing. I wonder how long she can stand like that. She'll get cramp in her arm soon, it's still stuck out in mid-air. She seems locked into that position."

"She is a damsel in distress. She is waiting to be rescued. This is great stuff, Emma – I haven't seen anything like this since the time we went to see Garth Brooks live."

"I think we have a taker on the rescue. Here come's the director. Ahh, isn't that sweet! He's taking her hand and helping her."

"He's probably afraid she'll get sunstroke."

"He's probably hoping he'll get a stoke."

Danny looked over and we waved at him. Julia came along the beach and Danny bent down and kissed her on the cheek. He pointed over to us.

She ran over.

"Can you believe Danny is the photographer? Everyone is talking about him. How great he is. They were dead impressed that I knew him. Jane was so nice to me, trying to find out all about him. If I powdered her nose once I powdered it a million times. Every time I powdered it she asked something else about him. She nearly got sick when I said he was your ex."

"You didn't tell her that, did you?"

"Yeah. She was dead impressed. Actually, she's not all that bad when you get to know her."

"Now that she's taken her claws out of Dylan." Abby laughed.

"She's only looking for something or someone. That's all."

"Aren't we all, Julia? Aren't we all?"

CHAPTER SIXTEEN

The whole film crew was having a final dinner in the hotel. Everyone involved was to be there. Plain Jane would have a field-day looking for something or someone. I was guessing that Danny would be the someone and a good ride would be the something.

As Abby and I had nothing to do with the photo shoot we decided to sneak off, on our own, up to the village.

'Gone up to the village for dinner. Back later. Have a good time at the dinner.

See you.

Ma and Mam.

PS. Will you tell Danny we'll meet him in the bar later?'

We pushed the note under Dylan and Julia's door.

In the lobby we caught a glimpse of Plain going into

the bar for a pre-dinner drink. She had painted her outfit onto her body. I suppose it saved on the packing. She only had to pack a very small pot of paint and a brush. Her blusher-brush could have doubled up as a paint-brush. The paint she brought must've been black gloss paint because that's the colour she had painted onto herself. She had only painted it to just below her bum and just above her boobs. It was probably very awkward for her to get the paintbrush around the other areas. She was wearing black patent shoes with heels like size 5 knitting needles.

"Plain is looking very smart tonight, isn't she, Abby?"

"Very smart indeed. Would you say she's wearing her interview suit?"

"Most definitely. I'd say she was all dressed to inter-view any or all eligible men."

"Do you detect a bit of bitchiness in the air, Emma?"

"Certainly not. I'm sure that's not bitchiness you detect, is it?"

"Certainly not."

"Certainly not."

"Good evening, ladies." Marco was all dressed up too for the dinner. He looked fantastic.

"Good evening, Marco."

"Good evening."

"Are you not coming to the big dinner, ladies?"

"No. We're off up to the village tonight. You look very dashing, I must say."

"Thank you, Emma. Will you be back for drinks later?"

"Yes. We'll join you all in the bar."

"I look forward to it."

The warm balmy breeze was glorious as we walked along the cobblestones.

"This is great, Emma, just the two of us. Didn't Marco look like a right ride all the same."

"Yeah. But you stay away from him. You're supposed to be saving yourself for Geoff, remember."

"Of course I will. You must think I'm a right slapper."

"No, I don't."

"Good."

"I think you're a right slut."

"Thanks. You're supposed to be my friend."

"I am. Only your friend would tell you."

"Speaking of sluts … if you're with Danny tonight I could sleep in the other room. The couch opens up into a bed. Just be careful, will you? Ronan might only be off licking his wounds. He might want you back when you get home. If you sleep with Danny he'll be gutted. He might forgive you for one indiscretion – he'll never forgive you for two."

"I'm telling you Ronan is gone. He will never come back. I know him, Abby he wouldn't have done what I did so he can't understand it. Anyway, there's no need for you to sleep on the couch tonight."

"Good. Now you're talking sense. Don't sleep with

him until you sort everything out in your head. I'm glad you've made that decision. It gets very confusing when you're sleeping with everyone at the same time."

"I never slept with everyone."

"Well, you know what I mean. It's all a bit confusing isn't it?"

"Would you look who's talking! You nearly had the knickers off poor Marco in seconds. Only Dylan came along you'd have given him loads."

"Well, that's different. I'm just glad you've decided not to sleep with Danny."

"I haven't. Danny has a room of his own, that's all I'm saying."

"Be careful, will you?"

"I will. It's great to be away from everyone for a while, isn't it?"

"Yeah. Just the two of us. I feel great."

She looked great. She was glowing. She was in love. It must be lovely to be in love with your own husband. It must be so safe. Abigail's life was on track and I was delighted for her. She deserved this moment. I was trying to be magnanimous. Being magnanimous is very hard sometimes. Especially when everyone is having a moment. Everyone except me. Dylan and Julia were having their moment and good luck to them. I was delighted for them. They deserved it too. Particularly Julia. I was really very magnanimous about that. Being magnanimous isn't such a struggle when your own flesh and blood is involved.

All the same, just because everyone was having a moment, did that mean that I couldn't have one? Was there some reason why I had to have crap when they were having their moments. Is there a limit to the number of people who can have moments at the one time in this world? What would be wrong with me having a moment too? Could we not all have one big, kick-ass, simultaneous moment, all together? A big Moment Fest. Every person in the world have a big moment at the same time. I could imagine the wonderful buzz it would be.

The evening was warm and the smell from the café made me hungry. I was delighted to see that the Dish of the Day was serving dinner. Maybe I could have a moment with him.

"Good evening, ladies. Is there anything I can do for you tonight?"

"Where do I start?" I knew I was being cheeky.

"Wine, please." Abigail wasn't a bit cheeky.

Dish went off to oblige. I was hoping he'd come back all cheeky.

"Don't tell me you're going to hit on poor Dish?"

"I just might, but it's too easy, isn't it? He has to know how good-looking he is. He has to know what we're thinking."

"What you're thinking. I'm thinking nothing only pure thoughts."

"You can't fool me. I know you're having unfaithful thoughts. I'm having impure ones. The great thing about impure thoughts is that no one can hear them. Unless of course you go straight from the impure thought to impure words and move on swiftly to the impure actions."

"Don't you dare!"

Dish came back with the wine and made a big production of pouring it. I sipped it.

"What else have you got on offer?"

"Well, if you like, I can show you our specialities. You can decide then what you want."

"That'd be lovely," said Abby.

"I can't wait," said I.

It was too easy. We knew we were acting like two teenagers.

He was wearing tight black jeans and a very tight tee-shirt with no sleeves. He was a poser and no mistake.

He came back with menus.

"Very tasty," I said.

"Thank you." He bowed slightly as he went back into the kitchen.

"One wink and we'd have him."

"It'd be like taking candy from a baby."

"He thinks we're gumming for it."

"He might be right, Abby. I am gumming for it. I'm dying for a bit of sex. I only nearly had it twice in the last few weeks. I'm gumming for someone to hold me. I think I'm lonely, Abby."

"You can't be lonely. You're here with me."

"Yeah. I'm being silly. Here, pour me another drink."

It was great being with Abby, but sometimes your best pal isn't enough. Sometimes you want more. But I'd never tell her that. I know she was wishing I was Geoff. But she'd never tell me that.

"Here comes Dish again," I said. "I don't care if it's easy, I'm going for it. You might be on the couch tonight after all."

"You wouldn't? Would you?"

"Watch me. Will we have a little wager? I'll have him before desert and you pay for the dinner."

"Are we ready to order yet, ladies?"

"Well, everything looks so mouth-wateringly delicious I just can't make up my mind," I said seductively. "Do you have any suggestions?"

"What are you doing? Stop, will you?" Abby was whispering to me. She turned and said out loud to Dish, "Can we have more wine, please? In fact, could we have a jug each instead of sharing one?"

She was so clever. A jug each. I was enjoying the effect the wine was having on me and the ambiance and the company and the chase.

"You can't. It's too easy," she whispered again.

"Sometimes, easy is good."

"You're mad or drunk or both. Go on then. I can't stop you."

"Watch and learn, girl."

I gulped back a full glass of the sweetest wine.

"I think I'm afraid to watch – you'll devour him."

"You're right."

"Go easy on him, Emma."

"Ah, the poor sod. Maybe I'll leave him alone."

"Sense at last."

"There's no challenge. It's too obvious."

She filled my glass from my wine and her glass from hers.

"I'm glad to see you're admitting defeat. I thought for a minute you were going to have him right here on the table. Does this mean I win the bet?"

She called Dish over again. "Can we have some more wine, please?"

"Are you ready to order your food?" I think Dish was getting a bit nervous of us.

"Not yet, give us a minute."

He withdrew.

"I'd never admit defeat," I said. "I need a challenge. Dish is too easy for me to waste my talents on."

"I bet you wouldn't mind wasting them on Danny all the same."

"Well, the lovely Jane is probably showing him her hidden talents as we speak."

"Don't be silly. You saw him today – he ran a mile from her."

"Well, tonight will be different. He'll have a few

drinks, she'll have a few drinks and one thing will lead to another."

"Will I take your food order now?" Dish was getting irritable.

"OK, will we just get a pizza between us, Abby? What do you think?"

"Yeah. Great idea. One large pizza with all the toppings. A real Italian pizza."

I poured us some more wine.

"Delicious! Do you know something, Abby? I think I'm losing my touch."

"You haven't lost your touch. You still have your touch, big time. This is the most delicious wine ever." She was knocking it back at a fierce rate I noticed because we both finished at the same time and I knew I was knocking them back big time. It was just great to be able to forget about everything and chill out.

"Na, it's gone, Abby. Just like *that* it went!" I tried to click my fingers, but they wouldn't click. "Look! I've even lost the touch in my fingers. I used to have great touch."

"You still have. I bet you could pull any man in this room."

"Well, I know I can pull Dish, but that doesn't prove I still have my touch. Anyone could pull him."

"Well, then go for … you know … a bit … of a … you know."

"You're pissed, Abby. You're doing that thing you do

when you're pissed. Forgetting to use proper words."

Abby gets pissed quicker than anyone I know. She doesn't build up to getting pissed. One minute she's stone-cold sober and the next she's legless. She was legless now.

"I am – not – pppp – whatever it was you said."

"Pissed."

"That too. Tell you what … I'll pick … a bloke … you hit on him. Then we … can see … if you still have … your whatever."

"Touch. My touch. That's a brilliant idea. I love games. Let the game begin. Now don't pick a dog, will you? Pick me a babe."

"Right, let me see." She looked all around the busy room. The tables were full. I was surprised to see how many men there were. Groups of men. Even men on their own. Outside more tables were full and again a lot of them were men.

"What about … your man … him over there? Him … with all the … whatsits … stuff … gold … around his … thing. The rich … one."

"Not Mr Slick. Him with the jewellery and the greasy hair combed back over his bald patch."

"The very … same."

"No, thanks. I get right of refusal on him."

"What … 'bout him?" She was pointing at a man who was sitting with his back to us. He looked good from the back. Blond hair to his shoulders, very tanned. Cream shorts and a cream shirt. I liked the look of him.

"Right. I agree. Now before I start, do I have to bed him or what?"

"Well … you're a big … girl now. That's … up to you. I only … want him … to want to … bed you."

"Good game, good game. I like this."

I opened my little black evening bag and took out my make-up. Well, if I was to succeed I had to give myself every advantage. I took out my mirror to give myself the once-over. I was sorry I didn't have a full-length mirror. That's the thing about little evening bags. Full-length mirrors don't fit easily into them. Very little fits into them. In the small mirror I looked good. The pearls in my ears and around my neck looked good with my tan. A bit of lip shimmer on my lips was all I needed. I attended to that and snapped the bag shut.

I adjusted my black halter neck and fixed the matching black skirt so all the seams lined up. I stood up and for a moment I was a little unbalanced. It was nothing to do with the wine. It was all to do with my high strappy black patent sandals.

"Well, wish me luck, Abby."

"I do … the best … of it … best of … luck … to … my best … pal!"

She raised her glass.

I sauntered over to the man at the table.

"Is there anyone sitting here?"

"No, I'm on my own."

He was as lovely from the front as he was from the back. He had a trim beard and moustache. It suited him. Lovely blue eyes. Behind his back I gave Abby the thumbs-up. I saw that she was ordering more wine. I did the same.

"You don't mind me sitting here, do you? I hate sitting alone when I go out to eat. Men always come on to me. If I can, I try to sit with someone who looks nice and won't bother me and is sitting alone. That way no one bothers me."

"What about the man whose table you ask to sit at? Doesn't he ever bother you?"

"If I minded him chatting me up I wouldn't have picked him to sit with in the first place, now would I? So I never mind that."

This was going well. I winked over to Abby. Dish was busy talking to her. She wasn't minding me at all.

"Who picks up the bill at the end of the dinner?" My new companion was still quizzing me.

I was hoping he wasn't a mean bastard.

"That depends on who wants to. Sometimes me, sometimes him, sometimes both."

For someone who was doing this for the first time I was bloody good. I looked over at Abby again. She was still talking to Dish. This wasn't fair. She was supposed to be supporting me not giving it loads to Dish.

"How's your friend doing?"

"My what?"

"Your friend. I noticed you when I came in, the two of you. You looked like you were having a great time."

I was mortified. I gulped back a glass of wine. Then another one. Only then did I notice that it was his wine I was drinking.

"I'm sorry. I thought it was mine."

I should have been more mortified, but I wasn't. The room was a bit fuzzy and I was a bit fuzzy too. I was hoping I'd be able to speak.

"No problem, we can share it. I'll get you a glass."

He handed me the glass and our fingers touched. He felt nice.

You feel nice, I was thinking.

"Thank you. You do too." He was reading my thoughts.

Maybe he's my soul mate – soul mates can read your thoughts, I think I thought or maybe I said it out loud. It was hard to tell the difference between my thoughts and my words. I was hoping my actions wouldn't join in. That would have been much too confusing.

"So you believe in soul mates?"

"Most definitely. Don't you?"

"Most definitely."

"Do I know you? You seem awfully familiar."

"You should update your chat-up line."

"I'm serious. I can't help feeling I know you. Do I?"

"I know this sounds corny, but I feel I know you too."

Jesus, maybe this was my soul mate.

"You're eyes, they're violet."

"Yeah. They've always been."

"I once knew a girl with violet eyes. It can't be you. Is it you, Emma?"

"How do you know my name?"

"You look different. Your hair, what have you done to it. It's blonde."

"Does it look that bad then?"

And then he laughed. It was only when he laughed that I recognised him. I recognised him immediately, once he laughed.

"Alex!"

I was stunned.

"Jesus! Emma! It is you. You're the last person I would have thought I'd see here!"

I was still stunned. I just kept staring at him.

"Are you all right, Emma?"

I just nodded my head.

"Don't tell me I have rendered you speechless?"

I nodded again.

How many times had I imagined this? How many nights had I gone to sleep with this moment as my last waking thought? The number of times I had rehearsed what I would say in this exact situation and here I was unable to speak.

"I used to imagine this," he said. "I used to imagine what I would say if I bumped into you somewhere. I had no idea it would be like this."

I opened my mouth to deliver the wonderful speech I had prepared for the last twenty-one years. Adding bits over the years. Trimming and culling the speech so it would only last for half an hour and not half a lifetime. It's hard to get half a lifetime into half an hour. Oh, if only I could find my voice! I only I could tell him what a shit he'd been to Julia. If only I could remember where my speech was supposed to start. Oh, yes. I was supposed to start with: how could you have walked out on me when I was pregnant? We both knew the marriage was a mistake, but you could have stayed around to support me. To support me during my pregnancy. To give me a backrub or at least come to anti-natal classes with me. It was your baby I was carrying. That's where I was to start.

All I had to do was start.

"How have you been, Emma? I have wondered how you were getting along over the years. I am sorry I left you when you were pregnant. It was so unfair. I have wanted to get in touch many times, but I thought you'd tell me to get lost. I really wanted to see Julia. How is she? Who's she like?"

And that was it. The dam burst. I found my voice. The trigger was Julia. He only had to mention her name.

"Don't you dare talk to me about Julia! You are not good enough even to mention her name. You have no idea what you did to her. Do you know she constantly asked about her father all through the years? Do you know what she would have given for a phone call, even one in all the years? A birthday card. A note. You're spineless, Alex. What the hell are you doing here anyway?"

"I live here. I paint now."

"Houses, fences?"

"Painting as in, I paint pictures. I have a little studio down on the beach."

"What sort of paintings do you paint?" I knew the answer before he gave it.

"Modern. I use strong colours. I always put a blue dot in the bottom right-hand corner."

"You bastard! You slimy bastard!"

I was shouting now. Standing over him. Shouting.

Abby came running over, suddenly sober.

"Emma, Emma, what is it? What did he do? This was a stupid game. I should never have –"

"This is Alex. My bastard of an ex-husband."

"Alex!"

He was on his feet now, stretching out his hand to Abby. She was a loyal friend – she ignored it.

I was shaking.

"You know the fucking paintings on the wall in my home. This bastard painted them and I have let them into my home. I hung them in my home. What sort of a gobshite am I?"

"Oh, Emma. Come on, let's get out of here."

Now I hated his paintings, my paintings. I hated him. I turned to bury my head in Abby's shoulder, but I had buried my head too long. I was sick of burying my head, in shame, in hurt, in pain.

Slowly I lifted my head and turned on him.

"The bloody nerve of you! Sitting in your ivory tower, hidden away from the world doing your painting. Letting Julia live a life with no father. It would have been better for her if you had died. She could have buried you and put flowers on your grave. She could have fooled herself that God had been responsible for her having no father. She could have fooled herself that you loved her. She wouldn't have had to face the stark reality that you didn't bother your arse to be around her."

"I'm sorry. How is she? Will you tell me?"

"No, you don't deserve to know how wonderful she is. How she has such a wild spirit and an energy. How beautiful she is. How gifted she is. You don't deserve to know that when she smiles she has a little dimple that would lift you on the saddest day. That she is kind, honourable and I love her to bits. You don't even deserve to know that she has brought something to my life that I'm glad you missed out on because you didn't deserve to have it. You have to put in the time, Alex, and you didn't. What you do deserve to know is that she is here with me. Only a stone's throw from your ivory tower and there is no way in hell that I will let you so much as lay eyes on her."

"Emma! Stop. This is ridiculous. Let me talk to you. There wasn't a day that went by that I didn't think of you and her. I never met anyone like you. The worst thing I ever did was leave. I was destroyed for years. I drank and just drifted. It's only in the last few years I have got my life back together. I thought when I had enough to make Julia proud of me that I would get in touch with her and you."

"Well, poor you! My heart bleeds for you. Do you think I'm being unfair to you? A little bit too tough maybe? A teeny-weeny bit bitter would you say? Well, too bloody right I am! You want sympathy from me? You've come knocking on the wrong door, buddy! I have changed since I was with you. I'm not the bleeding heart I used to be. I have had to put up with all the crap from everyone about being a lone parent. All the snide remarks about dysfunctional families. All the fucking sympathy votes. It has toughened me up, Alex. It's all thanks to you. I am a strong woman. A happy woman. I have lived a life that revolved around your daughter and I wouldn't change one single moment of it."

"Emma! I'm sorry. I really am. What can I do? Let me make it up to you and Julia, please. Just let us talk. Give me a chance."

"What chance did you give us?"

I noticed everyone in the café was silent. All hanging on to our every word.

Abigail was standing beside me holding my arm. Tears flowing down her face. I didn't cry. I didn't shed one tiny tear. I had no tears left for this man. I had cried them all away a long time ago.

"Do you know what's so funny about all this, Alex? I would have forgiven you anything at one time. You were only a kid. I could understand why you left. Kids make mistakes. I could forgive the young man who hadn't got the balls to stay and fight for his wife and daughter. As time went on, I thought 'He's not a kid any more – he'll get in touch with Julia now.' But you didn't. You haunted me, Alex. You were constantly in my life by never getting in touch. You were clever. You made me think of you. You made me wonder where you were. What you were doing. Every year you haunted me by not getting in touch. It's that man I can't forgive. The man who ignored us all through the years. Who still ignores us. The man you are now, Alex, that's the man I can't forgive. Don't talk to me about chances. You've had plenty of chances. You just never took any of them. Chances are dealt out all the time, Alex. All through the years. You have to take them, act on them. You didn't. You got all your chances. You blew them."

I turned to Abby.

"Come on, Abby, I want to go. Do you see this man? This piss-artist. Well this sorry little excuse for a man is Julia's ex-father."

Alex was standing looking after me. He didn't follow me. I didn't expect him to. That was the sort of man he was. Nothing was important enough for him to fight over.

Abigail linked my arm and we walked back through the cobbled streets.

"The next time you ask me to go away with you I will be saying no," was all she said.

"Can you get over it all the same? Can you? I can't get over it. I seriously can't, Abby. Can you believe it? Oh, Abby! What am I going to tell Julia?"

"The truth, same as always."

"I hope she won't fly off into a rage. This will come like a bolt out of the blue."

"She'll be fine. She's a strong woman. She's a good woman too, Emma, she'll handle it well."

"I hope she doesn't want to meet him. The bollocks."

"She might."

"I don't want her to."

"I know, Emma. I know."

"It was so weird. There I was chatting him up no end. Imagine you picking him out for the game!"

"I know, I feel so shit about it. If it wasn't for me none of this would have happened."

"Don't be so stupid. It was meant to happen. I actually fancied him while I was talking to him. He's changed so much. The beard. The manly figure. He's so different. That's the weirdest bit of all. If I'd never found out who he was I'd have really been into him. Whatever I saw in him in the first place must still be there. It makes my skin crawl that I was attracted to him, after what he did to Julia."

"Don't even think about it. You didn't know it was him."

Danny was in the bar when we got back to the hotel. He was alone. Sitting in an armchair with a drink in his hand. There was no sign of Plain Jane. It was just as well because I would have clawed her eyes out.

"Where did you two get to?"

"We went into the village for dinner. Did Julia not tell you?"

"She did, but I thought you'd be back ages ago. I've been waiting on you. Did you have a good meal?"

"Very liquid. Where's Julia? I have to talk to her."

"She and Dylan were out walking on the beach and –"

"On the beach? She's not still out there, is she?"

"No. They came in a while ago and went up to their room. There was definitely a touch of romance in the air. What's wrong?"

"I'd better go up to her. What the hell am I going to tell her?"

"I'll come up with you and take Dylan into our room until you're finished talking to Julia."

"Thanks, Abby. What am I going to say?"

"What's going on? What are you talking about? Say what about what? Sit down, Emma. You're shaking. Tell me what's wrong." Danny was rubbing my arm, almost automatically.

"I have to talk to Julia."

"She'll be asleep by now. She was exhausted. Dylan

was knackered too."

"The poor thing. I'll let her sleep. I'll tell her in the morning. What do you think, Abby?"

"If she's half asleep it wouldn't be fair to hit her with all this. Wait until tomorrow."

"Will one of you please tell me what's going on?"

"I met Alex."

"Alex as in Julia's father Alex?"

"Yes. He lives here. Can you believe it? The piss-artist is actually an artist living on Aronna. Now he wants to see Julia. Can you believe him? Well, over my dead body! He doesn't deserve to see her."

"Wow! Holy shit. That's weird. How do you feel?"

"Shite. You know that painting you bought me in Vienna? Well, Alex painted it."

"I don't believe you."

"He wants to meet Julia. I don't want him to."

"I think you better leave that up to Julia."

"I think I'll go on up, Emma. You'll be all right here, won't you?" Abby looked dead on her feet.

"I'll take care of her," said Danny.

"I know you will, Danny. Goodnight." Abby gave me a peck, goodnight, on the cheek and a big hug.

Danny put his arm around me.

It would be safe for me to cry now.

I didn't. I was determined not to waste another tear on Alex.

"Do you want to come up to my room. We could chat

and have a drink?"

I raised my eyebrows.

"I'm not taking advantage of you. I love you, Emma. I want to be with you. I've been sitting here for ages waiting for you. I wanted to ask you if we could try again. I just want to be with you. I'll make any commitment you want."

"I can't do this now, Danny."

"I know. I just want to let you know how I feel. Now come on, I'm going to take care of you."

It was easy to let him take charge. It was easy to let him bring me back to his room to hold me and cuddle me.

Right then I didn't want to be in charge.

I wanted to be cuddled and minded.

I wanted to have my moment.

CHAPTER SEVENTEEN

Danny's double room was much smaller than the apartment, obviously. But I didn't expect it to be as small as it was. Directly inside the door was the door to the bathroom. There was no bath in it, just a shower. It was white, the same as ours only the taps and fittings were silver not gold. The towels didn't look as plush either. The bedroom was painted white. There were blue tiles on the floor and a big blue and white rug in the centre. The bed wasn't very big either. It didn't really look like a double. There was a beautiful blue and white cover on it. The balcony looked out onto the cobbled streets that led up to the village. All the double rooms were to the front of the hotel. The apartments were to the back. A long corridor divided them. The door to his room was nearly opposite the door to my apartment. I was tempted to run across the corridor and climb into my big bed. All by myself. But I knew as soon as I did that I'd want to be here. Abby couldn't cuddle me the way Danny could.

"Which side of the bed do you want to sleep on?"

"The one near the door, thanks."

"Do you want another pillow?" He opened the wardrobe and got out a pillow. He remembered I liked two.

"How come you didn't get an apartment? Me and Abby have a huge apartment."

"There were none left. In fact the whole place was booked out. I only got this one because it was the other photographer's room. It was kept for me when he skipped off."

"I still think it's weird you ending up here all the same."

"Fate, that's what it is. We were supposed to be here together. Isn't it great the way it worked out? Aren't you glad I'm here?"

"Look, Danny, maybe this is foolish. Maybe I should just go back to my own room. Abby will be there so I'll be all right."

"Abby is knackered, she'll be asleep by now. I'll stay awake with you until you fall asleep. With all the best intentions in the world I don't think Abby will be able to stay awake to listen to you once her head hits the pillow."

"I should let her sleep. All right. But, if I stay here there's to be no funny business. OK?"

"I promise. No matter how tempted I am there will be no funny business."

"Well, lend me a T-shirt then and I'll get dressed in the bathroom."

He pulled a big T-shirt out of the drawer.

"Here, try this one. You change here. I'll go into the bathroom."

As he passed me by to get into the bathroom our bodies rubbed up against one another. The smallness of the room wasn't helping our promise of no funny business. I was dying for a bit of funny business. I was dying for someone to hold me and tell me everything would be all right.

I pulled off my clothes and it was a relief to get out of them. My body felt as if it had been released from prison. The wire in my bra had begun to conspire against me and had been digging into me. It was lovely to take it off.

I climbed into the bed and pulled the covers up around my chin.

Danny came out of the bathroom.

He was totally starkers. Not a drawers or a towel on him.

"That defeats the whole purpose of going into the

bathroom to get dressed, you big idiot!"

"No, it doesn't. The whole point of me going into the bathroom is that I missed the pleasure of seeing you getting undressed or undressing you myself. So, I think I showed huge self-control and I will be expecting a little reward. A kiss would be nice."

He climbed in beside me and gave me a soft kiss on the lips. I didn't respond. It took all my inner strength not to. I must have had a lot of inner strength that I never had before. That's what meeting ex-husbands does for you.

I felt Danny's arm around my waist. I left it there. I hadn't enough inner strength to remove it. He snuggled up tight to my back. I could feel every bit of him.

But things were complicated enough without letting him make love to me. I could feel that he wanted to.

"I can't, Danny. I just want to go asleep."

"Goodnight. I love you."

"Don't say that unless you mean it."

"I love you. I have always. Goodnight, Emma."

"Goodnight, Danny."

I must have fallen asleep instantly. But woke up again a few hours later in a panic. I drifted in and out of sleep all night. I kept rerunning the whole horrible mess over and over in my head. My brain was on overload.

I drifted in and out of dreams as well as sleep. My dreams went from me as a young girl with a baby daughter to cope with to me today with an adult daughter to cope with. Except in my dreams everything was distorted. Maybe my dreams were reflecting my life. My life was distorted. I kept having dreams of Alex. The way he was years ago. The way he was now. Of him and me together. Every time I closed my eyes I could see him. He had turned into a very good-looking man. I hated thinking he was good-looking. I hated thinking anything about him was good. Part of me wished nothing had happened between us and I could talk to him about his painting and his life. Part of me was upset that the other part of me wanted to know anything about him.

And now the sun was beating into the balcony and my head was aching.

My heart was beating in my chest.

I wished I was still asleep. I was like a well-tossed salad but not nearly as fresh.

I had been hoping that I would wake up and be at home. That, like Dorothy in *The Wizard of Oz*, I could have clicked my heels and arrived back home with Toto. A little puppy would be nice around the house. Julia would love Toto.

I had hoped that I had imagined the whole thing. That I had never set foot on Aronna. That I was in my own bed. But I wasn't in my own bed at home. I wasn't even in my own bed on Aronna. I was in Danny's bed.

Danny wasn't in the bed. I could hear the shower on full blast. Thank God. The morning after the night before is always awkward. I knew he wanted answers. I knew he wanted me to tell him that we could try again. That it would all work out. That we'd be fine. The thing about relationships is that it isn't enough for one person to say it will be fine. Both have to be capable of making it fine.

I jumped up and got into my clothes as quickly as I could. I left his T-shirt on the bed.

I had just opened the door very quietly and was just about to make my escape when Danny came out of the bathroom and saw me.

"Where are you going, Emma?"

"Back to my own room. I have to go, Danny, I have to talk to Julia. Thanks for last night. You were terrific. I'll talk to you later, I promise. I have to sort my head out. This thing with Alex has really upset me. I can't think of anything else at the moment. I know it's stupid to let him have this effect on me, but that's the way it is. I have to think of Julia too. I don't know how she's going to react."

"I understand, honestly. But will you think about you and me too, Emma? I know we can work things out. We're good together, you know that, don't you? We have something special, Emma. I'm sorry I didn't see it before, but I really do love you."

I went out into the corridor, but then I turned back to him. He was still standing at the door looking after me. He looked funny with his hair wet and the towel almost covering him. He looked lost and lonely.

I went back to him and gave him a kiss. A soft kiss. Not a big snog. Just a little one. On the lips.

"Emma!"

I spun around.

And my heart stopped.

"Ronan? What the hell are you doing here? How?"

He was looking right beyond me at the towel-clad Danny. "I followed you. I got a flight early this morning."

"Ronan!" Danny was looking Ronan up and down.

It was one of those moments where you hope the ground has that opening everyone always wishes for.

"Danny, this is Ronan – Ronan, this is Danny." I knew as soon as I did the introductions that it was stupid. I just didn't know what else to do.

They both exchanged grunts. The grunts were as good as pistols at dawn.

Danny seemed a bit pissed off with me.

"Danny, that's a nice towel you're nearly wearing." Ronan's nose seemed out of joint.

"So tell us what brings you here then, Ronan?" Danny was really aggressive.

"Will the two of you stop! It's wonderful to see you, Ronan, but what are you doing here? Don't tell me they needed some sort of a software genius and it's you?"

"No! No one needed me. I was hoping you might need me, but I can see you don't. I'm not in the way or anything, am I?" Ronan was annoyed. He was being bitchy. Both of them were being bitchy. Neither of them were usually bitchy. I felt like a right bitch. This was all my fault.

"Will you stop! So, what are you doing here then, Ronan?"

"I thought you might want me to be here, so here I am."

I couldn't believe it. He came all the way here for me. A big romantic gesture. I couldn't blame him for getting annoyed. This was not the way he thought his big romantic gesture would go. He had probably imagined himself finding me all alone and lonely on the beach or somewhere. He would have been able to march over and scoop me up into his arms, sweep me off my feet and carry me off into the most amazing sunset.

I was really charmed with his big romantic gesture even if it was a bit of a mess at the moment. I was so thrilled that he had followed me. It was just very hard to tell him in front of Danny. Poor Danny who was so good to me looked all annoyed too. This was not how he was expecting things to be going either.

It sure wasn't how I had expected things to go.

"I'd better go back to Abby and I need to see Julia. Ronan, you'd better come with me and I can explain everything that's happened. Danny, we'll see you later."

I was in complete control. This was a first. I wasn't waiting on a man to take charge.

"It really is great you being here." I waited until I got Ronan into the safety of my own apartment. I reached out and put my arms around him. He held me as if I was the most precious thing in the world. He ran his hands all over me. Then he kissed me. A loving, gentle, passionate kiss.

"What's going on, Emma? I have to know. What were you doing with Danny?"

"Shhhh! We'll wake Abby. First of all – tell me why did you come here? How did you get here? Tell me everything."

"It's all Madame Celeste's fault."

"Madam Celeste?"

"The very one. I missed you, so I started looking up your horoscope knowing you'd be doing the same thing. I laughed at some of them. Then I read this."

He took a newspaper out of his travel bag. There were two big red circles around two horoscopes. His and mine. I read mine first.

Madam Celeste
Scorpio
October 22 – November 23

Someone, somewhere follows their heart. It will bring you closer to them. Don't give up hope. Just wait for them.

Then his.

They're waiting for you. You have to follow your heart. You only get so many chances. Don't waste any of them.

"I thought you said that was all mumbo-jumbo."

"I still think it's mumbo-jumbo, but I know that you believe it. I knew when I read it that you would be reading it too. I imagined that if you read it you'd think I was going to follow you. I pictured you waiting for me. I couldn't have you waiting for me and me not turning up, now could I? I couldn't disappoint you."

"But how did you find me? How did you know I was here? Did Geoff tell you?"

"No, it was Julia."

"Julia?"

"She rang me last week to tell me you were going away. She was worried in case I'd try to get in touch and I wouldn't be able to reach you. She thought I might think something had happened to you both. So I knew where you were."

"She thinks of everyone, doesn't she?"

"Yeah. She was good to ring me. So when I read these I got a flight out as quick as I could. I just threw a few things into a bag and here I am. Have I made a total ass of myself, Emma? Have I left it too late? Are you back with Danny? Do you love him? Did he come here with you? Julia said you were only going to be with Abby and her and Dylan – she never mentioned Danny. Emma, talk to me. Are you sleeping with him?"

"No, he didn't come here with me. I didn't even know he'd be here. It's a long story, but he's working here. He's a photographer. He's been good to me, Ronan. He really has. I haven't had sex with him. I have slept in this room every night except last night. Last night I slept in his room and in his bed. I slept with him because I wanted to be with someone who cared for me. He does. I swear I didn't have sex with him. I didn't even want to. He held me and cuddled me and that was all. I needed it, Ronan, so if you have a problem with someone being kind and gentle to me when I needed it then you'd better go now."

He walked out on to the balcony and I could see he was hurting. I followed him.

"You weren't here. I needed someone. Danny was here."

"He has a knack of turning up just when you need him."

I smiled. I went into the kitchen and poured us some juice. He followed me. He pushed my hair back off my face the way he always did.

We sat at the table and I told him all about Alex.

"My poor Emma. I wish I'd been here."

"But you weren't."

"Danny was. I understand, now."

We moved out of the kitchen again and sat out on the balcony. The sun was shining again. It looked like it was going to be another terrific, day but I knew it was going to be a shit day for me.

"I better not put off telling Julia any longer."

"You're right. You better tell her before she finds out from someone else or bumps into him."

"I bump into who?" Julia was standing out on the balcony of her room, looking in at us. She was wearing a very sloppy T-shirt which I guessed was Dylan's. "Ronan! I thought it was you I heard. This is great. What are you doing here?" She was genuinely delighted to see him.

"I wanted to see your ma. How are you, Julia?"

"You flew all the way over her to see Ma?"

"She's well worth it, Julia. She's one in a million. It's just a pity it took me so long to realise it."

"I always knew. I could have told you."

"Well, why didn't you?"

"You never asked. Hey, are you going down for breakfast? I'll come with you if you wait for me."

"We'll go down in a while. Will you come in here? I need to talk to you. Can you come over? Where's Dylan?"

"He's asleep. What's wrong? What is it? You all look so morbid. Where's Abby?"

"Nothing's wrong. Abby's asleep. How she's still asleep with all this racket we're making is beyond me. Get some clothes on and I'll see you in a few minutes."

"I'll go and explore downstairs," said Ronan. "Unless you want me to be here. I'll come back up in a little while to make sure you're all right."

"I think this is something I have to tell her on my own."

I showered and put on my shorts and T-shirt in record time. Julia must have done the same because she was at the door in no time.

"What's wrong? Are you sick? Is Abby sick?"

"I'm fine, really fine."

I wasn't. I wasn't a bit fine. I was feeling very sick.

"What's wrong?" Abby finally woke up.

"Nothing, Abby."

"I dreamt Ronan was here. Can you imagine that? As if life wasn't complicated enough." Abby was rubbing her eyes.

"He is here. He's gone downstairs."

"Christ, this is turning into the holiday from hell."

"Ma! What is it you want to tell me? Will you get on with it and tell me!"

Abby ran into the bathroom, shouting at us as she ran, "I'll be out of your hair in two minutes."

"What's wrong with her?"

Abby appeared out of the bathroom in no time. "I'll just go down and get a coffee. Maybe find Ronan or Danny or Marco or anyone else who wants to cause me grief."

"Thanks, Abby. See you soon."

"I don't like this, Ma, what's going on?"

"Well, it's like this. You know your father, Alex?"

"Well, chance'd be a fine thing. Let's say I've heard about him." She laughed. "If you're going to tell me that he has died I have to tell you that I feel very sorry, but only the way I'd feel if I heard some stranger had died. So stop worrying. I'll do whatever you want me to do, but I can't grieve. I did all that a long time ago."

There was no alternative I had to just come right out and tell her.

"He's here Julia. On Aronna. He lives here. I had no idea. I saw him last night up in the village."

"Here? He's here? Oh, my God. Why?"

"He lives here. It's as good as anywhere else, I suppose."

I wanted her to tell me to take her out of here. To pack our bags and get a flight home as soon as possible. Get the hell out of this situation. I felt like a rat in a trap.

"Did you talk to him? What does he look like?"

"Yes, I didn't know it was him, at first. He looks different. He's older."

"Did he ask about me?"

"Yes. He wanted to know all about you."

"I bet he did, the fucker. I hope you told him to fuck off! If he wants to know about me let him find me and ask me. Let him do what normal people do, phone, write, e-mail – the fucking list is endless. He could have done that at any time, but he didn't bother his arse. That's the bottom line. What the hell is he doing here anyway?"

"He's an artist these days. He seems to have had a tough time during his life."

"Not as tough as ours though. An artist? What sort of artist?"

352

"He paints. Modern art." How was I going to tell her she loved his work?

"What do you mean? Modern paintings? I didn't know he was an artist. Is it like the ones we have at home? That type?"

"The very same. Exactly the same."

"He's not? No, I don't believe it? He's not the artist? Shit. The bastard! He wormed his way into our house. I hate him."

She was pacing up and down now.

"Yes, Julia. It's him. I couldn't believe it either. If I'd known I'd never have bought them, you know that, don't you?"

"How could you have known it was the bastard? The slime never signs them."

"The blue dot."

"The slimy git!"

"He wants to see you."

"Does he now? When would suit him? It would be dreadful for me to see him when it was inconvenient for him. Obviously it has been very inconvenient for him up to now. So now that it suits him I'm supposed to appear for an audience with him. He's whistled and I am to dance, is that it? Is that what he wants? Well, let's give him what he wants then. Let's give him exactly what he wants."

She jumped up and was gone out of the room before I could stop her. She stormed into her own room. I heard her shouting at Dylan.

"I'm off to meet my father."

"What? Come back!" Dylan was shouting at her.

Danny came out of his bedroom.

"What's happening?"

"It's Julia – she's stormed out and she's going to see Alex. I'm going after her."

I ran as fast as I could out onto the beach. I could see her ahead of me.

"Julia, Julia, don't do this! Not this way!"

But it was too late. I ran along the beach calling her name.

She was younger and fitter than me. I finally caught up with her at the door of the studio.

"Stop this, Julia! Come back with me. We should talk about this. I have already had a go at him. I don't want you to do this."

"Do you know how long I have imagined this? Do you know how much I wanted this? When I was five, ten, fifteen and all the years in between. One phone call – that's all I wanted. One phone call would have lasted me a lifetime. Something. Anything. I even rehearsed what I would say. When I was fifteen I convinced myself that he was in a coma somewhere being kept alive and that was why he didn't want to know me. When I was sixteen I stopped fooling myself."

"I don't want you to do it like this. You don't even have to meet him if you don't want to."

"Julia!"

He had come out of the studio and we hadn't noticed. She turned and froze. She was taking it all in. The stand of him, the look of him.

"I'm glad you came," was all he said.

"Well, you never came to me!" She was shouting. "Why? Why? That's all I have ever wanted to know. Why you didn't give a fuck. Why you never even bothered your arse to write to me."

"I'm sorry. I know I've hurt both of you. I know I can never make up for it. I wouldn't even try."

"That's what's wrong, Alex, or should I call you Daddy or Dad or fucker? You should try. You should have tried over the years. Look at you, you still couldn't be bothered trying. Even if we don't want you to try you should still try. If I had done to anyone what you did to Ma and me I'd spend the rest of my life trying to make it up to them.

But you're such a big fucking loser you won't even bother. Well, stuff you and stuff your trying. I don't need you. I never needed you. I hate you, do you hear me? I hate you. I hate your poxy paintings too."

"I thought you'd be better off without me. I knew I'd be a lousy father. I was only a kid. I knew I'd be a lousy husband. I thought the best thing to do was to just go away."

"My ma never had the luxury of being able to decide whether she'd be a good mother or not. She was a mother and she did what mothers do. She stayed around. She turned out to be brilliant at it. Amazing even. I don't know what I'd have turned into if she hadn't been there for me. She had no choice though, did she? She stayed."

"Julia, I really am sorry for all the hurt I have caused and I am still causing. I nearly got in touch with you so often. I knew, without a shadow of a doubt, that your mother would do her best by you. I knew you'd grow into a beautiful woman and you have. I was afraid if I did get in touch that you'd reject me. I couldn't bear that. Imagine, I couldn't bear it and yet it's the very thing I did to you. I rejected you. Can you ever forgive me?"

"I don't want to forgive you! Don't you get it? Fuck off out of my life. Ma and me are better off without you."

"I never stopped loving your mother, you know. She was the love of my life. You are just like her."

"Fuck off." She stormed off down the beach away from him. She put her arms around me. No tears. She was so angry. I was afraid for her.

Alex went back into his studio.

She watched him close the door.

She pulled away from me and ran up to the door. She pushed her way in through it.

"You fucking coward! You don't even have the balls to come after us now. You're quite prepared for us to walk off now."

I followed her.

She was standing in a large room with a glass dome in the ceiling. It was magnificent. The walls were all painted white and the floor was tiled white. It should have been clinical. It wasn't. Every wall was covered in paintings in vibrant, strong colours. It was a kaleidoscope. The colours danced off the walls. Julia stood staring at them. One by one going through each one of them. I was only able to take them all in together. Alex was watching her. He watched as the tears just flowed from her. She only moved from painting to painting. She never spoke a word. It was as if she were trying to get an answer somewhere in the painting.

A small corridor, again painted white and full of paintings, led to another room. This one had chairs and couches and was his living-room. In the corner was an easel, beside that a table full of paints and brushes. There were huge windows in this room and again a glass dome in the roof. There was only one painting in this room. A huge canvas that nearly filled the wall. It was a magnificent painting of a baby.

I knew immediately who it was.

"It's you," I whispered. She was very quiet.

"Me?"

"My father gave me a photo of you," he said. "I painted it from that."

"You had no right."

She walked around the room and stood looking at him.

"You had no right to see me every day and not see me at all."

She had it in her hand before I even saw what she was doing. The tube of paint was large and full. She squirted the paint all over the canvass. She spread her hands out into the paint and rubbed them all over the canvas. It went everywhere. The painting was covered in it.

"You had no fucking right!"

She ran out.

Alex was following.

"Leave it, Alex. She's said all she needed to."

"Do you think she'll forgive me?"

"I don't know."

I ran after Julia. All that I had held back poured from me. I cried as I struggled along the beach to catch up with her. I was struggling to walk. She was running ahead of me. She stopped dead in her tracks and stared out to the sea. She turned and waited for me. We held one another. Endless tears just fell from her. She made no sound. There are different types of crying.

There is the tearless crying of frustration and anger. There is the individual-tear type of crying from being badly hurt. Then there is the stop start tears that come from an even greater hurt.

But worst of all is the silent, flowing type of crying. It comes from some hurt deeper than you thought was possible. A hurt that never goes away. Very few people ever cry silent, flowing tears.

Very few people ever hurt that badly. My Julia was hurting that badly. I was hurting that badly watching her.

CHAPTER EIGHTEEN

There was no old black and white DVD for me and Julia to watch. There were no hidden treats for us to gorge ourselves on. It was just as well because this was too big a problem to be cured by *Madam X* and a bit of chocolate. We just sat talking for hours. At different intervals Dylan, Abby, Ronan and Danny came in to see if we were all right. They brought tea every time. I was all tea-d out.

Neither of us wanted to go to dinner that night. We weren't in the humour for being nice to anyone. We just wanted to be left alone with each other to wallow in our misery. We weren't allowed. We were bullied into going to dinner. It was the last one before we went home.

Abby gave us a good talking-to.

"Now you listen to me, the two of you. This man – I

will not call him either your husband or your father – this man has robbed you of enough all your lives. I will not allow him take another thing. I will not stand by and watch the two of you so upset by him. I know how hard it will be, I know you don't want to leave your rooms but, Emma, a man flew across the sea to be with you and another man's face lit up when he saw you were here the other day. You cannot stay locked up here and not include either of them in your pain – you never know they might even help you forget it for five minutes."

"But Abby –"

"But nothing. I can't do it, Emma, I can't see you both hurting like this. If you were at home and had the DVD and goodies I'd leave you alone, but I can't. This is the only way I know to make it better. I want you to go home remembering some nice things about this place. Julia, there is a very handsome, lovely man, who I might add was reared very well and has a lot of good stock in him, out there waiting for you. He wants to help you. He doesn't know how. Tell him what you want. Don't shut him out. He's a good kid. OK, so he might not always say the right thing, but I bet if you listen to him long enough he will. What do you both think? Will we knock the socks off 'em one last time for our last night?"

"How do you argue with that? And here was me thinking my ma was the bully of the two of you!"

"We're both bullies, Julia," I grunted.

"Well, I'm game if you are." She looked at me, hoping I'd say I wasn't game.

"I guess I could make some sort of an effort."

"Poor Dylan, all the same, I bet he thinks I'm a right sap."

"Well, come on then. Get yourself tarted up and let him see you're not."

"I am not admitting defeat here by the way. I'm still very pissed off with my so-called father. Very pissed off."

"That's good. Pissed off is good. What about you. Emma?"

"I'm pissed off too."

"Right, we can handle pissed off once it's only 'that man' that we are all pissed off with. Now come on, best bib and tucker tonight."

"Thanks, Abby."

"Yeah, thanks, you big bully. Poor Dylan, I feel sorry for him – you probably bullied him into eating all his vegetables when he was young."

"Aren't you delighted I did? Look at the big handsome hunk he turned out to be."

"Would it be a bit sick to have a group hug?" I was getting carried away.

"Yes."

"Most certainly."

But we did anyway.

I wore blue. Abby wore pink. Julia wore white.

We were all tanned and even if I do say so myself we

looked great.

We sang going down in the lift.

This time we made a grand entrance. We wowed them. Abby especially wowed them when she got the heel of her high-heeled pink sandals stuck in the gap at the opening of the lift. I thought she overdid it a bit.

"Oh look! My heel! It's stuck!"

"I'll get it out for you." Ronan grabbed a hold of her bare leg and started pulling her heel out. I thought he grabbed her leg a bit high up to be getting her heel out.

"No! No! I'll do it." Danny rushed forward and grabbed hold of her leg too. He was grabbing even higher.

"Let me do it! Stand back!" Marco grabbed hold of her leg too. He was grabbing her thigh.

Abigail was laughing.

She looked as though she was enjoying all the fuss a little bit too much.

"Thank you all," she finally said as she twirled her freed ankle around, showing us all how slim it was.

Ronan and Danny came over to me and they both handed me a drink. I know I said I wanted minding, but this was going to wreck my head. I took the glass off Ronan and gave it to Julia and the one from Danny I gave to Abby. Marco handed me a drink and I took it and sipped it.

I was delighted to see Ronan and Danny. I was delighted to see the way they were looking at me. Dylan was positively drooling at Julia and I knew that once Geoff had Abby home he would be drooling and delighted he was taking her away for a dirty weekend.

We had a wonderful meal: bruschetta, salad, pasta and chicken. But it was the sauce that was mouth-watering. It was laced with wine and very creamy. The fresh bread soaked up the sauce perfectly. Julia and I didn't eat as heartily as the rest of the group, not because we didn't like what was on offer, but because we were both feeling very sick in the stomach. We were good at covering up, Julia and I. We were masters at it. We looked good. We were going through all the motions of being polite and having a good time. Some might say we were having a terrific time.

We might even have looked as though we had forgotten all about meeting Alex, but that would have been a miracle and miracles must have been needed elsewhere that night. There wasn't a miracle to be seen. I hoped whoever was getting a miracle that night really appreciated it. Often you only get a miracle when you're so far into despair that you're on automatic pilot and don't recognise the miracle until after the event. I have had many miracles in my time. I have needed every one of them.

After the meal Marco and Maria asked us to join them for a drink down on the patio. It was a farewell drink and on the house. Well, on the patio actually, but it was free. Their treat. It was a lovely idea and a lovely way to spend our last night in Aronna.

"Will you come back to Aronna, Emma? For a longer stay. Maybe two weeks the next time. It would be lovely to see you again."

"Thank you, Maria, but I'm not sure. I don't think so."

"That's a pity. You didn't have much time here to yourself this time. I hope it wasn't too dull for you. There are great places to explore if you are here for two weeks."

"I assure you, Maria, my stay here was anything but dull."

I told her all about seeing Alex. I told her who he was. I left out all the cruel bits. I just gave her the basics.

"I had no idea. Poor Julia, it must have been tough on her. Poor you too. Poor Alex. Isn't it amazing the way some people can turn their lives around. He must be some man all the same. There must have been something about him you loved once. That something must still be there." She gazed along the beach up towards the studio.

"That was a long time ago, Maria. A lot has happened since then."

I think I saw her smile a half-hearted little smile. She wasn't even listening to me. She was thinking about Alex. Whatever it was that had attracted me to Alex was also attracting Maria.

"He's a wonderful artist. Maybe his paintings helped

him to heal himself. Maybe through painting he has turned his life into something good."

Such a load of bullshit. What is it with women? Why do they always go for the bastards. Alex was a bastard. Could no one see that? Was it only me and Julia that saw him for what he was?

"I don't know, Maria. I don't know if he has changed or not. All I know is that he never bothered with his only daughter."

"But maybe he is only getting his life together now. If given a chance he might have got in touch with her soon. He might have been working away here all set to do the right thing."

I realised that this was how everyone would think of Alex. He would stay on this little island and be sheltered from life. He would be the hero. The one who finally pulled out all the stops and got his life together. Like the reformed whore he would be applauded for going on the straight and narrow. I didn't hear anyone applauding for Julia and myself.

"But he left it too late, Maria. If Julia and I hadn't come here she would never have met him. I don't care so much for me, but I do care for Julia's sake."

"You don't know that he wouldn't have got in touch with her sometime. Maybe he was wondering how to do it. Maybe fate decided to take a hand in things. You seem to be very angry for someone who doesn't care any more."

I was very angry. I was angry with Alex. Now I was angry at Maria. How dare she imply I still cared about Alex!

"Maria. You really don't know what you're talking about."

"I'm only telling it as I see it. I'm not trying to hurt you. Don't you think you should at least talk to Alex. All this anger can't be good for you. You loved him once. Maybe you never stopped."

She stood up and walked away from me. I was gobsmacked. The hussy! The bloody hussy!

"Sing for us, Marco!" Maria shouted over to him. She was determined to get the party going.

First almost starting a fight and now a singsong.

Marco didn't need to be asked twice. I'd say Marco was one of the ones you'd hate to have at your wedding. Once he was up on his feet I thought he'd never sit down. He was good though and it lifted my heart a bit which was no mean achievement because my heart was like a lump of lead stuck in my chest. I knew it was my heart and not a big lump of lead I had swallowed inadvertently because it was beating away at a ferocious pace.

Marco was singing 'Amore'. We all joined in. He was good at getting everyone going.

Ronan and Danny sat on either side of me like two bookends. When I moved they moved. When one of them moved the other followed him. It would have been funny if I had been in the mood for laughing.

"Come on, Ma, give us a song!" Julia shouted over at me.

"Yes, Emma, come on!" Abby joined in.

I was just nicely merry without being a bit happy.

"Only if you sing with me, Julia."

"You're on."

It's amazing what a few drinks, a foreign place, a balmy night and a brass neck will do.

Elaine Paige and Barbara Dickson never sang 'I Know Him So Well' as well as we did. We belted it out. We gave it our all. We released so much tension within ourselves.

The small crowd applauded and Julia and I bowed.

Maria kept the party going. She kept on at Ronan until he sang 'Most of All I Love You Cause You're You'. He seemed to sing only to me.

He was good. The crowd erupted into a great cheer.

Then, just because Ronan sang, Danny had to sing. He stared into my eyes and sang 'Loves Changes Everything'.

He got a great cheer too.

Then just off in the distance around by the cliff path I saw a shadow. It was the same one I had seen the other night. I recognised it immediately this time. I got up and went over to the little picket fence that was on one side of the patio and leaned over to get a clearer view.

Alex was out walking again. All along the top of the cliff. I kept watching him. It was dark. He looked so familiar now. He looked like he used to. It was as if I had turned the clock back. I couldn't see how his features had aged. I could see the gait of him. The move of him when he walked. I wanted to call out to him. I don't know why. There was something pathetic about him out there all on his own. He looked lonely. As if he had been wondering all his life. Never finding anything. He was very close to the edge of the cliff. He could lose his footing, anything could happen, if he wanted it to. I hoped he didn't want it to.

I watched him walk all the way back to his studio. I turned to sit down again. I saw that Maria was staring right out where I had been staring. She had been watching Alex too. She saw that I was watching him too. We just stared at each other. Then she smiled. I didn't smile back.

Before I could get to my seat Marco came over to me.

"You have a wonderful voice. You are a woman of many talents, Emma."

"Thank you, Marco."

"I feel that you are restless? What is it?"

"Yes. I suppose I am restless. Maybe it's because I'm going home."

"Come for a walk with me on the beach. It's so beautiful when the moon shines down onto the sea."

It was late. I was nearly enjoying the party. I knew I shouldn't go with him.

"OK," I said. Now why did I say that?

I was wearing pale blue high sandals to match my short strappy dress. I took the sandals off and went barefoot. I saw Ronan and Danny move to follow me. Then they looked at each other, then they sat down again. It was like musical chairs. It was comical.

"I'll be back in a minute. I just want to get a last look at the sea. I'm going for a little walk with Marco," I shouted over to them.

They sat back. Eying each other up. Eying Marco up.

Marco led me down onto the firmer sand.

"Do you like our beautiful Island?"

"I love it."

"I'm glad you had a good time."

I decided not to tell Marco all about Alex. I decided that it was nice to be walking along the beach with someone who knew very little about me. Someone who didn't feel sorry for me.

"I had a terrific time, Marco. It was really wonderful. Your hotel is beautiful and yourself and Maria have been very good to us."

We walked along to the water's edge.

"It was my pleasure. It's lovely for us to have such perfect guests as yourselves."

"That's nice of you to say."

He was a nice man.

"I mean it. Every word of it. We get guests here from all over the world. Big important people and ordinary people, like yourself. It's the ordinary people I like the best. I have really loved you being here."

"So, I'm ordinary now, am I?"

"No, Emma, you are an extraordinary woman and very beautiful."

I thought he said I was beautiful, but I might have been wrong. He was such a gentleman. I blushed anyway. I thought it was the polite and ordinary thing to do.

He sat down on the sand.

"Come, sit down here beside me. Look at the sea. This is my favourite part of the day. Listen!"

I could hear nothing only the sea.

"This is the best time. When all you can hear is the sea roaring in."

"It's beautiful." And it was. It was so peaceful.

"I meant what I said – you are beautiful."

So I had heard him correctly. He really was a lovely man.

"Thank you, Marco. That's very kind of you to say."

"I'm only telling the truth. Do you like it here, Emma, I mean really like it?"

"Yes, Marco, I do like it here. You have a great life here. All the people living here must have a very good life." I was thinking that Alex must have a good life now.

"But it's lonely. I am lonely."

"You can't be lonely. You have a hotel full of guests and you have tons of friends in the village. You also have

Maria. It's great for the two of you to have each other. You can't possibly be lonely."

"I don't mean that I am lonely for people. You're right – I have lots of friends and I have Maria too. She is very good to me. We are a great team. But I am lonely for someone special in my life. Someone who wants to share all of this with me. Someone who would let me do all the little things for them. Someone who would let me mind them and spoil them. Do you know what I mean?"

"More than you know, Marco. Any woman would be lucky to have you in their life. I do know what you mean. I'd love someone special in my life too. Someone who loves me, warts and all. Who wants to be with me no matter what. Who'd do anything for me. Someone who just loves the bones of me."

"Yes, Emma, someone who just loves the bones of you."

"A handsome bloke like yourself will have no problem finding someone."

"But I don't just want any someone, I want the right someone. The someone that I love. I always said that one day someone very special would come to find me. I would be waiting and I would know instantly it was her. But I am a shy man."

"You're not a bit shy. Especially with women." I knew from Abby just how shy he wasn't.

"I am very shy with women I have feelings for. I love women. I love talking to them. I love the feel of them. I love all the womanly things. I love watching women doing all the womanly things they do. I think women are wonderful creatures. So with most women I am easy. I don't find it difficult to talk to them – it's easy and it's fun. I never promise them a happy ever after. They know that."

So Abigail was just a bit of fun. I decided not to share that bit of information with my dear pal.

"Well, I suppose there's no harm done if everyone knows where they stand."

"Exactly, we're all adults. There's no problem. However, there is a problem if I feel serious about a woman. When I am serious about a woman I am useless. I watch her from afar and never make a move."

He was beginning to sound plausible. I nearly felt sorry for him. I nearly had myself convinced that sleeping around with anything that came along was all right. Until the right thing came along. I nearly thought he had the right approach. Then I remembered that the reason I was in such a mess in my own love life was that I had nearly slept with two men. Not together, not at the same time. I could never do a threesome. Or could I? What an idea. Would they agree? Would I be able? I could do my best or die in the effort. It could be an interesting experience. I could jot it down to experience and add it to my many talents. Danny and Ronan would never agree. They just wouldn't. They'd end up having a jousting match with whatever weapons came to hand.

"So, you want to sleep with anything in a skirt even if they mean nothing to you? And you'd never let the woman of your dreams know she was the woman of your dreams just because you're shy?"

"No, that's what I'm trying to tell you. I am a changed man."

He hadn't changed very much when he was trying to get into Abby's knickers.

"Since when, Marco?"

He was playing with the sand. Letting it run through his tanned fingers. His nails were whiter than white.

"Since now. From now on, I'm not going to sleep with a woman just because she'll jump into bed with me. I don't want to do that any more. I want to be with one woman and only one woman. I want to spend the rest of my life with her discovering all the wonderful things about her. Enjoying her. Loving her. Exploring every bit of her."

"Sounds to me like you have someone in mind. Have you found this special woman, Marco? Have you found the one you think you could be happy ever after with?"

"I think I have."

Jesus, Abby was in for a bit of a surprise. Thanks be to God she was going back with me tomorrow. I'd hate to have to be the one who had to tell Geoff that she had stayed on an Italian island with a randy Italian. At least that was one mortification I was to be spared.

I started to laugh.

I don't know why. It was either because I was a little bit merry. Or the atmosphere of the place was making me even merrier. Or the thoughts of Marco and poor innocent Geoff fighting over Abby. Or the thought of Abby staying on the Island with Marco.

Marco started to laugh with me.

"Come for a swim with me," he said, gently pulling me up off the sand.

"Do you know I haven't been for one swim since I arrived here. I love swimming. Every time I tried to go for a swim something happened to stop me. I thought I'd be in the sea every day. Looks like I'll be going home without ever getting wet."

"Well, come on then. No time like the present."

"Are you mad? It's dark. It's probably freezing."

"It's not dark. The moon has the whole of the water lit up perfectly. It will be warm, I promise."

He was right. It wasn't dark. I was dying for a swim.

He started to strip off. His shirt. His shoes, he wasn't wearing any socks. Next his trousers. He wasn't wearing any underwear. There he stood starkers. In the pelt. All his bits glowing in the moonlight. His body was like a chestnut. Brown all over and shiny.

I couldn't stop laughing.

"I hope you're not laughing at me!" He was laughing himself now.

He ran towards the sea. He stood at the edge and stopped for a minute and then dived right into the water.

He swam out away from the shore. He looked good. He stopped and called out to me.

"Come on in it's wonderful. Come on. Don't be such a coward. It's warm, I promise."

I don't know what possessed me. I don't know why I did it. It was just there and I was just there and I knew I would never return to the island and anyway what harm could it do?

I peeled my dress off over my head and threw it up into the air. It landed softly on the sand. I ran in after Marco. I left my bra and knickers on. They were matching and looked like a bikini.

"It is warm. I didn't expect it to be. I thought you were only pretending."

"I never pretend. You should take everything off. Let the water go all over you."

"No thanks. I'm fine as I am." There was no way I was going skinny-dipping with a naked man.

It was wonderful in the water. I lay back and felt the waves carry me. The freedom of being in the sea was glorious. To feel the water lap around me. I was a good swimmer and it was a beautiful night.

Marco swam over to me. We swam along together. I dived in the water. I rolled and let the warm water roll all over my body. He was a stronger swimmer than me. He swam up ahead of me. He stopped just a little bit ahead of me. He scooped me up into his arms. Then he gave me a big slobbery, long, kiss. Tongues and all.

I didn't know what to do. I was gobsmacked. The worst thing about being gobsmacked is you are usually left with your mouth hanging open – which in this case Marco took full advantage of and saw as a sign for "Please, sir, can I have some more?". So he repeated the tongue-swilling kisses and this time put his two hands on my arse.

"Emma, Emma, it's you, you are the one I want! I love you! I don't want you to leave tomorrow. I want you to stay here. Stay here with me forever. I want to talk to you. I have to tell you how I feel. I love you! I will be good to you. I will look after you and treasure you always. Just say you'll stay here with me!"

"Marco!"

He grabbed me again and put his hand down my bra. He pushed his face into my boobs and started kissing them all over. He was desperately trying to fish out a nipple. I was up to my knees in the sea. It was hard to push him off and stay standing. I gave him one sharp shove and tried to run back to the shore.

He ran after me and grabbed at me. He grabbed at my knickers and pulled them down a bit. I pulled them up as best I could. I was stumbling and hoping I wouldn't fall.

"So, you want to play cat and mouse with me?" He was laughing. "Ah, come on, Emma, stop messing around. Come here to me."

There was no malice aforethought. He wasn't out to rape me or attack me. He genuinely thought that we

378

could be a couple. He thought I fancied him. He definitely fancied me. He thought we had a good thing going.

I stopped to grab my dress.

I turned around with the notion of explaining that I wasn't interested in him in a romantic way. He was running naked along the beach, trying to catch up with me. Only for the fact I was in the situation I was in and I didn't want to give him any encouragement, I would have stopped still and laughed uncontrollably. It was one of the funniest sights I have ever seen, his wobbly bits were so wobbly.

I ran again shouting back at him as I went, "Go away, Marco, you don't know what you're saying! You couldn't love me – you only just met me. It's Abby you fancy! I'm not Abby. It's Abby you were after, not me. But she's spoken for, Marco. "

"It's not Abby I want. It's you. It was always you."

I was nearly at the patio where everyone was sitting. Or at least when I left them they were sitting. Now they were all standing staring at the sight before them. I was nearly dry from running up from the sea. Danny and Ronan ran down towards me, each trying to get to me first. They pushed against each other in their haste. Both of them lost their footing for a moment. They steadied themselves and each of them grabbed one of my arms. Danny pulled me towards him. Ronan pulled me towards him. I was nearly pulled in half.

"Get off me, the pair of you! Is it not enough for you that I nearly drowned? Is it not enough that Marco is running after me naked as the day he was born, wanting to shove his tongue down my throat? Is that not enough? Now the pair of you want to pull me in two halves. Just get off me!"

"Are you all right?"

"Here, let me help you?"

"Oh shut up, the pair of you! You're like a vaudeville double act."

Julia, Abby and Maria were standing staring. Then Julia let out a snort and went hysterical.

"Poor Julia," I said to Ronan, "she's so upset. Do something useful and look after her. Tell her I'm all right. I'm grand. I'm not hurt."

"I'll look after her. Are you all right?"

"Yeah, I'm fine. Danny, will you go and talk to Marco? Stop him making more of an eejit of himself. God help him, he thinks he loves me. Get him some clothes and make sure he's OK, will you?"

"Stop worrying about him. He's fine. I'll take care of him. You just worry about yourself. Are you sure you're all right."

"I'm grand. Just a bit embarrassed, that's all."

Ronan ran over to Julia. I could see him holding her. I could see her very clearly now. She wasn't hysterical crying. She was hysterical laughing. Abby started to laugh too. I knew in their minds' eye they could see poor

Marco running up the beach naked as the day he was born. All his bits dangling, but not very far. Haven't I always said that there is something very unattractive about the naked body running?

I felt very foolish. I couldn't get out of there quick enough.

"I'm going to my room. I want a shower." I didn't want to see any more of Marco. I'd seen enough of him already.

"I'm coming with you," Danny said.

Fair play to him, he got in first.

"I'm coming with you too," Ronan added.

"Me too." Julia was still laughing.

"Well, I'm definitely coming with you. It's my room too." Abby followed me.

"I think I'll stay with Marco," said Maria. "I hope you're all right, Emma. He meant nothing by it. You know that, don't you? I'll have a good talk to him. He's just lonely and he thinks he's in love with you."

"Don't worry about it, Maria. I understand. We're all lonely. Tell him I understand."

Danny was at my side again. "I think it would be only right for me to come with you, Emma. You never know what he might do – after all, it is his hotel. He holds all the keys and probably a card or two up his sleeve."

"I don't think he has any sleeves," Ronan said. "What do you want us to do, Emma? Do you want to be left alone? If you need someone I'll come with you."

"Poor Marco is harmless. He's just lonely and humiliated. God love him, he's probably gone off to lick his wounds."

Danny and Ronan both fought all the way back to the apartment over who would look after me. Which one of them would win the prize of sleeping with me. Which one I would choose to stay with. I was sick of the two of them. So, in the end Abigail won and I slept in my own room in my own bed. I knew I'd have to talk to Danny and Ronan soon. They'd end up killing each other if I didn't. I couldn't leave the two of them dangling, waiting for me to decide which one of them I wanted to be with. If either of them. I was on the verge of telling both of them to shag off and leave me alone.

When I came to this island I had no one in my life. I had messed up and it was entirely my own fault, but I was partnerless. I was a free agent and all I did was whinge that I didn't have someone in my life.

Now I had Danny wanting me. Ronan wanting me. Marco wanting me. And I knew in my heart and soul that Alex wanted me.

I'd have to be an idiot to want to be with Alex. I couldn't even think about that. My brain wouldn't even go there. I was very proud of my brain.

Marco was definitely out of the question.

That left Danny and Ronan.

Both of them wanted a commitment from me. I had to decide which one I wanted to give that commitment to. If either of them.

I could have a happy life with either of them. Danny would always make me laugh. With his irresistible charm and rakish good humour I'd never feel my life was dull or pedantic. I loved the way he always seemed to know what I needed.

Ronan never gave up on me. He was safe, but not predictable. He would make sure I was always safe. He made me laugh.

Both of these men loved me. Both wanted to be with me. Both were overcrowding me and smothering me at the moment. That was only because I was pitting them against each other. That wasn't fair. Any one of the two of them would add to my life, not take over it or take from it. I could add to theirs. So either of them would be a good choice. I loved both of them in different ways.

But I was only madly in love with one of them and he was the perfect choice for me. I didn't even have to think about that. What was worrying me was how I was going to tell the other one that he wasn't the perfect choice for me. I didn't want to hurt either of them. It's hard to break someone's heart. It's even harder when you love them. I loved both of these men in different ways and for different reasons.

There was only one of them that I knew I couldn't live without.

And then there was the Alex factor. My brain kept letting me down. I wasn't proud of it any more. For some reason I kept thinking about him. I kept picturing him, a lonely lost soul wandering on the cliffs in the dark. Would that continue to haunt me for the rest of my life? Would he continue to haunt me? Would I let him?

CHAPTER NINETEEN

I woke up too early. I woke up too early because it was better to be awake than asleep. To sleep I had to close my eyes. When I closed my eyes I just saw the same picture running over and over again in my head. The only way to get rid of the picture was to open my eyes.

My bags were packed and waiting for the off. I was really looking forward to going home. I hadn't done much shopping except for the jacket and other little bits and pieces, nothing much. I hadn't needed to use my extra bag. I was disappointed that I hadn't bought any olive oil to bring back with me. Some of the local wine would be lovely too and fresh bread.

If I got up and showered very quickly. I could be up to the village and back before anyone would miss me. I would have enough time to go into some of the craft shops and pick up some of the local wares. Abby and Julia would kill me for leaving them behind, but I just couldn't wake them. It wouldn't be fair. I'd be back before they even noticed I was gone. I could buy them a little treat each. Julia would love some of the jewellery I had seen. I'd love to get Abigail the glasses she had admired. That'd be a great surprise for her. I had seen a hand-woven rug in a brilliant shade of blue that would be perfect for a job I was going to be working on over the next few weeks.

If I went exploring in the village I would be pre-occupied and I wouldn't be able to think about things. I didn't want to think about things. I was all done in on thinking.

I made myself a quick cup of coffee and went out onto the balcony to drink it and get some air and try not to think. I couldn't help laughing when I looked down onto the beach, remembering poor Marco running along in his birthday suit. Not a pretty sight.

I could hear Julia and Dylan talking. They sounded happy. Julia was giggling a lot. Last night must have done her some good. Abby was right, it had been the right thing to do. Although I think I might have been much better off sitting in my room moping.

I did manage to see the funny side of it all. Abby, Julia and myself hadn't laughed as much in ages as we did after the event. Julia had come in to make sure I was all right and found myself and Abby having a little nightcap and totally hysterical. Not being one to be left out she poured herself one and started laughing too. Poor Marco was the butt of our jokes. But what a butt!

"You should have seen Ronan and Danny's faces, Ma. They were so funny. They didn't know where to look. They couldn't believe that Marco was also showing his hand or his willy or indeed all of himself to show how much he loved you."

"Yes, they thought they only had each other to worry about. They nearly died when the naked, randy Italian come into the picture. You should have had a bit of fun with Marco."

"Will you stop, the pair of you! I'm bad enough as I am without introducing a third party."

We laughed well into the morning. Then Dylan stuck his head in around the balcony and told Julia he was going to bed. She said she'd be right in. Abby asked her to make sure the balcony doors were closed. Julia had the good grace to blush.

It had been lovely seeing Dylan and Julia together all evening. The way he looked at her and the way he cared for her. She was herself with him. He allowed her to totally be herself. There was no denying that Dylan really loved her.

I finished my coffee and was just about to get ready before leaving for the village. Then I heard Julia talking very seriously to Dylan. Their balcony doors were open again.

"I don't know if I can leave here like this, Dylan. I said some horrible things to Alex. I know he was horrible to me and Ma all our lives, but that shouldn't make me be the same way back to him. I am not my father's daughter. I don't know what to do. He is my father after all. No matter what he's done. It'll be awful if every time I think of him I think of all the horrible things I said and what I did to his painting."

I stayed where I was on the patio. I moved closer to the dividing wall. I needed to hear all of this. I didn't feel a bit guilty listening. Sometimes a mother's got to do what a mother's got to do. No matter how sneaky it is.

"You shouldn't be worrying, Julia. What you did was perfectly understandable. You got an awful shock. You had no warning, no time to prepare. I would have gone crazy if it was me. I'd have killed my dad if I hadn't seen him all my life then lo and behold he just turned up on this island having a great time for himself."

I imagined Dylan holding her and comforting her. It was a picture that didn't upset me. It was a lovely picture.

"I did go crazy, Dylan, that's the point. I don't know what possessed me to storm out like that and go and see him right there and then. I should have waited. But, if I hadn't done it there and then, I don't think I could ever have done it. Then again if I hadn't done it in that stupid impulsive way then I never would have destroyed his painting. It was a beautiful painting. I didn't tell him

388

that. It was such a beautiful painting of me. I was so angry. I was so jealous of the painting. He had minded it and looked after it and loved it. All the things he should have done for me. But he didn't do any of them for me and I hated him for that. I was so awful to him. I can't believe I attacked him the way I did. He kept saying he was sorry. He asked me to forgive him. I didn't. I can't believe that he wants me to keep in touch. I told him to fuck off. I have always wondered what he looked like and what I would do if I ever met him. How he'd be with me. Now, I'll never forget his face when I destroyed that painting. It was cruel of me. I should never have done it."

"Don't be torturing yourself, Julia! You can't keep thinking you're to blame for that. He was the one who left. Remember?"

"But I was the one who ruined the only chance I ever got to talk to him."

"He'll be in touch. You'll have another chance. You could always get in touch with him when you get back home, now that you know where he is."

"I should have taken the chance I was given. It's a mistake to let chances go, Dylan. Chances are all we have sometimes. I can't get in touch with him when I go home. It would really hurt my ma; I don't want to hurt her. She's already in bits. This must have brought it all back to her. All the trouble of bringing me up on my own and being a single parent. She's done everything for me. Part of me really wants him to keep in touch with me though. He won't even try now. Now that I have told him exactly what I think of him. He thinks I hate him. I do hate him. But I want to talk to him. I don't want or need him to be a father to me. He could never do that. I just want to know him as a person. I don't want my children not to know their grandfather. I think I'd even like to meet him again. I wouldn't ever be mean to him again. But how can I do that and not hurt my ma? How would she feel if I met up with him?"

"You should tell her how you feel, Julia. Emma is sound; she'll go along with whatever you want. She only wants what makes you happy."

"I know, that's why it's so hard. She'll go along with whatever I want even if she doesn't want it."

"Come on, I need some coffee. Do you want some?"

"Yeah, I'll make it with you."

They went silent. I guessed they were in the kitchen, making the coffee and talking. I couldn't hear anything.

Abby was still in bed, fast asleep.

I had a shower and washed my hair. I went through the motions of putting on sun cream. I put on a pair of shorts and runners and a sleeveless T-shirt. I left the trousers I was going to wear travelling folded over my suitcase. I got my bag and made my way out of the front of the hotel and headed for the village. I had made up my mind. I was going to get Abby the six glasses she had admired, Julia the coral jewellery, Dylan the painting of

Aronna and Danny and Ronan something lovely too.

I walked along the cobbled path. The sun was strong. I was weak. I was thinking again.

Halfway along the path I turned and went back. I had to make everything better. I had to be Ms Fix It. I couldn't let Julia live with this for the rest of her life. She'd always wonder if she had driven him away when she could have got to know him. She'd always blame herself if he never got in touch. The way I blamed myself that he never got in touch for all these years.

I ran down the steps of the hotel and along the beach without anyone seeing me.

I rehearsed what I was going to say. Each and every word.

He was sitting in a chair on the sand outside the studio. His hands covered in paint. He looked so lost. So lonely.

"Hi, Alex."

"Hi, Emma, how are you?"

"I think I'm all right. I'm not really sure." All the words I had rehearsed left me. They deserted me. I tried to find them, but I couldn't. I should have rehearsed a bit better before I spoke to him. I should have learned my lines properly.

"Will you be all right, do you think?"

"Yeah. You know me. I bounce back. I think I'll be all right."

"What about Julia? Is she all right?"

"No. She's hurting badly. It's all new and raw. But she will be all right."

"You don't know how sorry I am. I fucked up so badly, didn't I? Everything she said about me is true. I should have been in touch with her all her life. I should have made some sort of an effort to get in touch with her. God, I'm a fucking coward, amn't I? I'm going to keep in touch with her from now on, if that's all right. I'll write to her or mail her and keep writing and mailing until she answers. Have I left it too late do you think? "

"I don't know. I don't know what to think any more. To tell you the truth, I'm trying not to think too much. I hope it's not too late. For her sake."

"What about you, Emma?"

"Me? I'll be fine as usual. Once Julia is happy, I'll be happy. That's the way it has always been. I can't change now."

"Is there any hope for you and me? Can we ever put everything behind us and get to know each other as we are now?"

"I can't believe you'd ask me that after all that has happened."

"I had to. That old spark is still there, isn't it? It was there when you came and sat at my table in the café. I could feel it. You could feel it. Could we ever turn the clock back, do you think? Could I ever make up to you for what I have done? When I left I thought I was doing the right thing. I wasn't. I was just running. Running away from you, from the responsibility of a baby. From my mother, even from poor Harry. I lived the high life for a couple of years. Working at any menial job I could get and drinking my wages. I got into a scene. I thought it was what I wanted. I started drinking heavily and lost a series of jobs. I stole money from the last job I was in to pay for my drinking. I kept thinking of you and that photograph Harry gave me haunted me. She was so like you, Emma. She still is.

I kept wanting to get in touch, but I kept convincing myself that it was the wrong time. That it was better to wait until I was sober. So as time went on there was always another excuse and I was never sober. It got harder and harder to pick up a phone to try to find you. There was never a right time to get in touch. I was a drunk and a thief and a failure."

I let him talk. I listened to him and I have to admit I felt sorry for him. God forgive me after all he had done, but there was still something about him that I wanted.

"I got a job working on a ship and ended up in Italy. It's the country with the highest concentration of art, did you know that? I went to Rome and Florence and I felt at home. Then I heard of this place, L'isola Di Aronna.

"Do you know they say that real life begins here? No matter what age you come to the island at your life starts from that day. Whatever has gone on in the past is forgotten. The locals tell a story. They say that once upon a time there was nobody living here. It was uninhabited. A young sailor came ashore from a ship. He had some illness and was dying. He came here to die. He lay on the beach and asked the waves to take him out to sea. A beautiful maiden came out of the water to take him. She fell in love with him and she stayed with him on the shore. Her name was Aronna. The two lovers lived a long and happy life on the island. They are the direct ancestors of all the islanders. Some of the older people never even leave the island for a day. They fear that the spell will be broken if they leave.

I knew I could make a home here. I knew this was a place where I could begin again. Start a new life. I started to paint and a couple of my paintings sold. I wasn't drinking any more. Then I painted the one of Julia. It inspired me. Everything I have done since then has been because of that.

I've turned my life around, Emma. If I believed in fate I'd say it brought me to this place and you here, to me. I'd say it was written in the stars, if I believed in the stars. Whatever has happened in my life, all the good, all the bad, all of it has brought me here to this island to this time. To now. Whatever has happened in your life, all the good and bad has brought you to this moment, this time to be here now, with me. I'd like to get to know you again. Would you let me?"

I saw her before he did.

"Hi"

"Hi, Julia."

"I wondered where you had got to, Ma. I wanted to tell you I was coming here. I just couldn't find you." She started crying, again.

"It's all right, Julia. Don't get upset."

"I've caused all this," he said. "I'm sorry, Julia, truly sorry."

"I came to say that I'm sorry. I'm sorry about the painting. I'm not sorry I had a go at you, you did deserve that, but you didn't deserve me to destroy your work. I really feel so bad about it."

He held out his paint-covered hands. "I fixed it. It's all yours if you want it. You can take it home. It doesn't belong to me. You're right, I don't deserve it. Maybe you'd let me come and visit it one day." So, Alex had finally grown a set of balls. He was finally facing up to his responsibility.

"It doesn't belong with me. It belongs here with you. It's not mine. I don't think I can take it."

"I understand. Maybe someday, eh?"

Why did I feel sorry for him? Why didn't I still feel anger and hate? All I felt was sad. He had let go of something a long time ago and had wasted all his life looking for it. All those years ago he had turned his back on what he really wanted only he didn't know it was what he wanted until now.

"Julia, Alex wants to keep in touch with you if you want. I think it might be a good idea. Circumstances

sometimes dictate what we do. We were lucky, Julia –
our circumstances were a lot better than most."

"You're some woman, Emma," said Alex. "I know how
hard this is for you. Thanks for giving me a chance." He
touched me on the hand. He knew I was struggling. He
knew Julia was torn between hurting me and getting to
know him. He knew I was making it easier for her.

Julia looked at me. "Thanks, Ma." Even she knew
what I was doing – was it that transparent?

"I'll give you a chance too," she said to Alex. "If you
get in touch with me. I'll reply. That's all I can promise. I
can't say any more than that. I won't make the first
move though. The first move is up to you. You owe me
that much."

He reached out and rubbed her along the arm gently.
For a minute I thought she was going to pull away. She
nearly did. But she didn't.

"Thanks. I won't mess it up this time. I promise. I will
send an e-mail to you today. You'll have it by the time
you get home. Just to prove I am going to keep my
word."

Anyone walking along the beach would have looked
at the homely scene. Maybe even envied the three of us
sitting out in the sun, talking, getting along so well.
They would have assumed we were just another happy
family out for the day. Sometimes things aren't what
they seem. Sometimes they aren't what they first appear
to be. Sometimes it's worth taking a second look.

I was thinking that Alex had changed. Really changed and that Julia and he could build up some sort of a relationship. It didn't have to be a father/daughter relationship. I doubted if it would ever get to that. But they could become friends. All I wanted from him was that he'd never let her down again. I was thinking he could finally give me all I wanted.

"Come on, Julia, we have to go. The others will be waiting for us. You can walk us along the beach with us if you like, Alex."

"I'd like that. I'm going to miss you both."

"We'd better hurry – we have a plane to catch and there is nothing I like more than flying – isn't that right, Julia?"

"She's a natural. She just loves it."

Julia told him little bits about her life as we walked along the beach.

He left us at the bottom of the steps to the hotel. Julia just said a quiet good-bye to him. There was no last-minute hug. No dramatic farewell. No having to pull them apart. No empty promises of visiting each other. I don't know if she was crying, but I knew, if she was, she'd feel better soon. I was glad she had come down to see him. I was glad for her. She would have a different memory of him now. Nothing for her to torture herself about.

At the top of the steps she turned and ran down again. She was crying. I could see it now. He held his arms out and she gave him a hug. A gentle hug. Then she ran up the steps and disappeared into the hotel and into the arms of Dylan no doubt.

I turned to Alex. For a moment I saw the young man. The man I had loved, who had loved me. We were only recognising now, after all these years, that we had been madly in love. Life got in the way and we had let it.

He put his arms around me and hugged me.

"Goodbye, Alex."

"You never answered my question, Emma. If I try really hard to make it up to you and Julia, will you try to forgive me? Will you let me get to know you again? Do you think there's a chance for us? Tell me I have that chance, please?"

"It's too late for us, Alex. I know we could never go back, too much has happened. I don't even want to go back. I want to go forward. To see what is in store for me. What's written in the stars for me. Our past would only be hanging over us for the rest of our lives. You'd always feel that I wanted you to do more. You'd start to think that you could never do enough to make up for everything. I'd always feel that you were only with me to make up for what you did. It was all a long time ago, Alex. I'm not the one you have to make it up to. So, I'm giving you a clean slate with me. I forgive you for anything you ever did to hurt me. I do forgive you, completely. Now, it's only Julia you have to make up lost time to. You see, I got over you long ago. I am in love with someone else."

"I'm glad for you, Emma. I really am. I hope he's better to you than I ever was. I swear to you, I won't let Julia down ever again."

"I know you won't. She won't let you."

I walked up the steps. I didn't look back. This was a time for looking forward.

Everyone was waiting to leave for the ferry. Danny, Ronan, Abby, Julia and Dylan. Even poor Marco dared to show his face. He had shown us a little bit more than that last night, but everyone was kind to him and he was laughing about it in no time. Maria came out to wish us well too. I caught a glimpse of her as she watched Alex walk down along the beach.

"Look after him, Maria," I whispered as I gave her a good-bye hug.

She was surprised. "Do you think he would want me to?"

"He'd be a fool not to."

She smiled and there was something different about her. There was a twinkle in her eye.

"Goodbye, Marco." I hugged him. I was really getting into the hugging now.

"Goodbye, Emma. I am sorry. It was just a misunder-standing."

"Forget it, Marco. I was flattered. A handsome man like you chasing me along the beach! I will be telling that story for years. Keep watching out for the woman of your dreams. I have a feeling she's about to make an appearance any day now."

"I hope so, Emma. Good-bye."

The car pulled up outside to take us to the airport. At the same time a taxi pulled up.

"Well! Will you look at that?" Abby was gobsmacked.

"Can you believe it?" Julia was gobsmacked.

"I certainly can. I can believe anything." Nothing would gobsmack me ever again. Not even the sight of Plain Jane getting out of the taxi. She waved at us all.

"I just had to come back. I love it here!" she shouted. Marco stepped forward to greet her. He put his arm around her waist. She batted her overly long eyelashes at him. He was smitten, instantly. She even looked a bit smitten herself.

It wasn't too long before we were on the plane and everyone was having a great time slagging me.

"Someone strap her in."

"Knock her out."

"Don't let her out of her seat."

The whole plane seemed to be waiting for me to throw a wobbly. But I knew I wouldn't. I was safe. Madame Celeste had told me I was safe.

I opened the newspaper and looked at the horoscopes again.

I no longer only looked up my own horoscope daily. That was where I had been going wrong all the time.

Now, along with mine, I looked up Julia's, Abby's, Dylan's, Danny's and Ronan's. It was a lot of reading, but it was well worth it. You see, there's no point just knowing what the day holds for me. It's important that I know what it holds for all of us.

I read mine first.

I was delighted with it.

All the planets must have been in their rightful places today.

All must be very well with the world.

My horoscope was wonderful.

Madam Celeste was in top form and she knew what she was talking about today.

Madam Celeste
Scorpio
October 23 - November 22

You have followed your heart and found true, lasting love.
You're onto a winner and about to have such a wonderful life
– enjoy it.

Then I read Julia's.

Virgo
August 21 – September 22

Enjoy it all. Look forward to catching up with your past. You are one of the lucky ones. True love has found you. Young love is in your heart and you are all set to soar and enjoy it.

I was happy with Abby's.

Capricorn
December 21 – January 19

True love is waiting for you, exactly where you left it. You should trust it.

I left Ronan and Danny's until the last.

Sagittarius
November 23 – December 20

You followed your heart and now you have found true, lasting love. The future looks bright for you.

Leo
July 21 – August 20

Today is only a beginning. Remember to follow your heart. There is someone waiting for you. It's only a matter of time before you find them. Timing is everything.

I put my hand into Ronan's hand. He squeezed it. I snuggled up into his shoulder. Safe. All set for take-off.

402

All set to enjoy the journey.

I just knew it was going to be the journey of a life-time. I loved him.

"I love you, Emma. Will you marry me?" he whis-pered.

"Yes, Ronan, I will. I love you too. I thought you'd never ask."

He kissed me a slow passionate kiss.

The gang cheered.

We had taken off and I hadn't even noticed.

THE END